CARVED
IN
Ice

CARVED IN Ice

MADE OF STEEL SERIES - BOOK 3

IVY SMOAK

To the superhero in all of us.

CHAPTER 1
7 Years Old
Flashback

Silence. My eyes flew open. It was only ever this quiet when it snowed. That could only mean one thing. *Snow day!* I jumped out of bed and ran to the window. Small flakes of snow swirled in the wind. A smile spread across my face. It was more than I had even wished for. There was no way there was school today, but I still had to check.

I ran out into the hall. My socks slid along the wooden floor when I stopped in front of my parents' door. I was about to knock when I heard laughter outside. And not just any laughter. I'd recognize Miles' laughter anywhere. It was my favorite noise in the whole wide world.

I didn't want to miss one second of the snow or of playing in it with Miles. Maybe today he wouldn't ignore me. I ran past my parents' bedroom to the hall closet and pulled on my snow pants over my pajama bottoms. Miles had been pretending I was invisible for weeks. He wouldn't even acknowledge me when I spoke. But today would be the day I convinced Miles I wasn't invisible. I could feel it in my bones.

I heard my parents start to stir in their bedroom. If they came out to the hall before I was outside, they'd make me wash up and eat breakfast. But I didn't have time to do such frivolous things. I was losing precious time. I shoved my feet into my snow boots, grabbed my jacket and hat, and pulled them on as I ran to the back door. Thinking better of it, I went back to the closet and grabbed my pink mittens that matched my hat. They weren't waterproof, but they looked really cute. And if I was going to get Miles to see me, I needed to look my best. I adjusted my pink hat with the big poof on the top and opened up the back door.

I slipped outside before my parents could stop me and ran through the freshly fallen snow. "Hi, Miles!" I yelled from my side of the fence.

He didn't respond. He just continued to build his snowman.

I pushed on the fence door but it was too hard to open with all the snow on the other side. "Miles, the gate is stuck!"

He ignored me.

A fence was not going to keep me away from the man of my dreams. I grabbed the top of the fence and tried to pull myself up. I lifted my leg up once, twice, until I finally got my boot on top of the fence. All the extra padding made it even harder. "Miles!"

He ignored me.

That was fine. I didn't need his help. *Come on.* I finally hoisted myself to the top of the fence and unceremoniously fell into his yard on my butt.

Ooof. I slowly stood up and ran over to Miles. "Can I help build the snowman too?"

He didn't respond.

"Please?"

Nothing.

Why did he keep doing this? It wasn't very nice. "Miles, I'm not invisible!"

He ignored me.

"I'm not! I'm standing right here." I ran around the snowman so he couldn't possibly miss me. "Don't you see me?"

Nothing.

Maybe he was just tired of building the snowman. That was okay, I had loads of ideas for what we could do today. "Do you want to go sledding down the street instead?"

Nothing.

He was being especially mean today. "Do you want to have a snowball fight?"

Nothing.

I pressed my lips together. "Miles Young, you are not a very nice boy."

Nothing.

I wasn't going to let him ruin my snow day. He was such a meany face. I stomped my foot, hoping to get his attention. When he didn't look up, I started walking back toward my yard, hoping the whole time that he'd ask me to stay.

"Summer?" My dad's voice echoed into the silent snowfall.

"Over here," I said. "I'm stuck." I didn't want to climb back over the fence.

My dad came running over to the fence. He wasn't wearing a jacket. And he was wearing slippers in the snow. "Summer, you scared us. You can't go running off like that."

"I just wanted to play with Miles," I whispered. I felt like I was going to cry, but my eyes were too cold. I sniffed instead.

"I see. You know what?" He leaned over the fence and lifted me back over it. "Sometimes the best way to get a boy's attention is to give him a taste of his own medicine."

"What do you mean?"

"I mean if he's ignoring you, you should ignore him too." He carried me back into the house even though I was too big to be carried. I snuggled into his side. My daddy was my best friend, so it didn't matter that I was too big.

***

I ignored Miles all day. Right in front of him. I played on his swing set without annoying him. I danced under the snow, catching flakes on my tongue by myself. I even built a bigger, better snowman. The sun was starting to set and the sky was doing that orange thing it did whenever it snowed. But even though I'd be able to see in the dark, my parents wouldn't let me stay out much longer. Ignoring Miles hadn't worked. And I was running out of time.

I ran over to him. "Do you want to play now?"

Nothing.

"Miles please, who else are you going to play with? We're the only kids on the street."

Nothing.

"You're the meanest boy on the planet. There isn't anything you could do that would be meaner than ignoring me. I'm not invisible!"

Miles lifted up some snow in his gloves and patted it into a snowball.

Him throwing that at me would be meaner. I swallowed hard.

He finally looked up at me. Our eyes met. And I would have smiled if it wasn't obvious that he was about to throw the snowball in my face.

"Don't you dare, Miles Young!" I gave him the most serious scowl I could muster when I was trying not to smile. I had been hoping he'd play with me all afternoon. How could I be upset when he was finally looking at me?

He tossed the snowball straight up in the air and caught it.

"Really, Miles. Don't do it." *Please do.*

"Don't do what?"

I pointed at his hand. "Throw that snowball at me."

He immediately threw it right at me.

I screamed at the top of my lungs and tried to dodge it. But it made direct contact with my leg. *Ow.* I stifled a laugh. "I said not to!"

"No. You actually said, 'throw that snowball at me.' "

"I did not!"

He stuck his tongue out at me.

I stuck my tongue right back out at him.

He laughed.

And I laughed.

I wasn't sure how long we stood like that. But all I wanted to do was tell him how much I loved him. And how much it hurt when he pretended I was invisible. My babysitter, Julie, had told me that when boys were mean to you it meant that they liked you. But I told her that it wasn't true, that Miles was mean because he hated me. I hated that he hated me because I loved him with every piece of my heart.

This was the first moment where I thought Julie might actually be right. Miles wasn't looking at me like he hated me. He was smiling out of the corner of his mouth. He was acknowledging my existence. It felt like my insides flipped over.

I had one chance to make him keep smiling. "Do you want to make snow angels with me?" I asked.

"No."

Maybe I had two chances. "Do you want to go sledding?"

"No."

I guess I had no chances. I put my hands on my hips. "I've never done anything to make you hate me. Why are you so mean to me?"

"Because you're so annoying."

I glared at him. My babysitter was wrong. And Miles Young was a jerk face. "Well I don't want to play with you anyway."

"Good." He turned around and started to walk away.

I just wanted to be friends with him. Was that really so hard to ask? There were no other kids around. It was just the two of us. We were supposed to be best of friends.

And in that moment I hated him so much. I leaned down and packed a snowball together, lifted it up in my mittens, and threw it at the back of his stupid head.

It was glorious. The snowball made perfect contact and exploded into powdery dust. He immediately froze.

I clapped my mittens over my mouth so he wouldn't hear my laughter.

"Oh, it is so on," he said and leaned down to pack a snowball.

I squealed and started running. I didn't even want to retaliate. He was hitting me with snowballs. Which meant he could see me. I wasn't invisible anymore.

In a few minutes I was covered in snow. I was pretty sure if I looked in the mirror I'd think I was looking at a snowman instead of myself.

"I surrender," I said. I fell backward into the snow and started making snow angels.

He laughed and plopped down in the snow beside me. I smiled up at the falling snow when I heard him flapping his arms and legs. He *had* wanted to make snow angels. And I had convinced him to make them with me.

One of my favorite things was catching snowflakes on my tongue. I was about to tell him to try, but when I turned to face him, I stopped. He was still making snow angels. And his tongue was sticking out.

I had never seen it directed at anyone but me. There he was though, catching snowflakes on his tongue. And I realized that catching snowflakes was no longer my favorite thing. His smile definitely surpassed it.

I was about to tell him how much I liked playing with him when his mother called his name.

"The hot chocolate is ready!" Mrs. Young said. "Summer, do you want some too?"

I stared at Miles. All I wanted in the whole world was for him to invite me in. I had been in his house before, but always by his mother's invitation. He had always made it perfectly clear that he didn't want me around.

"I guess you can come if you have to," Miles said as he sat up.

I definitely had to. Yes, it was the rudest invitation in the history of invitations. But how could I refuse him? I loved Miles Young. The only thing I hated about him was that he didn't love me back.

CHAPTER 2

18 Years Old
Present Day – Sunday

I slowly opened my eyes. At first I wasn't sure what had awakened me, but it only took a moment to realize that the usual noises of the city had ceased. I stared up at the ceiling. A snow day. *Great.* I sighed and pulled the covers back up to my chin. All I wanted to do was curl back up in a ball and dream of simpler times. But time was a luxury I no longer had.

It had been four months since I had slipped the note under Miles' door, confessing who I was and telling him it was time for him to move on. When I wrote it, I thought I was going to die. In a lot of ways I had. I pushed the comforter off of me and stepped down onto the cold wood floor.

I stopped in front of the mirror and wondered if Miles would even recognize me now. I had ditched my Sadie Davis disguise. And with it, I had ditched the last piece of myself that made any sense…Miles. I'd cut my hair to right beneath my chin and dyed it dirty blonde. I'd stopped wearing my brown colored contacts. After dozens of fights with Liza, I had gotten a fake ID with my real name – Summer Brooks. The agreement was that I didn't contact anyone from my past. That I never actually used my ID for anything. And that I never left the house unless I could hide in the darkness or behind my new mask.

The rules should have been easy to follow. I was wanted for the murder of Sadie Davis. But every night, I came close to breaking the rules. I crept to a rooftop adjacent to my old dorm building and waited for Miles to come look at the stars. Every night I waited. Only…he never came. He stopped going to his favorite place. My letter had told him to stop looking for me. I shouldn't have been surprised.

My stalking tendencies didn't just stop there either. I watched his soccer games from afar. I watched his team win the division. I watched him celebrating with his friends. I watched him leave NYC to go home for the holidays. I watched him forget all about me.

And it hurt. Part of me thought he'd continue his search for me now that he knew I was alive. But it wasn't that simple. He would have seen the news. He would have seen that I was a murderer. Clearly he wanted nothing to do with me now. And even though I wasn't a murderer, I would be soon. Miles had made the right choice. I just hoped that I was about to make the right one too.

I pulled on my leggings and sweater and grabbed my gun off the nightstand. I had invested in a bra holster because when I kept the gun on my hip, all V could seem to do was glare at it. This way, I felt safe and he couldn't complain. What he didn't know wouldn't kill him. It wasn't like he had been anywhere near my breasts lately anyway. I had pushed him away. Just like I had pushed Eli away. And Miles.

Miles. He was coming back from winter session break today. I put my gun in its holster and adjusted my sweater. There was no reason to go to the roof to see if he would appear tonight. It was snowing. There were no stars in the snow. Besides, what if he did go to the rooftop? What if he brought someone with him? I couldn't watch that. Believing that he had moved on was one thing. Seeing it though? I couldn't.

I quickly washed up in the bathroom and stepped out into the hall. V was already sitting at the kitchen table. When we had all agreed to work together, I hadn't realized it would mean living together. Eli, Liza, V, and I were pretty much the worst group of roommates ever. Liza was a night owl. Eli hogged the shower for way too long. And V…it was just really hard living with V. He probably didn't enjoy it either. It never allowed him to take off his stupid mask. When I bought the apartment for our new headquarters, I should have invested in a bigger space instead of all the extra tech. It wasn't like our security was keeping Don Roberts away. And right now, all I wanted was more space.

"Good morning, Sadie," V said without looking up from his bowl of cereal.

That. That was why it was so hard to live with him. And it was one of the reasons I had pushed him away too. Right before the bomb went off in his secret lair, he called me Summer. He confessed that he loved me. And afterward? He went back to calling me Sadie right away. And never spoke of loving me again. People did stupid things when they were about to die. His lies stung. What was I supposed to say to him?

"Good morning." *Smooth*. I walked past him to the fridge. Nothing in the kitchen seemed at all appetizing. I grabbed an apple and sat down at the kitchen counter, basically on the other side of the room as V. We both ate in awkward silence. What it came down to was that we'd had a fling. And now we were living together. We weren't even friends really. He thought he knew me, but he didn't. And I barely knew a thing about him.

"Spring semester starts tomorrow," V said.

I looked up from my apple. "Mhm." For a moment, I let myself stare. I remembered how safe I felt in his arms. I even remembered how nice my name sounded on his tongue. He'd said he loved me, but clearly regretted it.

I stared back down at the kitchen counter. Miles was the one person I wanted to hear the words from, but he didn't say it. It felt like we had made love our last night together. I had told him that I loved him. But he had never actually said it back. And now he never would. I probably wouldn't have believed him anyway. Clearly no one ever meant it when they said it to me.

"Are you going to stay away from him?" V asked.

"Who?" I kept my eyes glued to the kitchen counter.

"Miles Young." His voice rumbled more than usual when he said the name.

I sighed and scooted off the stool. "I made Liza a promise."

"So you won't see him?"

I tossed out the rest of my apple and turned toward him. "When I say something, I actually mean it, V."

He pressed his lips into a thin line.

Maybe I should have felt bad, because technically it was a lie. They had told me to stop seeing Miles before and I went behind their backs and told him everything. I had betrayed V's trust. All of their trusts. But I didn't feel bad at all. I'm pretty sure all four of us were compulsive liars.

"What is that supposed to mean?" he asked.

"Nothing. Forget I said anything." I started to walk out of the kitchen, but he caught my wrist, stopping me. I immediately pulled my hand away.

"Would you please just talk to me? Something is clearly bothering you. If we could just talk…" his voice trailed off.

He regretted what he said four months ago. And I pretended it had never happened. I had assumed we had an unspoken understanding. "There's nothing to talk about. I'm sorry, I just…really hate the snow." It was true. It reminded me of what Don had taken from me. The last time I remembered enjoying a snow storm was with Miles. Both memories were just too painful.

"You hate the snow? That's why you've been pushing me away for months?"

No. "Yes."

"Why are you lying?"

"Me? Are you serious?" I could hear my voice starting to rise. "I'm not the liar in this equation, V." I put his name in quotes.

"I haven't lied to you about my name. I just haven't told you…"

"What's the difference?" I was losing my temper. I needed to go outside and feel the snow against my skin. I needed to remember why this conversation was insignificant, because right now it hurt. "I honestly don't even care what your real name is. That isn't what I'm upset about." I stormed past him, grabbed my winter jacket off the hook, and ignored the sound of him following me.

"So there *is* something you're upset about?"

Jesus. He was so dense. "What do you think, V? You called me Summer. You said that you loved me. And then literally less than 10 minutes after your confession, you started calling me Sadie again. You never spoke of loving me again. You backtracked so fast I thought I had imagined it. I've had to give up so much the past several months. I never thought I'd be forced to give you up too when you promised you weren't going anywhere." Everything I said was selfish. Because the whole time I was falling for him, I had already fallen for Miles and I was falling for Eli too. V shouldn't love me. I was a monster. And I was about to be so much worse.

He just stared at me.

It annoyed me even more that he had nothing to say to defend himself. "So there you have it."

He still said nothing.

I wanted to slap his stupid masked face. "Would you just put me out of my misery and tell me if you meant it?" My heart stammered against my chest.

"Sadie…"

I put my hand up. "That's all you had to say." I turned around. "Athena, open." The window made a whirring noise and started to rise.

"I meant what I said in the moment," V said from behind me. "It felt right to say it. I didn't want to die without you knowing how I was feeling."

I stepped outside onto the fire escape and turned back to him. *So he had meant it?* The gun suddenly felt heavy against my chest. I locked eyes with him. There was so much I wanted to say. I was just about to open my mouth when he started talking again.

"But I regretted it as soon as it came out of my mouth," he said.

The snow swirled around me as it danced in the wind. Nothing good ever happened in the snow. I wasn't even sure why I had gotten my hopes up. "Great. Thanks for clearing that up. See you later, V."

But I wouldn't. I strongly doubted that I'd see him ever again. I started to walk up the fire escape as the window whirred shut. Because today was the day. As soon as I heard the silence of the city I knew. Don Roberts had taken away my last hope in the snow. How great would it be for him to take his last breath in the silence?

CHAPTER 3
Sunday

I was going to kill Don today. I was finally going to do it. But there was one thing I needed to do first. I stared down at my old dorm building and waited. I needed to see Miles. Everything always came back to Miles. I shouldn't have been here. It was wrong, but I couldn't seem to stay away. Besides, it might be the last time I ever got to see him. If everything went right today, I'd be behind bars before sunset.

I watched as some blonde girl approached Miles and touched his arm. They laughed together about something I couldn't hear. He grabbed one of her suitcases for her as they walked toward the dorm. I couldn't hear their laughter, but his was easy to imagine. It was the kind that warmed my soul. The kind that made my stomach flip over. Coming here was definitely a mistake.

I exhaled and watched my breath mix with the snow in front of me, obscuring my vision of the two of them. I turned away from the dorm building. Miles was smiling again. *Good for him.* For years I thought he had forgotten about me. When I found out that he still wrote letters, all of that changed. I let myself believe in us again for the briefest of moments. But seeing him now? Apparently I was as easy to forget as I had originally assumed. The thought was numbing.

When I was far away from him, I felt strong. For the last few months all I'd been doing was training. I pretended that I was like freaking superwoman. Clearly I wasn't though. I was weak. Just seeing him laughing with another girl made me want to break down and cry.

Once upon a time, being with him would have been all my dreams coming true. That wasn't the case anymore. My dreams had become nightmares. And in every nightmare I had, it ended in one way: with Don taking his last breath.

I ran across the roof and leapt to the adjacent building. Running along rooftops was better than running through Central Park. Especially at night when it felt like I was running with the stars.

My feet slid along the slush that was forming on the roof. Running was going to be difficult today. It was going to take me longer than I anticipated to get to my post. I had spent too much time waiting for Miles to appear. If I missed out on my shot because of that, maybe it would finally get me to stop stalking him. Maybe I'd be filled with enough resentment to move on.

***

Did Miles like her? *Stop.* The gun shook in my hand. Miles didn't matter. Nothing mattered but my plan. Where the hell was Don, anyway?

I pulled up the sleeve of my winter jacket and glanced at my watch. I had been on time, but Don was late. Or had he left early?

It wasn't like it was hard to figure out the mayor's schedule. Especially one that was apparently as beloved as

Don Roberts. He'd won by a landslide in the polls a few months ago, and his first initiative was to clean up the city. He was pointing all the blame for the increased crime on the vigilante. Meanwhile, he was letting the mafia infect the city behind his constituents' backs. And somehow, only my team knew his secrets. He had the cops in his pocket. Hell, he had everyone in his pocket.

Today Don was doing some reading at a local elementary school. It was all so fake. A public service that he did to keep up appearances. He didn't care about children. For all I knew, he was scouting out his next victim. The thought made the gun shake in my hand again. *Get a grip.* My finger tightened on the trigger.

"Drop the gun, Summer," Eli said from behind me.

I didn't need to turn to know it was him. It was easy to remember what his voice sounded like whispering in my ear. My whole life was filled with memories, but in the present I had nothing. Nothing but this moment to hold on to. "No thanks," I said calmly. No one was stopping me today. Enough was enough.

"I'm serious, Summer. Don't make me do this."

I glanced over my shoulder at him. His gun was raised too, except his was pointed at me instead of the street below.

I laughed. "You expect me to believe that you'd shoot me?" *Yeah right.* I looked back out over the ledge again. *Where the hell is he?*

"It's an elementary school," Eli said. "You're putting innocent children at risk."

The irritation in his voice annoyed me. I would never put children in danger. "Luckily I'm a good shot."

"No one's a good shot from this distance with a pistol. This isn't the way. We're getting so close."

I turned back around. "*We*? Are you serious? You and I haven't been a we since you told V I was going to kill Don. You betrayed my trust. There is no we, Eli."

His gun was still pointed at me.

"I barely got away from him today. He watches me like a freaking hawk. Just let me finish this thing and then we can all move on." Saying the words out loud didn't make me believe them. How was I going to move past this? I was going to end up in jail or dead myself. The thought of Miles tried to crawl back into my mind, but I pushed it aside.

"If you kill Don, you're not going to get any answers. I agreed to help you do it when I thought we knew everything. When getting back at him for what he did to you was all that mattered."

"I have all the answers I need. He killed my parents. He *destroyed* me." My voice cracked. "To me, revenge is the only thing that matters."

"Summer…"

"We both know what this is really about, so stop lying to yourself," I said. "I stopped mattering to you. That's what happened. You don't give a shit about anyone but yourself."

"You really have lost it. I've been defending you this whole time. I'm on the run just as much as you are. I gave up everything for you."

I laughed. "And you've done nothing but regret it."

Eli shook his head. "I don't even recognize you anymore."

"It's probably the hair." The sound of a door closing made me turn around. I peered off the roof. There he was. And just like I had suspected, he wasn't surrounded by a bunch of kids. I lifted my gun.

And I immediately felt something hit the side of my neck. I reached up and felt the small feathers that accompanied the vial of serum that V used to knock people out. *Damn it.* I looked back at Eli as I fell to my knees. I hadn't even realized that he wasn't holding a regular gun. "I hate you," I mumbled as I fell onto the concrete. My gun fell from my hand and skidded away from me.

"Yeah, you've made that perfectly clear." Eli bent down and lifted me over his shoulder. "Luckily for you, you're not so easy to hate."

I would have laughed, but I was just so sleepy. "I don't really hate you," I said with a yawn. "How could I hate you when you have such a nice butt?" I put both my hands on his ass and squeezed.

He laughed. "I don't think you've said anything that nice to me in months. Maybe I should drug you more often."

"That's probably a good idea." I yawned again. "Maybe then I can be happy again."

"Summer?"

I drifted to sleep at the sound of his voice.

CHAPTER 4
Sunday

My head hurt. I went to reach for it, but I couldn't move my hands. The last thing I remembered was getting ready to kill Don. The feeling of my hands being bound made me slowly open my eyes. Had I been arrested? Had I done it?

"Good, she's awake!" Liza called and sat down in one of the three chairs across from me.

I blinked. "Liza, untie me." I hadn't been arrested. It was coming back to me. Eli had interfered. He had ruined my plans. I tried to stand up off the floor and realized my feet were tied together too. "Seriously, untie me."

"No can do, Summer."

"Why?" I tried to move my hands again to no avail.

"We're having an intervention," Liza said.

I stopped struggling. "An intervention? Are you serious? Why?" I watched as Eli and V sat down in the chairs on either side of Liza.

"Because you've been such a bitch recently."

I looked up at her. "Me? News flash, Liza, you're always a bitch. At least to me."

"Okay, that's enough," V said. "Both of you." He glared at Liza.

She shrugged and pushed her glasses up the bridge of her nose. "She asked."

"That's not what this is about," Eli said. "Summer, we're worried about you. You've stopped talking to us. You're shutting us all out."

"This is ridiculous," I muttered under my breath as I tried to twist my hands out of the rope. *Ow.*

Eli leaned forward and put his elbows on his knees. "Summer, look at me."

I continued to struggle without looking up.

"Distancing yourself isn't helping anyone. We need to be able to work as a team, and in order to do that, we need to be able to trust you."

I had nothing to say, so I kept trying to get loose.

"I've known you for a long time and..." started Eli.

My laugh made Eli sigh. It was one of those sighs when you're truly exhausted. When the battle seems too hard. I knew the type of sigh because I'd been trying to fight it off my whole life. I felt bad that I had made him sigh that way. That I had made him feel like giving up...on me.

"Summer, we've all been talking and we think maybe you should go to therapy."

That made me stop. "Really? And who should I go to therapy as? Sadie Davis? Summer Brooks? All of my identities are dead, remember? I'm wanted for murder, Eli. I can't exactly stroll up to the nearest psych ward and get admitted."

"I didn't say psych ward. Jesus." He ran his hands down his face. "We could bring a therapist here..."

"Despite what you all might think, I don't need therapy. I'm perfectly fine." I wasn't. Every morning when I woke up it felt like I was drowning.

"That's debatable," Liza said. "You did try to murder someone today."

"Not *someone*. I tried to kill Don. Why are you all suddenly acting like I'm crazy?" *Why can't I untie this freaking rope?* "Besides, no therapist is going to agree to come help someone accused of murder."

"I know one," V said.

"Well obviously a therapist that's willing to help a man who lives behind a mask isn't very good at what he does. No thank you."

"That's a little harsh," Liza said. "And before you throw something back at me, can we just remind you that you're not the only one that had to give something up the past few months? We're in this together, whether we like it or not. You could at least make it a little more enjoyable to be stuck with you."

"Are you comparing giving up your upscale Manhattan apartment to what I've been through? Cry me a river."

"You'd know I gave up more than that if you bothered to talk to me!"

"And what, Liza? You'd be able to tell me what true loss feels like? Everything was taken from me. Everything I've ever cared about!" I struggled against my restraints.

"That. That right there. How is that supposed to make us feel? Because I thought we all cared about each other." She glanced at V.

All she cared about was V. She was probably only sitting there pretending to care because he had asked her to be a part of whatever the hell this was. I wanted to scream at the top of my lungs. It was getting hard to breathe. "I need to go outside," I said. "Will someone please untie me?"

They didn't respond. The silence was so unnerving.

"Look, I'm not seeing the whack-job therapist that V uses who is clearly terrible at his job. And I'm not going to go find one on my own. Conversation over. Now untie me please."

"My therapist doesn't know I'm the vigilante," V said. His voice rumbled lower than usual. "He's good at what he does, it's not his fault that I've been lying to him. And you'll be using a fake name so he won't connect the dots."

I wanted to keep arguing with them. I wanted to prove that I wasn't insane. But there was a benefit to meeting V's ridiculous therapist. Maybe I could finally figure out who V was. "Okay, I'll meet him."

"That was easier than I expected," Liza said.

"Well, you guys are right. I've been hard to live with." *As if they hadn't.*

"Or you could just talk to us," V said. "Tell us what's really bothering you. We're your friends."

Friends. I swallowed down the lump in my throat. Wasn't that one of the problems? That we were once so much and now we were just friends? "No, I want to talk to your therapist."

"But if you…"

Eli cleared his throat. "Perfect. He should be here in about twenty minutes. We thought you'd need more convincing." He smiled at me.

I let my eyes focus on his lips. I barely remembered what it was like to kiss him. Why couldn't I remember?

God, maybe I was crazy. It felt like I couldn't focus on anything.

"Fine," V said as he stood up. "I'll be in my room so he doesn't see me."

"Or you could stay and take off your mask."

"Goodnight, Sadie," he said without turning around.

The name Sadie hurt even more than the word friends. Whatever we had was dead. Why had they suddenly decided I needed therapy now? Was it because of my question for V this morning? I hoped he hadn't talked to Liza and Eli about that. It was embarrassing enough hearing him say he didn't love me to my face. I didn't want anyone else to know and whisper about it behind my back. "Can you untie me now?" I asked no one in particular. I didn't want to go outside anymore, but I still wanted to be free. Really, I just wanted to curl up in a ball in my bed and dream. My dreams were the only place I could truly be happy.

Eli sat down beside me and started untying the ropes.

I looked up at him. "You really think I need therapy?"

"I don't know, Summer. Maybe it would help." He pulled the rope away from my feet.

"I'm the same girl I was when I lived with Don. The only difference is that I'm stronger now."

"That's not the only difference." He pulled the final rope away.

I rubbed my wrists as soon as they were free. "Yes, it is."

"The Summer I fell in love with had hope."

His words from earlier today came back to me. He said he didn't even recognize me anymore. "I do have hope. I'm just hoping for something different."

"Don's death instead of the hope to live your life?"

I shook my head. "You wouldn't understand."

"Try me."

My eyes locked with his. "Maybe that's the problem. I don't see a reason to try anymore. Wouldn't it be better if you were relieved when I died instead of missing me?"

Eli lowered his eyebrows. "No. And I think you're underestimating how much I care about you. Even when you've been pushing me away. If you died, I'd miss you every day."

I couldn't help but smile. It was nice to know that at least one person still cared if I was breathing. "But I've been such a bitch."

He laughed. "I never said that."

I leaned over and nudged my shoulder against his.

He nudged mine back. "I know all of this is hard. I lived undercover for over a year. It's easy to lose yourself."

"Yeah." But I wasn't sure that was my problem. If anything, I desperately wanted to forget who I was. I wanted to be able to let go of all the pain I was holding on to. I didn't want to tell Eli that, though. How could you tell someone who liked you that you wanted to throw up every time you looked in the mirror? I hated who he loved. "I hate the snow," I said to break the awkward silence that had settled around us.

"Why?"

I thought I knew why, but my confession held more weight than I imagined. I had lost my baby in a blizzard. Before that I had loved the snow. It reminded me of Miles. Now that I had lost him too? "Nothing good ever happens in the snow."

"Then maybe you shouldn't have been aiming a pistol from an insane distance. If you'd fired it, you would have added to the evidence that nothing good happens when it snows. You could have easily hit a child, Summer."

I wiped a stray tear away. "Maybe I have lost my mind. It just feels like the longer this goes on, the more I lose." I let my eyes meet his again. I had lost Miles. I had lost V. And I had lost Eli too. "No one believes in me anymore." That wasn't exactly what I meant. But how could I tell him that no one loved me anymore? That it felt like for one second I had everything and it was all taken away again?

"I'm not going anywhere."

It was like he could sense my true confession.

He scrunched his mouth to the side, the action that reminded me of Miles so much. My heart constricted.

"Dr. Miller is here." Athena's voice flooded the apartment.

Eli cleared his throat. "Dr. Miller thinks your name is Alison Montgomery. Talk to him, but try not to give him any information he doesn't need." He looked up to one of the cameras mounted in the corner of the living room. "Athena, secure the base." He stood up and put his hand out for me. I ignored the sound of the faux wall descending. It would hide our surely illegal security and training set up. I had thought it was an unnecessary and expensive precaution. But we were finally using it now. Besides, it didn't matter. I had all the money in the world and barely any time to use it.

I slipped my hand into Eli's and he helped me to my feet. "If you want to continue our discussion later, my bedroom door is always unlocked." He squeezed my hand and then dropped it.

I watched him disappear down the hall. Suddenly I didn't feel so alone. I was also very aware of the fact that his touch didn't feel scalding hot.

CHAPTER 5

Sunday

What was I allowed to say? It felt like Dr. Miller could see right through me. I glanced at the camera mounted in the corner of the kitchen. Was V watching me right now?

"Alison?"

I ignored Dr. Miller. How was I supposed to talk about anything with that camera right there?

"Alison?" He reached out and lightly touched my hand.

I immediately pulled away. "I'm sorry, I think agreeing to see you was a mistake."

"Agreeing was the first step, but you need to talk to me. Why don't we start from the beginning. Tell me about your parents."

Was he trying to make my heart bleed? "Clearly you already know all about me."

"On the contrary, Alison. I know nothing about you. My patient said he had a friend that needed help. So here I am."

"You know nothing about me?"

"Not a thing."

I wasn't sure why I was surprised. Why would V talk about me? I meant nothing to him. "The man that recommended I talk to you…" I wasn't exactly sure how to word my question without looking insane. What's his name? If we were friends I'd know his name. "He…"

"I'm not at liberty to discuss any other patients."

That was shut down fast.

"Let's go back to your parents." He jotted something down in the notebook in front of him. "Mentioning them upset you, why is that? Is your relationship with them strained?"

Strained? I clasped my hands together under the table. "My parents died when I was eight years old. I never even got to know what a strained relationship with them would be like."

His pen stopped. "Eight you said?"

"Yes. After that, I lived with my grandmother for awhile, but then she passed away. Then there were more foster families than I care to remember. Until one…stuck."

He put his pen down on top of his notebook. "Have you ever talked to anyone about any of this before?"

I shrugged. "Not all the details, no."

"You've been holding a lot of things close to your chest."

"Not by choice."

"And what do you mean by that?"

I wasn't fond of whatever mind tricks he was trying to play. But I did find it easy to talk to him. "My best friend growing up knew what I had been through. We stayed pen pals while I moved around between foster families. But he stopped writing to me eventually."

"Just stopped? With no explanation?"

"That's what I thought."

He stared at me, waiting for me to elaborate.

"I saw him again recently. He claimed he'd never stopped writing. My foster father must have hijacked his letters."

"Why would your foster father do that?" His voice was gentle. It made it easy to talk to him.

"Our relationship was rather toxic."

Dr. Miller lifted up his pen again. "How so?" He jotted something down in his notebook.

There wasn't really a way to sugarcoat it. "He abused me."

His pen stopped. "Mentally or…"

"Physically. Well, both really." I realized my hands were clasped so tightly that I was cutting off my circulation. I pulled them apart and rubbed them against my thighs.

"Physically how?"

Wasn't it obvious? "What do you think?"

"This isn't a guessing game, Alison. What did he do to you?"

Alison. This man had no idea who I was. So what did it matter if he knew the truth? "He beat me. He raped me. He made me believe that I was worthless." *I think he murdered my parents. He's manipulating this city just like he manipulated me. And he has a bounty on my head.*

Dr. Miller closed his notebook. "I'm not going to pretend to understand the pain you're feeling."

Something about the way he said it made tears well in my eyes. Everyone liked to pretend they understood what I was going through. But they didn't. I respected him for saying that he didn't understand. I closed my eyes to try to stop myself from crying.

"But I do want to help you work through that pain. If you'll let me."

"It won't go away. I can't even get over my parents' deaths. I can't get over anything. It's like I hold it close because I like being miserable."

"Maybe you feel like you deserve to suffer?"

I slowly opened my eyes. "Why?"

"Maybe it's easier to feel pain than taking a chance? Or maybe it's plain old guilt?"

"Guilt? I didn't do anything to deserve this."

"That isn't what I meant. How about we go back to the beginning again. This pen pal. Do you still have feelings for him?"

"Whoever said I had feelings for him?" I didn't like that he thought he knew me after such a brief conversation.

"It was the only time during this whole discussion that you smiled."

Was that true? It didn't matter. "At one point I think I loved him, but I was so young." I shook my head. "That's a lie. I still love him. But I'm not sure if it's because he's the last thing left from my past or because my feelings are real." I shook my head again. "It's probably both."

"And how does that make you feel?"

"Abandoned all over again."

"Why?"

"Because he's moved on with his life. Even though he stood there and told me he was still in love with the real me."

"The real you?"

"It doesn't matter."

"If these feelings are causing you pain, it does matter."

"Heartbreak is the least of my problems right now."

"I think that maybe a lot of the pain you're feeling is stemming from this issue of abandonment. Is there anyone else in your life that you feel has abandoned you?"

"Everyone. No foster family wanted me. I went from house to house. Do you have any idea what that's like when you're already barely holding on?"

He shook his head. When I didn't continue speaking, we just stared at each other. I wasn't sure for how long. But it was like he was examining my confession.

"Who else gave up on you, Alison?" he finally pressed.

"It felt like the state gave up on me. My grandmother died. My parents died."

"Death isn't abandonment."

"It is when you're eight years old!"

"I'm sure your parents loved you. I'm sure they wish they could be here right now."

"No, I don't think so."

"And why do you say that, Alison?"

"They'd be ashamed of who I've become."

"Are you sure it's not you who's ashamed of who you've become?"

I didn't even know what to say. He was probably spot on. But it didn't take away my feeling of resentment for everyone who'd left me on my own. It was my worst fears coming true though. I was terrified of becoming a monster like Don. What if it was too late?

"Even if I am ashamed of myself, it doesn't take away this feeling that I'm on my own. V…" I coughed. "I mean…the man that recommended you speak to me. He can't even stand me. It feels like he made me fall for him, and then as soon as he had my love, he pushed me to the side. It's not just in my head. No one ever stays."

Dr. Miller lifted up his notebook and slid it into his satchel. "I don't think he's going anywhere."

"Why do you say that?"

"Our mutual friend has greatly benefited from you being in his life. I don't believe he's trying to push you away. Have you ever considered that you just don't know him as well as you think you do?"

"I barely know him at all. He never talks about himself."

"Have you ever asked?"

"Of course."

He nodded. "Regardless, I truly believe he will not be abandoning you. It's not in his nature. Especially when it comes to you."

"Why do you say that?"

"It's like his heart thawed throughout the past 6 months. When you showed up in his life."

"I thought he never mentioned me?"

"That's true. He's never mentioned you, Alison. I need to get going. But we can meet again if you'd like. How about Wednesday evening at the same time?"

"I…um…"

"Your friend has my number. I'll see you then."

He walked away without waiting for my response. And I had an eerie feeling that he knew exactly who I was.

CHAPTER 6
Monday

Even though all the blinds were closed in the apartment, I still knew it was snowing. It was like I could taste the snowflakes on my tongue, like I could imagine making snow angels, like I could see the blood.

Stop. I wasn't sure I knew how to be alone when it snowed. My memories haunted me. Sometimes it felt like the good memories were just as painful as the bad ones.

I stepped out of my bedroom and closed the door behind me. My bare feet were cold as I tiptoed down the hall as quietly as I could. Eli had said his door was always unlocked. He hadn't invited me to spend the night in his room, he had just mentioned that we could continue our discussion. But I didn't want to talk. I just didn't want to feel alone. And Eli wasn't the person for that.

I stopped and stared at V's door instead. I had almost done something stupid today. A child could have easily gotten hurt. My behavior was becoming more sporadic and everyone could sense it. I was worried that I didn't remember what it felt like to be sane.

But for one night, I wanted to forget about everything. I wanted to feel safe. I wanted to feel loved. *Please be awake.* I tried to turn the handle and wasn't at all surprised that it was locked.

I lightly tapped my knuckle against the door. *Nothing.* I did it again, ever so quietly. "V," I whispered. I had this ridiculous notion that if I could thaw his heart, maybe he could thaw mine.

Mine wasn't frozen though. It was broken. It had been broken ever since my parents died. It shattered even more when Miles stopped writing. And it was irreparable after I lost my baby.

I felt that. In my head and my heart. There was nothing to hold on to. I stepped away from V's door. Two broken souls couldn't repair one another, no matter how much I wanted to believe they could.

I was about to retreat back to my room when I stopped. It felt like the snow was swirling around in my head, freezing every corner of my brain. A broken soul couldn't mend me. But there was one person who could help. Before I could talk myself out of it, I walked over to Eli's room and opened the door. It was unlocked, just like he said it would be. And he was doing exactly what any normal person should be doing at 1 in the morning. Sleeping. This was a mistake. I was about to retreat when he yawned and turned toward me.

"Summer?" He slowly sat up.

His voice sounded so innocent when it was doused with exhaustion. The 26-year-old man I had come to know looked more like a child than an adult. His hair was mussed up from the pillow and his eyes were hooded. It reminded me of how Miles looked when I woke him up in the middle of the night. *I really shouldn't be here.* But something kept me frozen in place.

I watched as he grabbed a pair of glasses off his nightstand. I smiled when he put them on. "I didn't know you wore glasses."

"Only when I'm not wearing contacts."

The air suddenly felt heavy, like there were a million things I needed to say if I wanted to be able to breathe again. Instead of saying anything, though, I closed the door behind me and walked over to his bed.

He pushed the covers back. "Just let me get dressed and we can talk."

"I don't want to talk."

He got out of bed anyway and grabbed a t-shirt off the ground. I watched his abs disappear beneath it. No one should have been allowed to look that good in pajama bottoms and a t-shirt.

"I mean…I do want to talk. But I just want you to listen. I need to get some stuff off my chest."

He stared at me from the other side of the bed. "Do you want to go for a walk?"

"No, it's freezing out." I looked down at his bed. I wanted to be curled up in it with his arms around me. V not opening his door was a blessing. My future was grim. And I didn't belong in the past. For once in my life I needed to truly embrace the present. Eli was the only person that seemed to know how to do that.

There was so much I needed to say. I took a deep breath. "I've been in love with Miles Young since I was six years old."

Eli lowered his eyebrows.

"I can't even explain why. When I was a kid, I was just convinced for no reason in particular that he was the one for me. And I think I held on to that for all these years because he reminded me of home. But he doesn't care about me anymore. Young love is supposed to fade. It didn't for me because I lost so much. My head is messed up."

"Summer…"

"But I don't want to love him. I don't. And I'm pretty sure a bigger part of me hates him for forgetting about me." I shook my head. I wasn't making sense. God, how could I make him understand? "He's my past. I'm so sick of living in the past.

"And I think I became infatuated with V because I knew it could never be more. He always talked about borrowed time or some stupid crap like that. You know how he is."

Eli pressed his lips together.

I shook my head. "But I think I hate him even more than I hate Miles." At least Miles had never told me he loved me and taken it back. "He's a murderer. He's a monster. And I'm so scared of becoming like him."

This wasn't coming out right. Why was I talking about everyone but him? "I've been so confused. And so…stupid. I was so consumed with living in the past and trying to embrace this darkness that no one should ever want to embrace, that I completely missed what was right in front of me the whole time."

The corners of Eli's mouth turned up ever so slightly.

"You were the first person I told the truth to. That I wanted to kill Don. There was a reason for that. I trust you, Eli. You see me for what I am."

He started to walk around the bed.

"I was happy in the past, I was. And it's nice to think that the future will be better. But this right now? This is me. I'm so tired of hating myself every day. There's nothing wrong with me. I don't need therapy. And I don't need to talk. I just need to learn how to be happy again. I need someone to remind me that I'm not as broken as I feel. Because I'm standing right here breathing. I think I pushed you away because I didn't want to accept all that I had lost. But I never meant to lose you in the process. I miss you, Eli. And I'm pretty sure you're the only person I don't hate at all."

He stopped right in front of me. "You never lost me. I was trying to give you space and hoping you'd forgive me."

"For what?"

"For not knowing that Don hurt you."

I looked at the pain on his face. The small lines on the outside of his eyes. The sadness in his eyes.

"I did my best every day to hide it," I said. "How could you have known?"

He shook his head. "It kills me, knowing that I missed the signs."

That was the other thing I loved about him. He actually felt bad for hurting me. I wasn't sure there was a better quality, besides for not hurting someone in the first place. And from my experience, that wasn't possible. "I forgive you."

The lines around his eyes faded and it seemed as though he exhaled the pain.

It was the most glorious thing I had ever seen. It was better than some dumb constellation in the sky. It was real and tangible and wonderfully had nothing to do with Miles. "I don't want to face any of this alone anymore."

"It's about time you realized that you don't have to."

I smiled. And when I exhaled, it felt like I let go of some of my pain too.

The awkwardness settled around us again.

"I like your glasses," I said.

At the exact same time, Eli said, "I'm glad you came."

Our words collided together and we both laughed.

Eli touched the side of his glasses. "I guess I should wear them more often then."

I nodded. "It's very Clark Kent of you."

"Except I'm not the superhero who lives here."

I sat down on the edge of his bed. "I've wished for a lot of things in my life. But I never wished for one of those. I've always preferred a knight in shining armor."

Eli didn't move forward, he stayed exactly where he was. "Summer Brooks, you are not some tortured girl that needs to be saved."

I pressed my lips together. Four months ago when I thought I was going to die, I had told him that I didn't want him to save me and that I didn't need saving. Had my words haunted him like so much haunted me?

"I'm not asking you to save me, Eli. I'm asking you to take me as I am." I realized I was holding my breath. For one second.

His eyes locked with mine.

For two seconds. He stepped forward.

For three seconds. He put his hand on the side of my face.

For four seconds. The silence settled around us.

For five seconds. I leaned into his touch. For the first time, it didn't feel like he was making my skin burn. Or maybe I had just lost the fire in me.

CHAPTER 7

Monday

For the first morning in months, I woke up with a smile on my face. I was surrounded by the smell of citrus and sunshine. It was one of my favorite smells in the world. Just from his intoxicating scent, I would have known I was near Eli even if his arms hadn't been wrapped around me. I slowly opened my eyes and found Eli staring at me.

"God you're beautiful," he said.

"Were you watching me sleep?" I tried to block my face from his view.

He pulled my hand away and placed a gentle kiss against my lips.

I laughed and squirmed away from him. "Don't kiss me, I have morning breath."

He caught me around the waist and pulled me back against his chest. "Try to stop me." His lips met mine again and I didn't resist him at all. I'd asked him to take me as I was. He seemed more than ready to do just that.

"You know what we need?" I asked as I smiled up at him.

"To stay in here all day?"

I laughed. "Yes. But we also need hot chocolate. What is a snow day without hot chocolate?" I managed to escape his grasp and climbed out of bed. God, it felt good to smile and laugh. I felt like a weight had been lifted off my shoulders. I would have said I felt like a kid again, but I didn't. I felt better. I was me, and for the first time, I was actually okay with that.

"How do you know it's snowing?" He pushed the covers back and yawned. "You haven't even looked outside."

"Can't you feel it?"

"Feel what?"

"That tingly feeling in your bones? The quietness of the city like it's wrapped up in a blanket? The buzz of excitement in the air?"

He laughed. "Oh those things. Normally I'd just look outside or at the weather forecast…"

I opened up the curtains and gestured without bothering to look. I knew it was snowing. I didn't need a weatherman or eyes to know it.

"Huh. You really could feel it."

I smiled and turned to look out the window. The snow danced in the wind. And it didn't bring back painful memories. It just made me happy. Today was about making new memories. I turned back to Eli. "So about that hot chocolate." I raised my left eyebrow.

"Two hot chocolates coming right up." He got out of bed and stretched.

"On second thought…" I left the window and jumped back onto the bed. "Maybe the hot chocolate could wait a minute." I gave him what I hoped was a seductive smile.

"A minute?" He shook his head. "I'm going to need much longer than a minute."

I laughed as he climbed back in bed with me.

***

"Are you sure you don't want my help?" I asked as I sat down at the kitchen counter.

"I know my way around a cup of hot chocolate." He grabbed two mugs out of the cupboard.

"Is that so?"

"There's a few secret ingredients that make my hot chocolate the best in the world."

I laughed. "Aren't you cocky today?"

"You'll see for yourself in just a few minutes." He twisted off the cap on the milk carton and started to pour milk into one of the mugs.

"What are you doing?"

He ignored me.

I slid off my stool. "You can't do it that way," I said and pushed the mug away from him before he could pour any more of the milk.

"What do you mean?" He slid the mug back into place.

I grabbed the milk carton away from him. "What on earth are you thinking? You can't make hot chocolate in the microwave, you lunatic."

"Why not?"

"Because it's best on the stove," V said from behind us.

I glanced over my shoulder to see him scowling at me. He tilted his head down so that his hoodie shadowed his eyes.

Suddenly I wasn't in the mood for hot chocolate anymore. My stomach felt like it had flipped over. "Right." I placed the milk on the counter. V looked upset. Why? And why did I even care? I grabbed a pan to distract myself and turned on a burner. "You have to do it on the stove." My voice came out as a whisper, like the past was trying to catch back up with me.

It wasn't V I was upset about. It was the reason why I preferred it on the stove. That was the way Miles' mom had always prepared it for us. The two men around me started to blur away in a memory. I closed my eyes and took a deep breath, willing the memory to go back to where it belonged.

"No, I like it just the way it is," I said and pulled my hot chocolate away from Miles.

"I know, but I'm telling you it's better with whipped cream." He stared at me like I was the dumbest person on the planet.

I was not an idiot. And he was being mean again for no reason at all. "It's better with marshmallows...doofus." It was the strongest insult I could think of off the top of my head.

He laughed.

I tried not to let the sound make me smile, but I felt the corners of my mouth lifting.

"Have you ever even tried it with whipped cream?" Miles asked.

I started tapping my heels against the wooden stool. "No."

"Then you stop being a doofus." He moved the can of whipped cream closer to my mug and I pushed it away.

He glared at me.

I glared back.

"You're a ridiculous human being, Summer."

For a moment I just let myself be happy that he had actually acknowledged me by name. "At least I'm a good human."

"What is that supposed to mean?" Miles set the whipped cream down on the counter.

"I care about all animals. I follow my parents' rules as best as I can. And my dad says I'm the sweetest person in the whole wide world."

Miles laughed.

"And I'm actually nice to everyone." I crossed my arms in front of my chest. "Unlike some people," I added under my breath.

He laughed. "Just try it, will you? And I'll try the stupid marshmallows."

"Never." I lifted up my hot chocolate with marshmallows and took a huge sip. "It's hot!" I started fanning my mouth. Ow. I stuck out my tongue and Miles took the opportunity to spray a huge dollop of whipped cream on my tongue.

It immediately cooled my mouth down.

"Good, right?" He stuck his tongue out and squirted some on it.

I laughed and some of the whipped cream flew off my tongue and into my hot chocolate. I looked down at the ruined beverage.

"Trust me, you're going to like it."

I looked back up at Miles. He was already sipping his hot cocoa like it wasn't scalding hot. And he was smiling. I really did like his smile. Maybe a little whipped cream wasn't the worst thing in the world. Especially if it made him this happy.

"You okay?" Eli asked. His hand on my shoulder finally pulled me back to the present.

"What?" I shook my head and turned off the burner. "Oh. Yeah, I'm fine. Actually, I want to try it your way. Microwaved milk and all."

"Yeah?"

I nodded. "I'm sure it'll be great." If I had been willing to try it Miles' way, I could try it Eli's way. Miles had been right too, hot cocoa was really yummy with whipped cream.

Eli started pouring milk into the mugs again. "Do you want any, V?" he asked.

When V didn't respond, Eli turned around. "Huh. Guess he's not a big fan of hot chocolate."

I looked back too, and V was gone. "I guess not," I said.

CHAPTER 8
Monday

Our daily meeting was about to occur. Liza and V would brief me on whatever small updates there were, most likely keeping out important details they didn't want to divulge. And I'd feel hopeless. I took a deep breath. I could feel myself sinking back into the darkness.

For a moment it was like Eli had fixed me. The memory of Miles had shaken my new resolve, though. It didn't help that Eli's hot chocolate wasn't very good. It was decent, but it was nothing like Mrs. Young's. I missed her. Would I ever see her again? Most likely not. I shook the thought away.

"Hey," Liza said and sat down beside me.

She usually never sat near me. Her seat of choice was right next to V. I took it as an olive branch. "I'm sorry about last night," I said. "I know you've given up a lot to be part of this and that you were forced into it. I really appreciate that you're here."

"You seem to be in a much better mood."

I shrugged. "The therapy session actually helped." I knew it was more than that, though. It was Eli. Why was I suddenly doubting everything?

"Good. And just for the record, I'm happy to be here. Spending this much time with V has been so nice."

"Mhm. How is that going by the way?"

She smiled. "Amazing. Today we went for a walk in the snow. Well, actually more of a stroll on the roof, but it was very romantic."

"Cool." I drew out the word to make it not sound cool at all. I cleared my throat. "Has he told you anything about who he is? Or his past or anything?"

"Look, I know you two had a fling, if that's what you're wondering. And I'm totally okay with it. There doesn't need to be any awkward tension between us. Especially because it's over."

"Is that what he said?"

She shrugged. "He didn't have to. You guys have been ice cold with each other for months. Thanks for stepping back. I know you knew I liked him. I really appreciate it."

"Mhm. He's all yours."

She smiled and pushed her glasses up her nose. "For the record, the only thing I had to give up to be here was my apartment. You were right."

"I didn't mean any of that. I was upset."

"But it's true," said Liza. "And I'm sorry about everything you've lost. I really am, Summer."

I nodded. I didn't really know what to say. It wasn't just V that had been cold toward me recently, it was her too. This was the first time it had ever felt like we might be friends.

"Hey," Eli said as he sat down across from me. "How are you doing, Liza?"

"Good. I like your glasses," she said with a smile. Her cheeks turned a little pink.

Maybe we weren't great friends yet. I was pretty sure friends weren't supposed to get jealous of each other. And I was certainly a little jealous now. She wasn't allowed to like V *and* Eli. But wasn't that what I had been doing?

God, what did I even know about friendship? The closest friend I'd had recently was my college roommate Kins and it had been months since I had spoken to her. She thought I had moved away. Maybe jealousy between friends was a normal thing. I smiled to myself. Maybe I was finally becoming normal.

V walked into the room and the floor immediately lit up blue. I wasn't sure how Athena knew that it was him, but she treated him like a rock star. He sat down across from Liza and dropped a folder on the table.

"What's that?" Liza asked.

V scooted his chair in. "I have some bad news, Sadie."

Liza grabbed the folder and opened it up. There was a picture of Mr. Crawford. I leaned over to look at it. He was surrounded by tall buildings and was looking over his shoulder like he could tell someone was watching him. Two people were walking beside him, but they weren't facing the camera. Their winter coats and hats covered anything that might help identify them. Although, from their heights, it looked like one was male and one was female. Snow was piled on either side of the walkway. The picture had been taken recently.

"He's alive?" My throat felt dry. We had been looking for him for months.

"Yes."

I grabbed the folder and pulled it toward myself. "How is that bad news? He's alive! Maybe that means Julie is too." We had thought that it was most likely that my old babysitter was dead. I pointed to the picture. "Is it possible that this is her and her fiancé?" The woman was wearing snow boots. Although I doubted Julie still owned her old converses. And if she did, she wouldn't wear them in the snow.

"I don't think that's Julie."

"But it could be. They could all be alive." I breathed a little easier at the thought.

He shook his head. "There's been buzz on the streets for weeks about a meeting of the Helspet Mafia. Known criminals have been flooding the streets. Mr. Crawford came back just a few days before it's going to take place."

"That's a coincidence. He was definitely trying to help me. He…"

"He's working for Don," V said, cutting me off. "I'm sorry, Sadie."

I looked back down at the picture. I remembered his kind smile. And his eyes. There was no death in his eyes. "You're wrong. He wanted me to have a fresh start. He kept saying that he hoped it would be the last time he ever spoke to me or saw me…"

"Exactly, Sadie. He expected you to die."

"That's not what he meant." God, what if that's what he meant?

"Regardless, it's about time we did that blood sample. We'll need to know how to engage with him if we come into contact."

V had been trying to get a blood sample from me for months. But I had no desire to know if I was related to

Mr. Crawford. "You want to know if you're allowed to kill him if you see him?"

V didn't respond.

"You're not allowed to kill him. I don't care if we're related or not. He's a good man."

"He's working for Don. You remember Don, right? You tried to put a bullet in his skull last night. This is no different."

"But Mr. Crawford didn't rape me!" My words bounced off the walls and echoed oddly.

All three of them stared at me. The silence stretched around us, making it hard for me to breathe.

"I do not need a blood test," I said as calmly as I could. "No matter what, Mr. Crawford isn't my father."

"But what if he is, Sadie?"

"Like I said, I wouldn't want you to kill him either way. You're wrong about him. He's not working for Don."

"Summer's right," Liza said. "This is circumstantial evidence at best. He could have come to the city for a variety of reasons."

Thank you, Liza.

"And why didn't you talk to me about this on our walk earlier? This was clearly taken last night, V."

For some reason I wanted to take back my silent thank you. Maybe it was the way she had said V. It made me nauseous.

"He's recruiting," V said and tapped on the image. "I'm sure of it."

I looked back at the two people. V couldn't possibly know that from a picture. It did appear that they were all walking together, that had been my first thought too. But looking at it again? The other two people were walking much closer together. There was a gap between them and Mr. Crawford. "It looks like those two are together," I said. "They probably don't even know Mr. Crawford."

"They were speaking to him right before I snapped the picture."

"Oh, okay. In that case you should have just shot them all on sight then." *You maniac.*

"I needed to talk to you first…"

"I was joking, V! You're not allowed to go around killing people you don't even know. Have you completely lost it?"

"Me? You almost shot a child."

"That…that's an exaggeration."

"You've completely lost control, Sadie. I vote that you can no longer leave the apartment. All in favor?"

"Fuck you, V." My words were icier than I had meant for them to be. "I'm not some animal that you can keep caged up in your secret lair."

"It's *your* apartment."

Why was he acting like a stubborn five-year-old? God, I wanted to strangle him. "I'm going out." I needed some fresh air before I did something I regretted, if it wasn't already too late.

"No you're not," he said. "We haven't voted yet. All in favor?"

"Don't bother voting on my freedom. Because even if you do say I can't go, I'm leaving anyway." I stood up.

"Maybe you shouldn't leave right this second, Summer…" Eli's voice trailed off when I glared at him.

Was he seriously agreeing with V? I thought we had been on the same page today. And last night. Screw him too. "I'll even leave my gun here so you can all feel better." I reached into my sweater and pulled it out.

Liza immediately put her hands into the air and her eyes grew wider than usual, if that was possible.

Did she really think I was going to shoot her? I set my gun down on the table. "Have fun with your vote. Obviously I vote nay, not that my vote ever seems to matter." I stormed past them and the ground lit up red underneath my feet. *Screw you too, Athena.*

CHAPTER 9
Monday

The happiness I had finally just grasped was slipping through my fingers. It was one thing to be ignored. Venom being thrown at me for no reason was completely out of line. What the hell had even set V off? According to Liza they had a super great date earlier. He should have been chipper if anything.

I balled my hands into fists and stared out at the city. The blanket of snow should have been calming, but it wasn't. It made the taste of blood fill my mouth.

I took a deep breath and watched my exhale fog the air in front of me. Mr. Crawford was alive. I wanted to feel relief. But what if he was working for Don? I exhaled again and stared at my breath. What if he was my father?

"I thought you hated the snow." V stepped up beside me and stared out at the city street.

"Yeah, but I didn't used to."

"What made you change your mind?"

I kept staring out at the snow. "Why did you come up here, V? I know it wasn't for pointless small talk."

He sighed and the air from his breath collided with mine. "Eli and Liza both voted with you. You're free to do as you please...under the other rules of course."

"Right. Only come outside at night unless I'm wearing a disguise. Now if you'll excuse me, I want to be alone."

"Do you though?"

I finally turned toward him. "Yes."

"Liza told me that you said the therapist helped."

"That's perfect. How about the two of you keep talking about me behind my back and leave me alone?"

"Whatever you want, Sadie." He started to walk away.

God, it hit a nerve every time he called me that. "Would you just call me by my real name?"

He kept walking away from me.

"My name is Summer Brooks, you psychopath!"

"You are not Summer Brooks." His voice rumbled lower than usual as he turned back around.

My heart stammered against my chest. "What do you mean by that?"

"Nothing." He turned back around and kept walking.

"V, what do you mean?"

He didn't respond so I started running after him.

There was only one reasonable explanation. "Did you know me when I was a kid?"

He was almost to the fire escape.

I couldn't run any faster in the snow. "V!" My feet slipped on a sheet of ice and I landed hard on my ass. *Ow.* I tried to stand up but my feet slid again. And that was why you didn't wear converses in the snow. Before V completely disappeared, I made a snowball and tossed it at him.

It made direct contact with his upper back. He immediately stopped. A laugh escaped his throat. "You're so going to pay for that." He bent down and started making a snowball.

Shit. I shifted to my knees and was able to get up just as a snowball hit me.

"I knew you loved the snow," he said. He grabbed my arm before I was able to make another snowball.

I tried to search his face. "You knew me."

"A lifetime ago." He lowered his head so I couldn't see his eyes.

"And you won't call me Summer because…"

"Because you're nothing like her."

I had been trying to hold on to my past for so long. But there was no point if I held no resemblance to the kid I used to be. It hurt. I had been ready to give up my past last night. But now that there was no way to bring Summer Brooks back? I swallowed hard. "When did you know me?"

He didn't respond.

"Did you love me then?" I moved closer to him.

Nothing.

"Is that why you said it when you thought we were going to die? Because it used to be true?"

His silence was driving me crazy. I got close enough to breathe in his exhales. *Tell me the truth.* "What about now? Do you hate me?"

"I think I hate you more than I ever loved you."

For some reason, I didn't believe him. I smiled. "I hate you more."

He laughed. "Is that why you're trying to kiss me?"

"I'm not trying to kiss you." But I didn't step back. Was I trying to kiss him? There was such a small space between us that snow could barely fall through it. "I've decided to see how things go with Eli actually."

"What?"

"I'm going to date Eli."

"You can't."

"This isn't something you can vote on, V." I tried to take a step back but his grip prevented me from moving. "You said yourself that we don't end up together, remember?"

"That doesn't mean you end up with *him*." There was venom in his voice.

"I don't see why you care."

"You're mine, Sadie."

The way he said it made my heart race. "To hate?"

"Just until I'm able to love every part of you again. The space between us doesn't have to be the way it has been. I'll show you tonight. I'll give you whatever you need. Don't go running back to Eli. I just need more time."

"To fall back in love with me? I don't even know who you are."

"We're not running out of time anymore. You'll find out when we're both ready. Besides, if I recall correctly, you love when I fuck you." He released me from his grip and walked away in the snow.

I didn't want to be hated. I wanted to be loved. He couldn't have been more wrong. So why hadn't I corrected him?

CHAPTER 10
Monday

I pulled on a different pair of pajama bottoms. *No.* I ditched all my clothes, pulled on a silk robe instead, and stared in the mirror. This was so stupid. It didn't matter what I wore. What mattered was who I went to. I sat down on the edge of my bed and put my face in my hands.

Eli loved me. V hated me. What was I even debating? Yet, I couldn't make myself leave my room. It was tempting to just lock the door and not decide at all.

"It's like his heart thawed." Dr. Miller's words came back to me. Why had V's heart needed to thaw in the first place? All I could think about were the different foster kids I had lived with. V must have been a boy I used to know. Was he one of them?

But none of them stood out in my head as liking me. Let alone hating me. I was never chosen at any of the foster homes for adoption. There couldn't be resentment there. I was missing something. Maybe he was older than I realized. I needed to talk to him again in order to figure it out.

I stood up and wandered into the hall. For just a moment, I hesitated in front of V's door. Yes I needed to talk to him. But that wasn't what he was offering me. And I definitely wouldn't find any comfort in V's arms. It used to feel like he was absorbing my pain, like he truly was a superhero and that was his power. But I knew he didn't have any powers. My pain went away when I was with him because he understood it. And I didn't want to be with someone who understood my pain.

I wanted someone who was able to rid me of my pain completely. Someone good. Someone happy. Someone who made me feel normal. I could talk to V in the morning. Nothing good would happen if I stepped into his room. I kept walking down the hall and opened up Eli's door.

He set down the book he was reading. "I wasn't sure if you were coming."

"Where else would I go?"

He stood up and walked over to me. "V left shortly after you did. I was trying to give you some space, but...I figured he might have gone to talk to you."

I hadn't moved from his doorway.

Eli stopped walking when he was right in front of me. "I thought he might try to convince you to be with him again." His words were so honest. And I could feel his hesitancy.

Did he think I was here to say goodbye? "So you wanted to see what I'd do? You could have just come after me too." I smiled up at him.

"I needed to know. I don't want to share your heart with V and Miles. I want you all to myself. Because despite what you think, I love all of you. Every single piece of you."

I blinked away the tears in my eyes. "V did try to get me to choose him." I closed the door behind me and locked it. The sound of the lock clicking echoed around the small room. "And he failed."

"Is that so?"

Eli was so close that I could smell the citrus on his skin. It reminded me of summer and sunshine. I was choosing to live in the light, and I didn't doubt my choice for a second. "I love you, Eli. And only you." I undid the sash on my robe and let it fall open. "Every single piece of…"

His lips colliding with mine drowned out my words. I pushed up his t-shirt, letting my fingers wander over his six pack. He grabbed his shirt and pulled it the rest of the way off before grabbing my thighs and lifting my legs around his waist. He was about to carry me over to his bed, but I grabbed the doorknob. I didn't want that. I wanted him right this second. "I want you right here."

"I'll always give you whatever you want."

I kissed the side of his neck and listened to the sound of his zipper. And the sound of foil ripping.

But instead of the feeling that I was craving, his fingers slowly traced my wetness.

"Please, Eli. I need you."

"You just told me that you loved me, Summer. Let me cherish you." His eyes wandered to my breasts. "Every inch of you."

"I know how you feel. But right now I just need to feel you."

He placed the tip of his cock against me. "Is that so?"

"Stop teasing me," I said with a laugh. "Please."

"Hmm." He shifted slightly forward, driving me crazy.

I tightened my legs around his waist, forcing him to thrust into me harder than I think we both expected. *God.*

"Fuck," he groaned into my mouth.

I grabbed the back of his neck, ensuring that his lips wouldn't leave mine. I never wanted to stop tasting him. Or feeling him. Or loving him. "I love you."

He unwrapped my hands from his body and pressed them against the door. "I love you too." He moved his hips faster, hitting me in all the right places.

I believed his words even though what we were doing screamed fucking not making love. It's what I wanted. The roughness of the door and the soft silk somehow made it even better. It was raw and real. This was the best way to feel.

And the longer I spent with him, the more I realized that he was able to take away my pain. Love was so much stronger than hate.

He tilted his hips at just the right angle.

"Yes, Eli!"

He kissed the side of my jaw and tightened his hands around mine. "Say my name again."

"Eli!"

I felt his cock pulse just as I exploded into a million pieces. And for the first time in years, it actually felt like someone loved every single one of those pieces of me.

***

Eli reached forward and brushed a strand of hair out of my face. "Can I ask you something?"

I stared into his brown eyes and willed him not to ruin the moment. "Anything."

"Last night you said that you hated both V and Miles. But that wasn't always the case. Did something happen? That made you change your mind?"

I thought about my conversation with V from the other day. Where he said he never meant to say he loved me. I thought about Miles laughing with the blonde girl outside my old dorm building. "Honestly? I think I finally saw both of them for what they were: memories. And I needed to move on."

He searched my face. "I don't want to be your third choice."

I put my hand on the center of his chest. "Eli, you couldn't be a consolation prize even if you tried."

He smiled.

"I'm sorry if I made you feel that way. I can't even express how happy I am right now. I don't even remember the last time I smiled this much. And I know I changed my mind about them. But I don't intend to change my mind about you, Eli Serrano." His last name sounded strange out loud. I think it was the first time I had ever said it.

He raised his eyebrow. "Still getting used to my real last name?"

"I'm just so used to thinking of you as Eli Hayes. But Serrano has a nice ring to it. Summer Serrano." As soon as I said it, I pressed my lips together. Crap, had I really just said that out loud?

He laughed.

"God, please pretend I didn't say that. I didn't mean it. I was just trying to say Serrano out loud a few times to get used to it."

"Mhm."

"I was!" I lightly nudged his shoulder.

"Actually, I think Summer Serrano has a nice ring to it."

"You do?"

"Once we get out of this mess, maybe we can make it official. I know how much you like changing your name."

I wanted to laugh at his joke. But he'd kind of just proposed. Hadn't he? It felt like my heart was going to beat out of my ribcage. I had only ever dreamed of marrying one boy. My heart used to beat for Miles. Now? I exhaled slowly. Now I could picture it with Eli. I could as clear as day. Eli wasn't just some childhood fantasy. He was real. He had moved to New York to help me. Hell, he had given up his career to help me. He wasn't some childhood dream, but that didn't mean he wasn't the man of my dreams.

"I do like changing my name," I said. "Sometimes I forget that you're 26 and ready for so much more than boyfriend and girlfriend labels."

"I'm patient. There's no rush, Summer."

But I wanted that happy ending. I felt like I deserved it. Like I had waited my whole life to get to smile again. The white picket fence. The kids. It felt like a knife cut through my heart. "You're really okay with the fact that I can't have children?"

"We've already talked about this. We can adopt. Some cute little kid that needs us."

I loved that idea. And I loved him. I truly did. Why had I spent so much time pushing him away? He was so much better than sad memories, so distant and cold. My future finally felt bright. "I'd really like that. And maybe we can move back out west? I hate New York."

He laughed. "Me too. We can go to some small little town and start fresh. Maybe I can even get reinstated eventually. Or we can do something together. I know how much you like hot chocolate. We could open a bakery or something."

"Very funny. But that actually sounds kinda perfect. We'll have a hot cocoa shop with several little kids running around." It was not at all what I originally pictured for my future. But it sounded fantastic now.

"Several, huh?"

I laughed as he pulled me on top of him.

CHAPTER 11
Wednesday

"The Helspet Mafia meeting is confirmed for tomorrow night," Liza said as she switched off her laptop and pulled her earbuds out of her ears. "I was able to pick up audio at the deli down the street. We have a location and everything."

I had thought she was listening to music during our whole meeting. That made a lot more sense.

"Perfect. So our plan is to find William Crawford and extract him," Eli said.

"Peacefully," I added.

"Right. This is it, Summer. We're finally going to get some answers." He gave me a reassuring smile.

I had felt relaxed for the past couple of days. But hearing Eli say that made me feel even better. I smiled back at him. Everything was finally coming together. My mind was no longer consumed with thoughts of revenge. It was filled with thoughts of a future that was actually bright.

"Great," V said. "We can go through particulars tomorrow morning since Sadie has an appointment in a few minutes."

"Actually," Eli said. "Summer and I have been talking and we think it's best if she stops seeing Dr. Miller. She said last time wasn't very helpful. And we've been talking a lot of things out. She definitely doesn't need him."

I grabbed Eli's hand under the table. I had asked him to help get me out of my next appointment. *Thank you.* I squeezed his hand.

V looked down at Eli and my intertwined fingers beneath the glass table. "The two of you have been talking it out?" he asked.

"Mhm," I said. "Really, I feel so much better about everything. It's like a weight has been lifted off my shoulders."

"You do seem happier," Liza said. "I've never seen you smile so much."

"Thanks, Liza." *I guess?*

"So let me get this straight," V said. "You're just magically mentally stable after a chat with Eli…the disgraced detective?"

"Look, V…" Eli started.

"I'm not talking to you, Eli. And the answer is no, Sadie. Dr. Miller's already on his way. It's too late to cancel."

"She said no, man," Eli said and dropped my hand. "We don't take orders from you. Get it through your thick skull."

"Sadie," V said, ignoring Eli. "Please."

"Why don't you just take the appointment? He's your therapist. And I'm doing better. Really."

"So that's it? You've been in a terrible mood for months and all you needed was to fuck Eli to feel magically better, like a common hooker?"

Eli stood up. "If the next words out of your mouth aren't an apology, I'm going to beat the shit out of you."

"Stop." *Jesus*. "Both of you just stop. I'll talk to Dr. Miller, alright? And thanks, V." I didn't say it sarcastically. I meant it. If there had been any doubts in my mind that I was making the right choice by being with Eli, they had just evaporated. *A common hooker. Fuck him.* I stood up and started walking away from them.

"You're welcome," I heard his voice rumble from behind me.

It made the tiny hairs on the back of my neck stand up.

***

"There you are," Eli said as he walked into his bedroom. "I've been looking all over for you." He sat down next to me.

The mattress sagged slightly which made me fall into his side. I snuggled into his shoulder as he wrapped his arm around me.

"I told him if he ever talked to you like that again that I'd kill him," Eli said.

I laughed. "Thanks, but I'm pretty good at handling his wrath."

"You don't have to talk to Dr. Miller if you don't want to. No one is making you."

I looked up at him. "Actually I was hoping you'd see him with me. Talking to him actually was kinda helpful. And maybe we could learn a little more about each other too."

"Yeah, of course." He pulled me closer.

"I do need to tell you a few things. Before we meet with him. Just in case it comes up. I don't want to blind-side you."

He didn't respond, he just waited.

"I've slept with V. It was a while ago but…"

"I know, Summer. And if I'm being honest, I'd really rather not hear the details. All I care about is that it's over."

"It is." I swallowed hard. "There is one more thing. I also slept with Miles."

"What? When?" He dropped his hand from my shoulder.

"The night before the explosion. I thought I was going to die. It meant nothing. I mean…I thought it did. I guess I hoped that it would. I've always had a special place in my heart for Miles. But it was completely one-sided. I gave him a letter about who I really was because I thought I was going to die. I wanted him to know the truth. And he hasn't given Summer Brooks a second thought since. I'm pretty sure he's dating someone new."

"You told him you were Summer Brooks? That was incredibly dangerous. We all agreed…"

"Yeah, but it didn't even matter. He doesn't care. Whatever we had when we were kids is over. It's been over for years now. I was just trying to hold on to something from my past."

"I don't know what you want me to say."

"I want you to say you want us to work." I straddled him on the bed. "I want you to say that you forgive me. I want you to say that you still love me."

His hands settled on my waist. He pushed his mouth to the side in the way that reminded me of Miles. But this time I just liked the way it looked on him.

"If Miles showed up outside our door saying that he always loved you, would you take him back?" Eli asked.

I shook my head without even thinking. "It's too late." I stared into Eli's eyes. "It's definitely too late."

"Same with V?"

I laughed. "God yes."

He smiled. "I want us to work. I forgive you. And I love you."

I was pretty sure he was the sweetest man on the planet. "Any secrets *you* want to share before we talk to Dr. Miller?"

"I'm an open book," he said. "But he is waiting if you want to get this over with."

"Oh, I didn't realize he was already here." I climbed off his lap. "I am sorry," I whispered as we walked out of his room.

"I already forgave you." He kissed my temple.

Dr. Miller was sitting at the kitchen table like last time. He was clicking his pen opened and closed and looking at the false wall that hid so many secrets. When he saw us, the clicking stopped.

"Alison, it's good to see you again. And…"

"Eli," Eli said and stepped forward to shake his hand. Eli sat down in one of the chairs across from Dr. Miller.

"Nice to meet you, Eli. Alison, is there someplace we can go that would be a little more private?"

"I was hoping Eli could join us today." I sat down at the kitchen table too.

"I see." Dr. Miller glanced back and forth between us. "And how do you two know each other?"

"Eli is my boyfriend." I smiled at the thought. I remembered when we first started dating and I didn't know what we actually were. It was nice to be sure now.

"Oh. You didn't mention a boyfriend last time we spoke." He looked taken aback.

"It's new," I said. "And you didn't ask me if I was in a relationship last time."

He nodded. "Right, right. Well, I don't specialize in couple's therapy, so unfortunately Eli will need to leave."

Maybe Dr. Miller didn't look taken aback. He kind of just looked upset. And I didn't understand why. "Eli's just here for moral support," I said.

Dr. Miller opened up his notebook and jotted something down. "That's highly unusual. I want you to be able to talk freely, Alison."

"You can just pretend I'm not here," Eli said.

Dr. Miller frowned. "If that's really what you want?" He was looking at me, not really engaging with Eli at all.

"I'm most comfortable if he's here with me."

Dr. Miller nodded. "Very well. There are a few things I wanted to dive into deeper this time." He flipped through his notebook. "We talked a little about your childhood pen pal. I think we should start again there."

"There's nothing left to say."

"I would have thought so too." He glanced at Eli and then back at me. "But given this development, I believe we should dive back in. You said you still loved your pen pal."

"I didn't say that."

Dr. Miller cleared his throat as he turned to a page in his notebook. "And I quote, at one point I think I loved him, but I was so young. That's a lie. I still love him. But I'm not sure if it's because he's the last thing left from my past or because my feelings are real. It's probably both."

I could feel Eli's eyes on me.

"Alison, it is my clinical recommendation that you are not ready to be in a healthy relationship with anyone."

"I'm not asking for your opinion."

"It's not an opinion. I'm a licensed..."

"I don't love Miles." I turned to Eli. "I don't." I couldn't read Eli's expression at all.

Dr. Miller tapped his notebook. "But you said..."

"I didn't mean it. I don't love him."

"I believe you do. I believe you still harbor feelings after all these years. And I think..."

"I can't love him because I hate him!" My voice seemed to echo around me. "I hate him so much," I said more quietly. I blinked away the tears that were forming in my eyes.

"Hate and love are very strong emotions. Usually you can't have one without the other."

"That's not true."

"You loved this boy. And your abandonment issues turned your strong feelings into hatred instead of love."

"Your theory is bullshit. You can hate without love. I hate my foster father. I despise every bone in his body and I always have."

"But is it possible that you craved his love at one point? That you desperately needed the support of a father figure..."

"I didn't *need* anything from that man. I had a father. A wonderful, perfect father. And no one can replace him. I don't need to talk to Mr. Crawford or anyone else. My father is irreplaceable."

Eli put his hand on my knee and I immediately stopped talking. Shit, what had I just done?

"Who is this Mr. Crawford?" Dr. Miller asked.

"No one."

"Alison, I can't help you if you don't talk to me."

It didn't seem like he was trying to help me at all. It seemed like he was trying to throw my new relationship into oncoming traffic for no reason. "Are you trying to help me? Because it seems like all you're doing is trying to break up my new relationship. And our mutual friend doesn't exactly want me to be dating Eli either."

"You know I can't discuss him. Doctor-patient conf…"

"And what about all the things you shared with me before you left last time? Like how I thawed his heart? Like how he'd never abandon me? It almost seemed like you were pushing us together."

"Hmm." Dr. Miller flipped through his notebook. "I don't have any record of that. Is it possible that you have unresolved feelings for him as well as your old friend, Miles?"

Eli's hand fell from my knee.

I turned toward him. "Eli, he's twisting my words. You don't believe anything he's saying, right?"

"You told him that you were still in love with Miles when you just told me that you only loved me. Which one is it?"

"I just said I hated Miles. Isn't that enough proof?"

"Hate him how? Like you want to put a bullet in his skull like your foster father's?"

"No." I shook my head. "Not like that."

"Why?"

I was somehow guilty even though I hadn't done anything wrong. "Because I would never want anything bad to happen to him."

"Because you love him?"

It felt like my heart was about to beat out of my ribcage. "Because I care about him. I want him to be happy."

"I think it's important for you to talk out your feelings with your childhood friend, Alison," Dr. Miller interjected. "If for no other reason than closure."

"I don't need to talk to him."

"I agree with, Dr. Miller," Eli said. "Maybe you could benefit from some closure."

"I'm not allowed to speak with him," I said. Eli knew that.

"Not allowed?" Dr. Miller asked. "Is that how it feels? Like you're not allowed to do certain things in your current relationship?"

Oh. My. God. "Are you even a psychologist?"

"I can assure you that I have my credentials."

"You're manipulating everything I'm saying. You're jumping to wild conclusions for no reason. This isn't helpful. At all. And I'm done." I stood up and marched toward V's bedroom door before Dr. Miller could say another word. I was going to kill V.

CHAPTER 12
Wednesday

I pounded on V's door with my fist. No answer. *Son of a bitch*. I grabbed the handle and it shocked me. *Ow!*

It was like Athena knew she couldn't talk with Dr. Miller there, so she had electrocuted me instead. I looked up at the camera mounted in the hallway, gave her the finger, and resumed my pounding until my hand started to hurt.

"Summer." Eli's voice was soothing.

I slammed my palm against V's door.

"Summer." Eli's hands on my forearms were even more soothing.

"He's trying to ruin my life," I whispered. "Why is he doing this to me?"

Eli's gentle kisses on my neck made me melt backwards into him.

"He's hell-bent on ruining us."

"I'm not going anywhere, Summer." He wrapped his arms protectively around me and kissed my shoulder. "I promise."

I closed my eyes and let myself relax. Eli's strength was radiating into me and I was able to breathe a little easier.

"Dr. Miller is gone," he said with another gentle kiss against my skin. "And I asked him not to come back. I've never been to a therapist, but that seemed a little invasive and pushy. And don't worry, I'll handle V."

I nodded.

"But I do want to talk about what he said."

"Can it wait until tomorrow? I'm exhausted."

He lifted me into his arms and I laughed into the fabric of his shirt.

"Yes, it can wait until morning." He opened his door with one hand and then closed it with a kick before placing me down on his bed.

I snuggled into his chest as he joined me under the covers. "Actually, I want to get everything out there. Any questions. All of it."

Eli ran his fingers through my hair, but stayed silent.

So I launched into the story of Miles. How we met. How I fell in love. How he left me. I told him everything about my foster families. And Don. I told him about how broken I'd felt since I was a child. I told him how I thought V understood my pain. I told him everything.

And Eli held me when I cried. He held me as I let my past go.

***

I woke up drenched in sweat. I had been dreaming about when I found out Joan was working with Don. It had been so easy to trust her. And I couldn't have been more wrong. I could still feel the gun pressed to the back of my head in her diner. Her words came back to me so easily: "The only person Don wants dead more than you is that pesky vigilante."

It had been disturbing my sleep for months. I needed to tell them. For some reason, it was easier to take all the blame for Don being here. It was like I wanted everyone to hate me. But tonight was going to be dangerous.

I closed my eyes even tighter. I needed them to know in case things went south. There was no choice. I had to tell them today. And maybe it would make things better. Maybe Liza wouldn't hate me so much. Maybe all the resentment would disappear if her beloved V was the one she was risking her life for. Regardless, they deserved to know the truth. And I was trying to let things go. Forcing them to hate me and only me wasn't healthy.

I reached out and felt empty sheets. I slowly opened my eyes. The light filtering through the blinds let me know it was morning. I stopped mid-yawn when I heard hushed voices outside of my room.

"You're hurting her right now," Eli whispered. "Don't you see that? She's trying to be happy but you're interfering."

"She's looking for happiness in the wrong place," V said.

I should have let them know I was awake. I should have called for Eli. I should have done anything but eavesdrop, but I couldn't seem to stop.

"That's not your right to tell her how and with whom she can be happy," Eli said.

"Yes…actually it is."

"No, it's not."

"If she would just go home…"

"She is home." Eli's whisper was gone. "Why do you always say that to her? This is her home. Here. With me and Liza and you…even though I'd rather you not be in the equation."

"This isn't her home. She needs to stop lying to herself."

"It is! New York City is her new home. There is nothing left for her in Colorado or Wyoming."

"You're wrong," V said. "About everything. Home isn't a place, it's a feeling."

A feeling. The words sunk into my mind slowly. *Home is a feeling.* I pictured myself laughing at the kitchen table with my father. I pictured my mother grabbing his hand to dance. I pictured my perfect little family. And I pictured blood on the asphalt.

"Don't you want her to be happy?" Eli asked. "If you love her, that should be your ultimate goal. And I make her happy. You need to stand down."

"I can't do that, Eli. I can't."

Eli sighed. "Well, she's not going back to your therapist. He's just pushing your agenda on her. If you refuse to stand down, at least stop playing mind games." I heard the door start to open.

"What we have is bigger than you could possibly understand," V said. "She belongs to me. She always will."

Before Eli closed the door, my eyes locked with V's. And for a moment, it felt like his words couldn't possibly be wrong. Like my heart would only beat with him. Like I could only breathe if he was still breathing. Like he was home to me.

The door closed and the feeling instantly vanished. *Mind games.* That's what Eli had said. And that's what they were. I didn't know V. And at the rate we were going, I never would.

"Sorry about that," Eli said as he climbed back in bed with me. "I tried to get him to let up, but I'm guessing you heard that he doesn't plan to."

"Sorry about eavesdropping."

"It's fine." He ran his fingers through my hair. "We weren't exactly being quiet. He really knows how to crawl under my skin."

"Yeah, it's kinda his thing."

Eli laughed.

I stared into his eyes. No, I couldn't picture my parents when we were together, and I couldn't picture my home in Wyoming. It had been so long since I had a home. I could picture starting a family with Eli eventually, though. I felt like he could become home to me.

"We need to go over the plan for tonight," Eli said. "Everyone's meeting in a couple minutes over breakfast."

"I really don't need to talk to Mr. Crawford," I said. "Maybe we should just try to take down Don tonight instead."

"You're very trigger happy."

"I'm not," I said.

He raised his eyebrow.

I laughed. "Fine. Maybe you have a point. We could just capture Don instead, though."

"That would be much harder. Hopefully Crawford doesn't have a security detail."

I didn't respond.

"No one is going to ask Crawford if he's your father, Summer. That's a conversation you can have with him if you choose to. No one is forcing you."

I nodded, my cheek sliding along the soft pillowcase.

"But if he is your biological father, it doesn't change anything. You had a father." He placed his hand on my other cheek and stopped the movement.

I hadn't even realized I was still nodding.

"Crawford wouldn't replace that relationship. No one could replace your dad. But if you have any family that's still alive...that's something to hold on to."

He had a point. A really good point, actually. "I'll think about it."

He placed a soft kiss against my lips.

CHAPTER 13
Thursday

"How was your therapy session last night?" Liza asked as Eli and I joined her at the table.

"Unproductive," I said. I watched V's back as he flipped pancakes at the stove. Did he know that Don wanted him dead? It seemed like he knew everything. Maybe my revelation wouldn't be a shock.

"Oh, that's unfortunate." Liza adjusted her glasses as she stared at me. It felt like she was trying to read my soul.

"Um, what's up?" I asked as I drummed my fingers against my knee. She was making me incredibly nervous. Or maybe it was just the fact that I had been lying to them for months. *No, not lying.* Withholding information was different. V couldn't exactly argue with that logic.

"Were you planning on…you know…dressing up to-night?" Liza asked.

"I'm planning on wearing all black, if that's what you mean." I knew the rules. I wasn't allowed to leave the apartment unless I was in disguise.

"Well, yeah," Liza said. "But are you going to like put on some makeup? Wear a pushup bra? That kinda thing?" She pointed to my breasts.

I quickly folded my arms across my chest. "No, Liza, I wasn't planning on dressing up for the extraction tonight."

"Oh." She pushed around a piece of pancake with her fork as she kept staring at me. "I think you should reconsider that. A little mascara maybe…"

"Drop it, Liza," V said as he placed a plate down in front of me.

I didn't look up at him, I just continued to stare back at Liza. "Why?" I doubted Liza even owned mascara. So why was she badgering me to put on makeup? I needed the momentary distraction. Soon she'd be rapid firing questions at me.

She looked down at her food. "I just think that it's important to always look your best."

Really? I was pretty sure she hadn't combed her hair in a week.

"Liza, I said drop it." V's voice rumbled lower than usual.

Liza pressed her lips together, like she wanted to continue talking and the only thing preventing her was V's disdain.

"What's this about?" Eli asked. "We agreed to talk about everything during our nightly meetings. The two of you going behind our backs and discussing…"

"Us?" V said, cutting him off. "What we've been doing doesn't exactly compare to what you and Sadie are doing together behind our backs."

"What?" Liza's voice was almost a whisper. "What have they been doing behind our backs?"

"Nothing," V said and handed Eli a plate too. It clattered against the table. "Nothing important."

I could feel V's anger radiating off him as he sat down across from me.

Liza looked back and forth between V and Eli. "Okay. But, V, I still think it's a good idea…" her voice died away when V glared at her.

"Really, I'm curious," I said. "Why would it be a good idea for me to dress up tonight?"

"I just think that if things go south it would be nice if you could distract Don or at least bait him into not hurting us or to maybe even tell us something important." Her words came out so fast that V didn't even have time to clamp his hand over her mouth. Which he did. One second too late.

Liza's eyes got wide, but she didn't look upset. She looked oddly happy that V was touching her.

"I doubt that I could distract him. V, would you please let me have a conversation with Liza?"

"You don't need to listen to her, she doesn't know what she's talking about."

That seemed to snap Liza out of her stupor. She shoved V's hand away. "And why not? Don loved Summer's mom. Maybe he loved her aunt too. And Summer looks just like them. He probably loves her too."

Loves me? The thought made a chill run down my spine.

"He literally blew up her aunt," V said.

"Regardless. Don's physically attracted to her. Obviously. I think we should use whatever we can to our advantage. Besides, she's his target, not us. And if things go south tonight, I don't want to die."

"You just want me to die?" I asked.

Liza sighed. "That's not what I said."

It didn't matter what she said. It's what she meant. Suddenly my news didn't seem so bad. At least I wasn't wishing death upon any of them. "I'm not," I said. "I'm not his target."

Everyone turned to me.

"Of course you are," Liza said. "Don followed *you* here. You're the only reason any of us are in this mess."

"Maybe he came here because of me. But I don't know if he stayed because of me. Don loves a challenge. And what bigger challenge is there than to take the turf of the New York City vigilante?"

V laughed. The low tone made my stomach flip over. "I don't think so, Sadie."

I hated when he called me that. And I hated that he dismissed my thoughts so quickly. "I don't *think* it, I *know* it. Before they kidnapped me, Joan said there had been a change of plans. She said Don wanted you dead. They were hoping I could lead them to you. Yes, Don wants to kill me. But he wants V dead more."

V's smile vanished. "And you didn't think that was important to tell us? What the hell, Sadie?"

"Despite what you all think, I've been protecting you guys too. So don't sit there and tell me to look pretty when I'm putting my life on the line for him." I pointed to V. "Maybe we should be serving him up on a silver platter instead. Maybe Don would like it if you wore mascara and a pushup bra." I pushed my plate away and stood up. "If you'll excuse me."

"Eat your breakfast," V said. "You need your energy for tonight."

Was he joking? I was decidedly not hungry after that conversation, or lack thereof. "I lost my appetite." I walked away to the sound of their whispers.

CHAPTER 14

Thursday

"Everyone in place?" Liza's voice sounded shaky in my earpiece, even though she was the farthest away from any action that would be happening tonight. She was sitting safely on the roof of the building scanning the premises through her computer.

"Yes," I whispered my reply into my watch. I listened to the other yeses come through and exhaled slowly. Everything was set.

Despite what I had said earlier, I *was* wearing a bit of makeup. And a pushup bra. I knew Liza was partially right. No, Don didn't love me. But he did love hurting me. Or using me. Or something. He had always looked at me like I was a piece of meat. Like I belonged to him. If things went south, I wouldn't want anyone else to get hurt. Maybe I would be able to distract him while the others got away.

"Thanks, Summer," Liza said. "For listening to me. About the makeup and stuff."

I assumed she was talking to only me. But I didn't know how to respond to only her. So I didn't respond at all.

"And it's just in case," she said. Her voice sounded far away. "Good luck."

Thanks, Liza. I heard the sound of footsteps and my heart started beating in rhythm to the echoes. I peered around the column I was standing behind and looked down at the abandoned theater. Don just had to choose the creepiest meeting place ever. It didn't look like the theater had been used in a decade. The red fabric on the seats was torn and stained. There was a slash through the screen up front. It was depressing, like dreams came here to die. Maybe that's why Don liked it.

A chill ran down my spine. I could feel Don's presence, but I couldn't see him. Something wasn't right. *Where is everyone?* I could hear the footsteps, but there were no bodies or voices to accompany them. The meeting should have started by now.

I stepped out from behind the column and approached the railing, keeping low. I could just make out V on the other side of the balcony from me. Eli was nowhere in sight.

"Stand your ground," Liza's voice flooded my ear.

"I need a better view," I whispered into my watch.

I crouched down in front of the railing and looked down at the theater. Still nothing. But the echoing of distant footsteps continued. It was disorienting, like the sound was all around me.

And then all the lights turned off.

Fear crept into my bones. I was frozen. I couldn't see anything. My heart pounded against my chest. I was hyperventilating.

"No one move," Liza said. "Something's interfering with my feed."

I gulped. None of this was right. Don was here, I could feel him. I looked behind me, but couldn't see a thing. The echoing of footsteps grew louder.

There was a burst of light and Don appeared larger than life on the theater's ripped screen.

"Hello, Summer." His lips curled into a smile. Don's voice was all around me, booming from speakers.

I swallowed hard.

"You failed the game," he said.

The air in the theater was suddenly stale. I took a huge gulp of air, but it felt like my lungs didn't expand.

"Liza, where is he?" V's voice sounded in my earpiece.

"Shit," Liza said. "He scrambled my surveillance. I don't know…"

Seeing Don so large made it seem like he was all powerful. Like whatever he wanted would happen. Everyone's voices died away but his. And I couldn't look away. His eyes were focused forward, not on me, but it felt like he could see me.

"This was supposed to be fun, Summer," Don said. "But you've never made anything easy."

My bottom lip trembled.

"I sent people after you." He ran his fingers downs the scars on his face. "A face for a face."

"Summer, get back in position," someone said into my earpiece.

But I couldn't move. All I could do was watch the movie unfold.

"And I'm sorry about that, doll," Don said. "I changed my mind. I could never destroy your beauty. You know that."

I felt nauseous.

"You're everything to me. A living, breathing replica of your mother. I could never hurt you. But you were supposed to make this fun."

"Summer, you have to move!"

I ignored the voice in my earpiece.

"You left me," Don said. "Do you know how much that stung? No, killing you isn't an option. But I can take everything from you. Until you come crawling back to me on your knees. I always loved you on your knees." His smile grew crueler by the second. A leering scowl that took up too much space on his face.

I swallowed down the vomit that was threatening to come up.

"I'll keep playing this game until you can't trust anyone. Until you realize your mistakes. Until you willingly hand me who I want. He's here, right? The infamous V. Hello, V. Guess what? I know your secret." Don laughed. "I know exactly who you are. It's going to hurt her when she finds out. Whatever game you're playing, you've already lost."

"Damn it, Summer," Eli said as he grabbed my arm. It seemed like he had been trying to get my attention for awhile. "We need to go, we were set up." He pulled me to my feet.

And then all the lights came back on. I blinked as my eyes adjusted to the light. I tried to blink away the image in front of me. But no matter how many times I did, the image didn't go away.

The real Don was standing in the middle of the theater. With that same stupid smile. And his gun was pointed right at us.

"He's in the theater," Liza said. "But I guess you already know that…"

I barely heard her. I reached for my gun.

"Don't move," Don said. He made a disgusting tsking noise with his throat. "Oh, it's so good to see you, doll."

I could feel his eyes scanning my body.

The movie stopped playing and it sounded like the movie roll was continuing to spin in the projector.

"And Elijah Serrano," Don said. He turned his gun to Eli. "I see you've found something better to do than sit outside my house spying on me. I'd apologize for ruining your career, but weren't you trying to do the exact same thing to me?"

Eli stepped in front of me, blocking me from Don.

No. "Don, stop." I ran to the balcony, blocking Eli. "I'll do whatever you want. Please just take me. I'll go with you. Please."

"Weren't you listening to what I said?"

His gun fired faster than I had time to react. All I could do was close my eyes and wait to die. I expected an impact. I expected to feel the bullet pierce my flesh. I was prepared for death. I had been ready for it since that first night Don put his hands on me.

But I didn't feel anything. I was alive. *God, I'm alive!*

"Eli, Summer, get out of there!" Liza's voice sounded in my earpiece. "Now!"

Sirens wailed in the distance. I turned around and grabbed Eli's arm. I nearly tripped when he didn't move.

"Eli, we need to go." I intertwined my fingers with his and tried to pull him.

A horrible gasping noise escaped his throat.

"Eli?" I turned back to him. Something was wrong. His face was pale. "Eli?" I said again, but it was like he didn't hear me.

He coughed and blood sputtered out of his mouth.

"Eli!"

I held my breath as he fell to his knees, pulling me down to the ground with him. For one second.

His free hand was pressed against his stomach. For two seconds.

Blood was seeping into his winter jacket. For three seconds.

So much fucking blood. For four seconds.

No. The sound of the sirens were drawing closer. For five seconds. It took me five seconds to realize that my life was still a nightmare.

I pulled my hand out of his and touched the side of my watch. "Eli's been shot! Someone help!" I put my hand on top of his, hoping to stop the bleeding. "You're going to be okay, Eli. We're going to get you out of here."

"He needs medical attention," Liza said through my earpiece. "You need to leave him."

Leave him? I can't. I looked down at his face. His eyes were focused so intently on mine.

"Go," he whispered. More blood dripped out of the corner of his mouth.

It was so soft, I thought I imagined him saying it.

"Summer, you have to go."

"I'm not leaving you," I said and touched the side of his face, smearing blood onto his cheek. *God.*

The sirens were getting closer. He'd be arrested. What did it matter if I was arrested too? I wasn't going to leave him like this. I'd never leave him.

He gasped for air.

"You're going to be okay," I said as calmly as I could muster. But it didn't seem like he was going to be okay. He was growing paler by the second. The life was draining out of him.

"I will always love you, Summer." His voice was raspy. He took a huge gulp of air. "Always." He gasped.

"Eli, I'm not going anywhere. We're in this together remember?" *Stay with me.*

He didn't look like he was focusing on me anymore.

"Eli?" I touched the side of his face again and his head fell to the side. "Eli?" He blurred in front of me as the tears streamed down my cheeks. "Eli! You can't leave me." My body started to shake as I let my fears take over. "Please, Eli, you can't. I love you."

V grabbed me around the waist, lifting me away from Eli. My fingers slid off Eli's cheek, leaving lines of blood against this neck.

"No!" I shouted and struggled in V's grip. "Eli!"

But Eli didn't move. His body was so still.

"Let go of me!" I thrashed in V's arms. Months of training proving useless against his strength.

"We have to go," he whispered in my ear.

"Not without him! We can't leave without Eli." I kicked and screamed.

"It's too late," V said. "It's too late," he repeated.

If he thought his words were soothing they weren't. His words echoed around me as he carried me away from Eli's motionless body.

CHAPTER 15
Thursday

I held my breath for one second as I watched the cops swarm the theater.

For two seconds. Why had I moved out of formation in the first place? I should have stayed behind the pillar.

For three seconds. Why hadn't I listened to what Don was saying? He wasn't there to hurt me. He was there to take away everything I loved.

For four seconds. My last thread of hope had been cut.

For five seconds. It was my fault that Eli was dead. I tried to take a deep breath, but it felt like I was choking.

V carried me farther and farther away until I couldn't see the red and blue lighting up the sky. The whole time I reached out, trying to get back to Eli. Trying to remember what his eyes looked like before they went blank. *No. No!*

The wind swirled, blowing some of the fallen snow around us, like it was trying to pull me back into my memories. Trying to pull me back into everything I had lost.

"They'll find him," Liza said from beside us. "They have to." But there was doubt in her voice.

It's too late. Those were V's words. And I had seen Eli's face. He was staring into nothingness. It should have been me. It felt like my tears had frozen against my cheeks.

"I need to go back," I said and kept trying to struggle out of V's grip. "I have to…I need to be with him…"

"I'm the only one that isn't a wanted criminal," Liza said as she stopped running. "I'll go figure out what I can."

"It's not safe, Liza," V said.

"He's our friend, V."

"The cops are going to recognize him. They'll link you two together. You can't."

Liza shook her head. "He's one of us. I'm going back. I'll say I heard a gunshot. I'll point them in the right direction before he bleeds out." She started running toward the fire escape.

Before he bleeds out. I saw the death in his eyes. "V, please," I said and tried to push V's arms off of me. "Let me go with her. They're looking for a brunette, not a blonde. Let me go."

But he continued to carry me farther away from Eli.

"He needs me!"

V didn't say a word.

"He needs me," I sobbed. I wasn't even sure if it was true. But I needed him. I desperately needed him.

***

"Put the apartment on lockdown, Athena," V said.

A few seconds later, Athena's voice came over the speaker system: "The apartment is on lockdown."

He lowered me to my feet. As soon as he did, I collapsed to my knees. The tears were back, raking through my whole body. I didn't even know I could cry so hard.

"Sadie, get up. You're stronger than this."

I lifted my head and looked at V. I couldn't get up. And I couldn't explain it to him. I had just lost everything. If he didn't see that, then he couldn't possibly understand.

"We failed the mission. We won't next time." He stared at me. "You just need to sleep it off," he added when I didn't respond.

Sleep it off? "This has nothing to do with the mission. I watched Eli die! I love him. And I watched him die. How…how can you be so cold?"

"You don't love him."

I swore he rolled his eyes. "Fuck you, V. If you have something to say, just say it. Don't roll your eyes and minimize my pain."

"I just said it. You don't love him." His voice rumbled lower than usual.

"I love him! I love him more than you could possibly understand. He sees the real me. I'm not living behind a mask! I have real emotions and…"

"You don't love him! Your heart is shattered into a million tiny pieces. It's broken, Sadie. And no one is going to magically put it back together in a few days. You don't love him. You love the idea of him, nothing more."

"You're wrong." I pushed myself up to my feet. Nothing was going to stop me from going back to Eli. Definitely not a self-entitled prick. I pressed the button to open the window.

"The apartment is on lockdown," Athena said.

"Athena, let me out!" I hit the button again.

"The apartment is on lockdown," Athena said.

I slammed my palm against the window. "It's my apartment, Athena!"

"The apartment is on lockdown," Athena said.

I hit the window again before turning around. "Let me out," I said to V.

"No. And you're right, I do have more to say. If you loved him so much, you shouldn't have left your position. None of this would have happened if you could have listened to directions for once in your damned life."

I didn't need him to tell me that. I already knew it was my fault. "Is that all?"

He walked toward me. "You should have realized as soon as Don said he wasn't there to hurt you that he was going to hurt one of us. You put us all in jeopardy by being careless!"

Screw him. I actually wasn't the only one to blame. "And what about you, V? You were on the other side of the balcony. You had a clear shot. You could have saved his life!"

"Taking out Don wasn't the plan…"

"You could have prevented him from shooting Eli!" I closed the distance between us.

"Liza told us to abort the mission. So I left. I followed protocol."

"You wanted him to die!" I poked him in the middle of the chest. "Right? You wanted him out of the way? You're a murderer." I poked him again. "I've seen you kill someone with my own two eyes. And just because you didn't pull the trigger, don't think for a second that you're not at fault for this death too."

"You really are nothing like Summer Brooks."

I slapped him across the face. Harder than I meant to. Or maybe not hard enough, because he smiled at me.

"Do you feel better now? Less guilty?"

I went to slap him again, but he grabbed my hand before it reached his cheek.

"Because this isn't on me. It's on you. And I wasn't minimizing your pain. I was reminding you that you've experienced worse. That you're stronger than this."

"That's not what you were doing." I tried to slap him with my other hand, but he grabbed that too. He pushed me backward until I was pressed against the window.

"Let go of me, V. Or I swear to God, I'll…"

"You think I don't know what it's like to lose the love of my life?" he asked, cutting me off. "Why do you think I became this?" There was pain in his voice. It was real. It was raw and full of emotion.

I believed him. But this wasn't the time or place for this conversation. And he was hogging my air supply. "I'm serious, V, let go of me."

"My heart is shattered into a million tiny pieces too, Sadie. It's broken. I know better than anyone else that it doesn't heal that quickly. Maybe you want to love him. But you couldn't possibly love someone when your heart only beats for one person."

"If your heart only beats for one person, then go torment her instead of me." I tried to wiggle out of his grip.

He released me with an exhale.

I rushed past him. I needed my phone. If I was going to be stuck in this prison of an apartment, I needed to call Liza to see if she'd heard anything. But I knew. I just knew Eli was dead.

V wasn't right. Maybe my heart was shattered, but every fragment loved Eli. And now it felt like the pieces had shriveled up and died.

"It's you," V said from behind me. "I love you."

I stopped at Eli's bedroom, my hand on the knob, and turned to look at V. "Are you kidding me, V? Just a few days ago you said you didn't love me. You drove me away. What the hell do you want from me? I'm not just some pawn that you can play with. You don't love me. Trust me. And the only reason you even like me a little is because you can't have me."

He looked exhausted. "It's always been you." He shrugged his shoulders. "And it always will be."

Why now? In what maniacal way did he think this was okay to talk about after what just happened? "The whole city thinks you're brave," I said. "But they couldn't be more wrong. You're a fucking coward." I walked into Eli's room and slammed the door.

The smell of citrus hit my nose, causing another round of tears to escape. I found my phone and called Liza as I collapsed in Eli's bed. I let Eli's scent engulf me as Liza's voicemail beeped on. I called again and again and again. Nothing.

Love was pain. And I was never going to fucking love again. I pulled Eli's sheets up to my chin. If I closed my eyes tight enough I could picture him beside me. But it didn't stop my heart from feeling like it was bleeding.

CHAPTER 16
Friday

I wanted to be dead, if this wasn't already death itself. I couldn't sleep. I couldn't eat. I couldn't move.

A knocking on Eli's door made me open my eyes.

"Sadie?" V called from the other side.

"Go away," I mumbled.

He opened the door and stared at me. "Get up, Sadie." He stepped into the room. "This is ridiculous."

"Don't come in here!" I imagined his stupid cologne permeating all the surfaces, removing Eli's presence from existence. "Get out!" I yelled it again and again when he didn't move. I chucked my phone at him and he finally left, closing the door behind him.

I sobbed into Eli's pillow, until I had nothing left.

CHAPTER 17
Saturday

I felt weak and small. All those months that I had pushed Eli away, I could have been making him happy. Us happy. I regretted everything. At least the last time I saw him I hadn't been pushing him out the door like I did with my parents. At least Eli knew I loved him. I hoped he knew. I wiped the snot away from under my nose.

Regret seared in my mind regardless. I lived a life of awful choices, one after the next. Anger seeped into my bones until it felt like my body was on fire.

When a knock sounded on the door, I glared at it, daring V to come in and face my wrath.

"Alison?" I heard from the other side of the door.

Hell no. I didn't respond. I couldn't handle seeing Dr. Miller with his fake motives. He wouldn't be as cocky as V. He wouldn't come in here.

But apparently this loony psychologist thought silence was consent, because the door slowly opened anyway. "Can you come out here and talk to me?" His voice was overly soothing like he was speaking to a child.

"No thank you."

"I heard your friend got shot in a mugging," Dr. Miller said.

"Is that what our mutual friend told you?"

"He did."

"Did he tell you that it's his fault that Eli got shot? That he could have stopped it?"

"No. Actually he said that you pulled Eli into a position that made him vulnerable and that you were blaming yourself for his injury."

"Injury? I don't even know if he's alive." My voice sounded as weak and small as I felt.

"How about you come out here and talk about that? Unless you'd rather me come in?"

"Or you could go away."

"You've been holed up in there for a day and a half. This behavior is unacceptable. You haven't been eating. Come on. I brought food." He lifted up a takeout bag that I hadn't noticed before.

My stomach growled, betraying me. "Are we alone?" I asked.

"I believe so. I'll be waiting in the kitchen for you." He retreated out of the room, leaving the door ajar.

If V wasn't here and Dr. Miller had been able to get in, the apartment was no longer in lockdown. I pushed the comforter off of me, jumped out of bed, and ran out of the room. No one was stopping me from seeing Eli. I grabbed my winter jacket off the hook and shoved my feet into my boots.

I wrapped my hand around the doorknob and it immediately shocked me. *Ow!* I glared at the camera that was pointed directly at me. I grabbed the handle again and it shocked me even harder. "Screw you Athena and V," I said under my breath. Apparently I was on lockdown, not the apartment.

The smell of greasy goodness floated into the hall. I hung my coat back up and kicked off my boots. I didn't bother to change. I was wearing one of Eli's t-shirts, but it was big on me, coming down to mid-thigh. If Athena hadn't locked me in, I'd be walking the city streets in it. So Dr. Miller could deal.

I sat down across from him at the kitchen table.

He pushed one of the bags at me. "So why aren't you at the hospital visiting him?"

I ignored him and unwrapped a juicy burger. It was almost angering how he knew exactly what I was in the mood for. I took a big bite and tried to swallow down the resentment.

"Alison? Why aren't you with him?"

I cleared my throat. *I'm a wanted criminal. I'm not allowed to leave the apartment.* "It's family only."

"I see. You could sit in the waiting room."

V won't let me. "I can't. I'm a mess." I gestured to myself. Hopefully that would do the trick.

He didn't say anything.

"Look, thank you for bringing food, but I'm really not in the mood to talk."

"I'm sorry, I just think it's odd that you have such a fear of abandonment, but you'd be so willingly able to abandon a friend in need."

I set the burger down. "He's not just a friend. I love him."

"Even more of a reason to go to him."

"You don't think I want to be there?" I shook my head. "But it doesn't even matter. I saw him die. He's gone."

"You don't know that for sure."

"I've seen more people die than I care to remember. I'm not going to sit here and have you judge me too."

"Who else is judging you? Our mutual friend?"

"Yes, who else would I be talking about? The one that you can't talk about yet you're always bringing him up."

"I didn't bring him up," Dr. Miller said. "You did."

I took a huge breath and exhaled slowly. "Well I don't want to talk about him, or Eli, or anyone else. I just want to sit here and eat in silence."

"I think it's important that you go to the hospital, Alison. You don't want to regret this choice."

"It's not a choice! I'm being held here against my will!"

"Emotionally? Or…" Dr. Miller's voice trailed off. He was looking at me like I was insane.

Screw V. Screw the secrets. If I was being forced to see a therapist, I could say whatever I damned well pleased. And he was my doctor. He couldn't tell anyone what I said. Right? Fuck it. "I'm not abandoning Eli. There's nothing in the world I want more than to be with him. But I'm not allowed to leave the apartment because it's on lockdown. I tried to leave and the doorknob literally shocked me."

He just stared at me. He clearly didn't believe me.

"Your patient isn't who he says he is." I put patient in air quotes. "He's the New York City vigilante and he's holding me against my will. I don't even know his real name. You're the only one that does and the fact that you refuse to share it is infuriating."

Dr. Miller didn't say a word.

"He's a murderer, Dr. Miller. He killed someone right in front of me. He needs to be locked up, not me."

No response.

I stood up and walked over to the fake wall. I pressed my thumb against a button and the wall started to ascend, revealing our headquarters. I stepped into it and the floor lit up red. "This is his secret lair." I gestured to the computers and the target on the wall. The glass table spread with documents. A bulletin board filled with pictures and yarn connecting images.

Nothing.

"My name isn't Alison. V lies about everything. He lies to himself about his feelings. He lies to me constantly. He's certainly lied to you about his true identity. And he's holding me here against my will."

Nothing.

"We're part of a secret team to take down Don Roberts. You know…our beloved mayor? He was my foster father. He's the one that raped me. He's the one that broke me." My voice cracked. "And I think he has my old babysitter, Julie, hostage. I think he killed my parents. I know he killed my aunt, even though I'm wanted for her murder. And he certainly killed me. Because as much as I wish that I could be myself again, that part of me is dead." I sat down. "I died when I was 8 years old and I've been trying to hold on to someone that doesn't exist anymore. I'm so tired."

Dr. Miller smiled. "Now we're finally getting somewhere, Summer."

CHAPTER 18
Saturday

I stared at Dr. Miller and the smile on his face. Had I just heard him correctly? "How do you know my name?"

"My patient never talked about Alison. That was true. But he always talks about you."

"Your patient…"

"V. And he's never lied to me. Despite what you seem to think. I've been very aware of his extracurricular activities."

"But he said that you didn't know…"

"I never said he didn't lie to you. Although, I strongly advised him against it. He has it stuck in his head that you need to love both sides of him equally before he tells you the truth. Which makes no sense. Most people fall in love with one person at a time. He's asking too much from you."

"Both sides of him?"

"The darkness and the light."

"So what's the other side? All I've ever seen is the darkness."

"The one without the mask of course. You're not looking hard enough, Summer. The answer has been right in front of you the whole time."

I thought about how V always spoke in riddles. How he always made me think. How he seemed to know everything about me and my past.

Dr. Miller was young. Mid-thirties maybe. I stared into his eyes. They were brown, just like V's. My gaze wandered to his lips. Could it be him? He clearly had access to this apartment. Apparently more so than I even had. It didn't seem like anyone had let him in. He just…appeared.

Like V always appeared when I needed him. And lots of times when I wished he wouldn't.

If I could get a few more answers from Dr. Miller, maybe I could piece it together. Maybe I'd be able to see whatever was apparently right in front of me. "V always calls me Sadie. Why?"

"Because that side of him didn't know you when you were Summer. Calling you Summer would violate his…psyche. He feels like it would be a betrayal."

It was all starting to make sense. "So it's the other part of him…the light part that loves me?"

"I believe so, yes. It's hard for people who have been hurt to open themselves up to love again. He's been cut deeply."

That's why he was so torn when he said he loved me. The darkness wasn't supposed to love me. "So he's crazy?" That was really the only conclusion to all of this.

"Aren't we all a little crazy?" He smiled.

I sighed. "You know what I mean. V clearly has a split personality…"

"No. He doesn't. He might feel as though he is insane, but he's not. I just think that when he hides behind a mask, it's easy for him to hide a part of himself. But he's all one person. The hate and the love. It's hard for him to hold on to all of it. So he separates it. The real him loves you to the ends of the earth. And the masked part of him…he loathes your existence."

"He hates me?"

"Yes. Very much so. To the point where he finds it hard to be around you."

"So why is he helping me?"

"Because love is stronger than hate, Summer. You know that."

"I don't. Hate rules this world. Just look at our city. Everyone voted for a mayor who is the leader of the Helspet Mafia. A rapist. A murderer. He's vile."

"People see what they want to see. And Don knows how to give a good speech. You can't blame this city for believing a lie that's presented in such a nice way."

Presented in a different way. *Behind a mask.* It felt like I couldn't breathe. "Is it him? Is Don V?" It would make sense. He hated me, but a part of him loved me. He always fucked me instead of holding me close. He wore a mask so I wouldn't see the real him that I wanted dead. And he knew about our extraction plan. It was like he had inside information.

Dr. Miller laughed.

The sound calmed me.

"No. I can assure you that Don Roberts is not V." He shook his head like it was the most ludicrous thing he had ever heard.

"So who is V?"

"It's not my place to say."

"But you just told me all that other stuff. Just give me his name. A letter from his name. Anything. One tiny hint is all I'm asking."

"He'll tell you when he's ready. Until then, look a little harder, Summer. See if you can't find his light."

There were the riddles again. I swallowed hard. "Is it you?"

Dr. Miller smiled. "I need to get going."

"Is it you?" I asked again.

He stood up. "You're my patient. That would be crossing a line, don't you think? Go visit Eli. I'll see you again in a few days."

"V won't let me. He won't listen."

He tilted his head to the side as he stared down at me. "He's jealous. You must see that."

"Can you please just talk to him? I need to see Eli. I need to know if he's okay."

"I'll see what I can do. Until next time." He nodded at me and walked away.

I heard the whirring sound of the window opening. No scolding from Athena. No doorknob shock. Like he could come and go whenever he wanted. Like he had access to this apartment.

Dr. Miller never said he wasn't V. He basically said it was unethical for him to have a relationship with a patient. But everything V did seemed unethical to me.

CHAPTER 19

Saturday

"Athena, please," I said and let the back of my head fall against the window. "I don't know if you have feelings, but…I love Eli. He needs me. Please."

She had stopped responding to me half an hour ago. Right after I called her a slut. It was a moment of weakness. I didn't think she'd ice me out, but she hadn't responded since. I was just talking to myself in the empty apartment. Like a lunatic. Maybe I had lost my mind as much as V had.

My phone ringing pulled me out of my pity party. *Liza.* I ran my thumb across the screen. "Liza, is he okay?" I held my breath as I waited for her to respond.

"He's…stable. He lost a lot of blood…"

He's alive! "Is he going to be alright?" I put my hand on the center of my chest.

"I don't know. I wanted to wait to call you when I knew, but your millionth phone call finally swayed me."

"So you don't know anything?"

"I didn't say that," she snapped. "I'm sorry, I'm just exhausted. He was in surgery a long time. He only just got out."

"That's good, right? They wouldn't have done surgery if there was no hope." It felt like my heart started beating again. *He's okay. He's breathing.*

Liza sighed. "He's been mumbling your name. The only reason that they let me in his room is because I said I was Summer."

"He's asking for me?"

"Not exactly…he…he's repeatedly saying your name in his sleep. I'm holding his hand, hoping he thinks it's you. But it's so cold…" her voice cracked. "You need to get down here, Summer."

"V won't let me leave the apartment. I can't."

"You need to find a way. There's cops standing outside his door. As soon as he's alert enough, they're going to take him away, I just know it. You need to come now so you can say goodbye."

Goodbye? "Because he's going to be arrested or because you think he's not going to make it?"

"Summer…"

"Just tell me."

"He doesn't look like he's going to be okay. They won't tell me anything because I'm not related to him. But he's so pale. And cold. He's not holding my hand back."

"Can you put the phone up to his ear?"

There was a rustling sound and then light breathing. It was him. I could tell.

"Eli? Can you hear me? I need you to listen to me. You're not allowed to give up. I'll try my best to get to you. But you can't give up." My voice was shaky. "Do you hear me? I love you. And I need you to keep breathing. I don't know how to keep going without you." I took a deep breath. "I thought I lost you. But you held on. And I can't. I just can't lose you, so don't you dare make me right."

"I have to go," Liza sounded alarmed. "They want to question me." The line went dead.

I took a deep breath. Eli was alive. That was all that mattered. And I was going to get to his side no matter what. Not that I wanted to believe he was running out of time. He was a fighter. I pushed myself to my feet.

Liza was with Eli. V was who knew where. Probably masquerading as a shrink all over the city. And Athena wasn't speaking to me. Hopefully she wasn't watching me either.

I was all alone. I needed to break out. There had to be a toolkit here somewhere. Or an Athena manual.

***

I threw the hammer at the target. The side of it hit the bulls-eye and then fell to the ground. "Athena, let me out!"

I had tried everything I could think of. All I had managed to do was accidentally scratch myself with a screwdriver.

"When was the last time you got a tetanus shot?"

I turned around and glared at V. "I don't know."

"You need to clean that." He gestured to my hand.

I looked down at the dried blood on the side of my hand and wrist. "I don't need you to take care of me, V."

"You could get tetanus and die. Just…stay right there."

I watched him disappear into the bathroom. *Freaking lunatic.* I wasn't the one whose life was in jeopardy. And where the hell else would I go? He had locked me in this apartment like an animal. *Ass hat.*

I sat down, rummaged through the toolkit again, and bit back a scream when my cut rubbed against something sharp.

V lifted up the bottle of peroxide as he walked back over to me.

I didn't want tetanus. And I had no idea when my last shot was. Probably sometime when my parents were alive. Certainly I was due for one. I put out my hand for him.

He sat down beside me and poured some peroxide on a cotton ball.

"I really need to see him, V."

"Eli will live or die regardless of whether you give yourself over to the cops."

"I'll wear a disguise."

"Sadie, dying your hair doesn't change your appearance at all. I knew who you were the first moment I saw you." He dabbed the cotton ball against my skin.

Ow. I bit the inside of my cheek and tried to ignore the pain.

"They knew he was in New York to watch you. They're probably waiting for you to show up outside his hospital door."

"I don't think so." I inhaled sharply when he applied more peroxide. "Liza said he was mumbling my name. She's pretending her name is Summer and she hasn't been arrested yet." I left off the fact that she was being questioned. I hadn't heard back from her since she had hung up on me. All my calls to her had gone straight to voicemail.

"Then they're idiots."

I laughed.

He smiled as he put some Neosporin on my cut and then placed a Band-Aid on top of it. "You're all set. Now are you done trying to break all my tools?"

I sighed. "Please just let me go to him."

"I just opened a bottle of wine. It'll help numb the pain." He stood up and put his hand out for me.

"That's something an alcoholic would say. You do realize that, right?"

V didn't respond.

I stood up without the help of his offered hand. "Seriously, V, just let me go. I'll wear…sunglasses."

"It's 7 o'clock at night. That would be incredibly suspicious."

I followed him into the kitchen. My wrath was gone. I was just exhausted and depressed.

V slid a glass of wine down the kitchen island.

"You could lose your license for this, you know." I caught the glass before it teetered off the edge.

"What?" He took a sip of wine from his own glass.

"Isn't that what it's called? For you to practice medicine or something like that?"

"What the hell are you talking about?"

I took a huge, ungraceful gulp of wine. "I know who you are, V. You don't have to play dumb anymore."

He just stared at me as I downed the rest of the glass. Numbing my pain didn't seem like such a bad idea.

I cleared my throat. "Dr. Miller," I said with a wink.

"What about him?"

"He's you."

V laughed.

"I told him all about you being a superhero and all that and he already knew all of it. Because he's…you." I walked over to him, grabbed the bottle off the counter, and took a sip straight from it.

"I'm not Dr. Miller."

"Right." I winked at him again.

"Why the fuck do you think I'm Dr. Miller?"

"Language, good doctor. They're going to strip you of your license if you go around talking to patients like that."

He just stared at me.

I took a swig from the wine bottle. "Of course…we both know you're not too worried about your license. You slept with a patient after all." I pointed at him with the wine bottle.

"I'd say you were drunk, but you literally only started drinking a few minutes ago. So clearly you're just insane."

"Take off your mask."

"No."

"But I paid attention. I did just what Dr. Miller said and actually listened. To all the clues. To all the signs. So now you can show me the light in you."

"What are you talking about?"

"Dr. Miller said that this side of you," I waved the bottle at him, "is the dark side. Which is obvious. You ooze venom. And then he said that you didn't think I was ready to see the light side. But I am. So just take off the stupid mask."

"Does he talk about me during your sessions?"

I shrugged. "If by talking about you, you actually mean talking about yourself, then yes."

"What did he tell you about me?" He set his wine glass down.

I said the most memorable thing that Dr. Miller had said about V. The first thing that popped into my head. "That I thawed your heart."

V laughed. "Well what he forgot to mention was that it probably wouldn't have needed thawing in the first place if it wasn't for you."

"You mean…*you* forgot to mention that fact."

"No, Sadie. I don't fucking mean me. And he had no right to talk about me to you. That wasn't our deal."

"So you're not…"

"No!" He put his hand up to his hood like he wanted to run his fingers through his hair, but stopped.

How I wished he had done it and accidentally pushed back his hood. I wanted to see him. I needed to see him. This was insane. We had known each other for six months. Enough was enough. And I didn't believe him for a second. There was no way he would have told Dr. Miller he was V. There was no reason for him to trust a strange doctor over his friends. Which meant he was Dr. Miller. The charade was over. I took another swig from the wine bottle, as if I needed liquid courage to keep confronting him with the truth. "V, I know you're him. Stop hiding. Please. We can have a real conversation without all this," I waved my hand at his outfit.

He walked over to me and grabbed the bottle from my hand. "Did he tell you that I dream of you?" V asked. He set the bottle down behind me, caging me against the kitchen island with his arms.

It felt like my heart was going to explode. And guilt crept over me. I shouldn't have felt excited by his proximity. I was in love with another man. Despite what V thought. "No, he didn't mention that."

"Then what else *did* he tell you about me?" he asked.

I needed him to step back. "That you've been cut deeply. Which is why it's hard to open yourself up to others."

"Oh. Well in that case, he's clearly told you everything you need to know about me, right?"

"I didn't say that."

"You should be able to easily guess my true identity now that you've talked about me with Dr. Miller. And you still don't see it. So maybe that's why you're not ready to know."

"I'm not the one that hurt you, V. Why are you shutting me out as punishment for something I didn't do?"

"You're the one…" His throat made a deep groaning noise and he pushed himself away from me. "Drink some water and then get some sleep." He walked away, leaving me alone in the kitchen.

I'm the one? I rolled my eyes. Yeah right. *You hate me.* I grabbed the bottle of wine and took another sip. His stupid façade was done. And I was going to prove it.

I stumbled into Eli's room and collapsed on his bed. Even with my bloodstream pumping more alcohol than blood, I knew I wasn't going to be able to sleep. I pulled my laptop onto my lap and typed in Dr. Miller's name in a Google search. After adding a location and his medical distinction, I was able to find his practice. He was a real doctor. For some reason, I was a little surprised. But that didn't exactly squash my theory. I jotted a few things down, like where he went to school so that I could quiz V. Maybe he'd slip up and admit something he didn't mean to.

But Dr. Miller wasn't my only suspect. There was the issue of Mr. Crawford. He hadn't shown up at the extraction. And V had been there. Maybe Crawford couldn't show because V literally couldn't be in two places at once. V had denied being Mr. Crawford once. Although, his word meant nothing as far as I was concerned.

But V had disappeared during the extraction. I lost sight of him right before that creepy movie had started playing. I finished the bottle of wine and set it down on my nightstand. That was enough time for V to take off his disguise and put on a nice suit. I could picture Don standing in the center of the theater with the scarred skin on the side of his face. Scarred skin would be a good reason to wear a mask.

And really, what other reason? I didn't care who V was as long as I knew he wasn't Don. A chill ran down my spine. So why hide it otherwise?

I climbed out of bed and locked Eli's door. Could V really be Don? Did that even make any sense?

V had appeared in this city as soon as I did. Like he followed me here. He watched me. *He hates me yet loves me at the same time.*

I started pacing back and forth. Crime escalated as soon as I came here. *As soon as V appeared.* Being Don, V, and the mayor seemed like a big load. But not an impossible load.

Dr. Miller had said that V was the dark side. Which meant Don was the light side? My laughter sounded strange in my throat. Or was him being the mayor the light? I pinched the bridge of my nose. It felt like I was hung-over already.

Mr. Crawford hadn't shown up at the meeting. No one from the Helspet Mafia had. It was like they knew about our plans so they changed theirs. Like they had someone on the inside of our group. Obviously we had been compromised. We had a mole.

It felt like I couldn't breathe. God, what if V was Don?

CHAPTER 20
Sunday

My phone buzzing pulled me out of my drunken stupor. I had lost my mind last night. The proof was in the fact that I had fallen asleep with my back against Eli's door and my gun laying beside me.

The buzzing sounded again.

Liza. I crawled forward and grabbed my phone off Eli's floor. I didn't remember why it was there. Wait. That was a lie. I put it far away from myself last night because I thought V had bugged it. I had completely lost my mind. And I wasn't sure I was going to find it again anytime soon.

My phone buzzed again in my hand. I saw Liza's name on the screen. "Liza?" I said as soon as I answered it. "Tell me he's okay! Tell me everything you know!"

"Are *you* okay? Why are you screaming?"

Was I screaming? *Ow.* I put my hand on my forehead. Why did it matter if I was okay? I wasn't the one sitting in a hospital bed. "I'm fine."

"You don't sound fine. You sound like death."

"I had too much to drink last night. Just tell me how he is."

There was silence on her end. "So let me get this straight. While I've been sitting here with your boyfriend, you've been…partying?"

"No." I heard the sound of a hushed voices. "Is that him? Is he awake?"

"I stepped outside to call you. He's sleeping and I needed some fresh air."

"How is he?"

"A little better. He was even awake for a little while this morning. He asked for you several times. I told him you were trying to come."

"Thank you." I sighed. He was awake. He was healing.

"So are you? Still trying to come?"

"Of course." I pinched the bridge of my nose. It felt like my head had been run over by a truck.

"So the party…"

"A pity party for one? Trust me, I wanted to be there rather than imprisoned here." I yelled imprisoned, hoping V could hear me. If he had bugged my phone and was listening in, maybe I had just split his eardrum.

"Alrighty then," said Liza. "So aren't you going to ask me what the cops wanted to question me for? I'm sorry I didn't call back last night, you must have been worried sick about me."

I hadn't been worried about her at all. She was much safer there than stuck in this miserable apartment with V. "I was just about to ask you," I said, even though I hadn't been and I had forgotten about it completely halfway through the bottle of wine. I couldn't think of anything but the searing pain in my head.

"Sure." She laughed. "Well, they tried to arrest me."

"What?"

"I mean, I said my name was Summer in order to get into his hospital room. It wasn't exactly my smartest move."

"Jesus. So what happened?"

"I told them that I just pretended that my name was Summer in order to visit his room since they weren't letting me in. They weren't blind so…they let me off the hook. It's probably good you weren't here though. They were clearly waiting for you ever since he started mumbling your name."

"I'm glad you're okay." I guess V was right. The hospital was definitely a trap.

"Thanks. So…" she let her voice trail off and cleared her throat. "I also lied and said I was his fiancé, which helped them believe me. Eli was a little disoriented when he woke up. He kept asking for his fiancé. So I just pretended that was me to help clear up the whole Summer thing."

I swallowed hard. Fiancé? Was that what he was referring to me as? My insides felt like they flipped over. I liked the sound of that. We had talked about getting married after all this. "Good. I'm glad you're allowed to be with him still."

She didn't respond.

"Liza, are you still there?" The reception was terrible in Eli's bedroom. Much worse than it was in my room.

"Yes." She sounded annoyed now, like she usually did when talking to me.

Had I missed something? "Is everything okay?"

"No, everything's not okay! How could you not tell me that you two are engaged? You're my best friend."

Her words hung in the air awkwardly. *Best friend?* I thought she hated me. "Eli and I aren't engaged… he didn't like get down on one knee or anything like that. There's no ring on my finger." I shook my head. Not that a ring mattered to me. I didn't need anything like that.

"But you talked about it." She sounded so accusatory. Like I had killed her puppy or something awful.

"Yeah, we talked about it."

"Well, he's on a lot of painkillers but clearly he thinks it's a done deal. You should have told me right after it happened."

"I would have if I thought it was official. You'd be the first person I'd tell."

"Really?"

"Of course." Who the hell else would I tell? I wasn't allowed to leave the apartment. I wasn't allowed to see Kins or…anyone else. Miles had popped into my head, but I dismissed the thought of him. Why would I tell Miles anything? He was the freaking worst.

"I hope you know how much I value our friendship," Liza said.

I did now. And the fact that Liza didn't hate me made me smile through my splitting headache. "I do. We should do a girls' night soon," I said, knowing she wouldn't take me up on it. Despite what she said, Liza did not like being around me. She preferred hanging all over V. I eyed the door. I needed to get out of this apartment.

"Um…yes! How about tonight?"

Huh? "How about what tonight?"

"Our girls' night, of course. We should make it a weekly thing. Saturday's are probably better, but it can be Sunday just this once."

What the hell had I just done? "Liza, you should probably stay with Eli. He needs you."

"Why? He's not my fiancé. I'll be home tonight for dinner. I'll get takeout. This is going to be so much fun!"

"Okay, but how is Eli doing?" I stepped to a different spot in the room to try to get better reception. It sounded like my call got dropped. "Liza?" The call had definitely ended. *She hung up on me!* I still had so many questions for her. Was Eli feeling better? Was he going to be arrested? Would it be safe for me to go to him soon?

I sighed and sat down on the edge of Eli's bed. I didn't want to have a girls' night with Liza. All I wanted was to be snuggled up to Eli.

I stared at the door to his room. Not believing that V was Don would be nice too. And my headache vanishing. And Don being behind bars. Or dead. Really I wanted a lot of things to change.

Ow. I massaged my forehead with my fingers. If girls' night involved drinking I was going to have to pass. I should have listened to V and drank some water last night. I hated that he had been right.

But maybe tonight wouldn't be a total loss. If there was one person who was as eager as me to figure out who V was, it was Liza. Tonight could be more of an investigation instead of being filled with pointless gossip. Besides, two seconds after spending time with me and Liza would remember that we weren't friends. We were acquaintances at best. Who lived together. And ate most meals together.

And… my train of thought stopped. *When the hell did Liza become my best friend?*

CHAPTER 21

Sunday

"I'm so excited," Liza said and set down the Chinese take-out containers on the coffee table. "I just need to go change real quick." But instead of leaving, she just stared at me.

"What?" I lifted up one of the containers. "Thanks for bringing the food." It came out as more of a question than a statement because she was making me feel uncomfortable under her scrutinizing gaze. "I'm excited too," I added. What did she want me to say?

"Aren't you going to change too?"

I looked down at my sweater and jeans. "What's wrong with what I'm wearing?"

"It's girls' night."

"I know…" I let my voice trail off. Did she want me to put on a dress and stilettos and pretend we were the cast of Sex and the City? That wasn't happening. I broke a pair of chopsticks in half.

"So you have to put on pajamas."

I laughed. "It's not a slumber party."

"I'm pretty sure junk food, pajamas, and reality TV is *the* definition of a girls' night."

"Really it's probably going out and getting wasted. But alas I'm not allowed to leave the apartment."

No response.

"Is the whole junk food, pjs, and TV thing what you usually do with your friends?"

"Um…yeah."

The awkward silence made me look back up at her face. Liza stared down at the ground instead of at me.

A pang of guilt seared through me. Had Liza ever had a girls' night before? I wasn't really one to talk. The number of friends I had were limited at best growing up. Kins had been my first real friend in years and she thought I had moved back home. All Liza and I had were each other now. There was no reason for me to act like a stuck up bitch. Besides, I wanted tonight to be fun. "Your friends know what's up," I said. "Let me get out of these uncomfortable clothes. I'll be right back."

"Yeah?"

"Absolutely. What show did you have in mind?" We started walking down the hall together.

"Well, we have a few options," said Liza. "American Idol, Real Housewives, The Bachelor…"

"I'm really good with whatever. How about you choose."

"Are you sure?" She pushed her glasses up the bridge of her nose.

"Mhm. I'll be back out in a sec." I walked into my bedroom and closed the door behind me. The only time I ever seemed to go in here anymore was when I needed clothes. I expected my room to be dusty and depressing, but it wasn't. The bed was even made, which I hadn't remembered doing. *Weird.* Regardless, the room felt empty. Eli's room felt lived in, even without him there. It felt like home. I smiled to myself as I quickly changed into a pair of plaid pajama pants and a tank top.

I wanted to give Liza whatever girls' night she'd dreamed up in her head, but I really needed to talk to her about how Eli was doing. Maybe she'd have an idea about how to sneak me out of here so I could go visit him tonight. And I definitely needed to team up with her to uncover V's secret identity. I had a list a mile long and none of it involved watching Real Housewives and gossiping like teenagers.

I laughed out loud and it sounded sad in the empty room. Technically I was a teenager. But I had never really felt like one. Not in an "I'm an old soul" sort of hipster way. Just in a "my childhood was robbed from me" kind of way. Maybe tonight would actually be fun.

Regardless, I needed to give her a little bit of us time before I started asking her all the questions I needed to. It seemed like a fair compromise. When I walked back out, Liza was sitting on the couch in bright pink flannel pajama bottoms and a matching top. There were cute little panda faces all over them. She had the top buttoned all the way up to her neck, which couldn't possibly have been very comfortable. But she looked happy enough.

There was a box of chocolate doughnuts already opened on the coffee table and there were two cases of Mike's Hard Lemonade. I didn't know much about girls' nights, but this was definitely not a Sex and the City kind of girls' night. This was one for teenagers who didn't really like the taste of alcohol yet. Which was technically me. But there was no way I was drinking tonight. My headache had only just gone away from last night's escapades.

"How'd you score those?" I asked as I sat down next to her and lifted up a chocolate doughnut. I was down to eat dessert first at least.

"I'm 23."

"Oh. Right." How did I not know that?

She laughed. "Shut up, slut, you had no idea how old I was."

Slut? Rude. I laughed it off. "Yeah, I guess we never really talked about that."

"Well, you're eighteen. But I only know it because of the background check I ran on you after we first met. Although, your birthday is coming up in a few weeks. The big one-nine." She winked at me.

Why was she being so weird? "Yup." I didn't want to talk about my birthday. It was the last thing on my mind.

"Do you have any special plans for it?"

"No, not really. Although, Don's head on a platter would be nice. Or Eli getting out of the hospital. Or seeing V's face."

Liza laughed. "I feel like we're still a long way off with Don. Eli's not leaving the hospital anytime soon. And I kind of like the whole sexy masked man thing V has going on. If you know what I mean." She winked at me, lifted up one of the Mike's Hard Lemonades, and tried to hand it to me.

"Oh, no, that's okay."

"You have to drink."

She was a stickler for these random girls' night rules she had made up in her head. "I had some wine last night and I only just got rid of my hangover. I really shouldn't.

Besides, we have lots of work to do tomorrow. We need a new plan for Mr. Crawford and…"

"No work talk," Liza said, cutting me off. "That's why I closed the wall to the headquarters. There's girls' night rules."

I glanced to my right and sure enough, the apartment could have passed for any other one in this building. "Liza, I have so many questions about Eli though…"

"We can talk about all that later. I know that sometimes it's fun to break the rules. Technically I could be arrested for serving someone underage alcohol." She whispered alcohol even though it was only the two of us in the room. "But I've been breaking lots of rules recently and I've found it very liberating. I bought these with the sole purpose of serving them to a minor." Her eyes suddenly got huge. "Oh my God. That sounded *so* bad. I did not mean that in a sexual way. At all. I just literally meant that you're under the age of 21 and therefore it is illegal for you to drink libations."

"I got what you meant."

"Good." She popped off the top and this time forced me to take it from her. "I'm feeling very rebellious ever since I joined this group. But girls' night is sacred and we are not breaking any rules tonight. Drink up."

"I really shouldn't…"

She got the same look on her face as when I told her it wasn't a slumber party.

"You know what, you're absolutely right." I took a tiny sip. Honestly it was a whole lot better than the red wine I'd had last night with V. Not that I really drank it with him. I kind of stole it from him and drank it alone in Eli's room. I shook away the thought. "We only live once, right?"

"Exactly." Liza grabbed the remote and brought up the recordings on the DVR. There were several episodes of The Bachelor and she clicked on the oldest one.

"Since when do we have DVR?"

"Chill, slut. You have a ton of money. You're not going to miss ten bucks a month."

"Can you please stop calling me a slut? I'm not a slut."

Liza laughed and took a sip from her drink. "I don't mean it in an actual slut way. I mean it in a girl, you funny way." She pulled her legs up on the couch. "Although, you have slept with quite a few guys. Way more than me. Don, V, Eli, Miles…"

"Who told you that I slept with Miles?"

"Eli talks a lot in his sleep."

I had been sleeping over in Eli's room. He had never talked in his sleep before. Had they been talking about me? "Don doesn't count," I said.

"I'm sorry, I know. I don't know why I included him."

"Thanks. And for the record, three guys isn't exactly a lot."

"Mhm."

She didn't sound convinced though. "Well how many guys have you slept with?"

"None of your business."

"You literally ran a background check on me. The least you can do is tell me your sexual history. Slut," I added.

Her smile grew tenfold. Apparently she enjoyed being called a slut. Me on the other hand? Not so much.

"I don't have one."

I laughed. "You know what I mean," I said. "I know it's not technically history." I put history in air quotes. "Just tell me your number."

"Zero?"

No one? Seriously? "Is that a question or a fact?"

"It's zero." She took a huge sip from her bottle and turned to me. "That's bad, right? No one wants to sleep with a virgin. And I'm not just a virgin. I've never even kissed a boy. Let alone given him my flower."

Her flower? Really? She was so naïve. Or maybe I was just bitter. Because I never got to give anyone mine. It got taken from me. "Don't call it your flower, that makes it sound creepy."

"Oh. Okay."

"You've really never had sex, Liza?"

"No." She pushed her glasses up her nose. "I knew it was bad. What 23 year old has never had sex?!" She pressed her lips firmly closed and looked behind her down the hall. "God, do you think he heard me?"

"Who? V?"

"Who else?" She lifted up a pillow and put it over her face. She started talking into the pillow, but her voice was so muffled that I couldn't even hear her.

"Liza." I grabbed the pillow and yanked it down from her face. "You shouldn't be embarrassed. Honestly I still wish I had my…flower." I tried not to cringe at the word. It was laced with such innocence that it made me feel sick to my stomach. Nothing about my first time had been innocent. But I did mean what I said. I wished I was still a virgin.

"Really?"

"Yes, really. I never got the chance to choose, you know. And I always had one person in mind." I pictured Miles' face and tried my best to squash down the feelings threatening to emerge.

"I want to give V my flower. Desperately." She hugged the pillow to her chest.

"V? I feel like you should choose someone who's comfortable enough to let you see his face."

"V doesn't wear a mask because he's uncomfortable with himself. He wears it because he's uncomfortable around you. But I know him really well. He's sweet and caring and…"

"And cruel."

"No, not at all. He's one of the nicest people I've ever met. And he cares so fiercely for those in his life."

"He doesn't care about Eli," I said. "V hasn't visited him in the hospital. He hasn't let me leave the apartment to go visit him either."

"That's not true, V has visited Eli."

"What?"

"He came last night after all the nurses left for the evening. Eli was sleeping, but he sat with us. I'm telling you, Summer, V is a stand-up guy."

He was nice to everyone but me. Was it really because he was uncomfortable around me? There were more reasons why Liza shouldn't sleep with him. The most important being that V confessed that he loved me a couple nights ago. But I didn't want her to know that. We were just starting to get along. "Liza, I really think you could find someone sweeter."

"Like Eli? He really is the best. No one's ever listened to me like Eli does. He doesn't grow impatient with me or anything or call me names. We've had such nice conversations about life the past few days. What we'll do after this whole thing is over and everything. It's easy to talk to him because he's not still in the college scene like some people I know." She smiled at me and then took a sip from her drink. "But girl, haven't you heard? He's taken! My bffl just got engaged to him." She looked down at my hand even though I'd already told her we weren't actually engaged.

I laughed. "Seriously, we're not engaged."

"Did you talk about getting engaged?"

"Yes, but…"

"Did you talk about the future?"

"Yeah, but that doesn't…"

"Do you want to marry him?"

I swallowed hard. "Yes."

"Oh my God, you hesitated."

"I didn't hesitate."

"Yes you did. You waited several seconds before saying yes."

Had I? I took a sip from my bottle. And then another as her eyes scrutinized me.

"You two are good, right?" Liza asked.

"Absolutely. And I miss him terribly. All I want to do is visit him."

"You really should. He asks about you all the time. I think it's been hurting his feelings that you haven't come."

"Could I call him next time you're there? You can give him your phone?"

Liza shook her head. "No, they won't let him use a cell phone near all the machines, but he's dying to talk to you."

"What about the other day when you called me by his bed?"

"I told you I recently got into breaking the rules. But I got in so much trouble. The cops caught me red-handed. I'm lucky they didn't confiscate my phone like they did with his."

This was my chance to find out more information. And I wasn't even the one to bring it up. *Perfect.* "How did that conversation with the police go? You told them you were his fiancé, but did they tell you anything about what would happen to him? Is he going to be arrested once he gets better?"

"I was waiting for tonight to tell you so that we could properly celebrate." She leaned forward and tapped her bottle against mine. "He's in the clear."

"What? How?"

"It was all my idea really. We told them about how he was undercover for so long and didn't want to blow it because he was really close to getting the information he needed."

"Information?"

"Mhm. Getting you to confess to everything. The murder. All that. They totally bought it. I think they're even considering letting him go back undercover. I'm pretty sure we convinced them that his cover wasn't' blown. They said they'd let us know soon."

He turned the tables on me? My throat constricted. I guess it's what I would have wanted him to do in order to get out of this mess. So why did it sting? "So he's not going to be arrested?"

"Nope. The guards that were outside his room were even dismissed. You could totally come visit now."

"Tell V that."

"I'll tell V that if you describe oral to me."

I choked on the Lo Mein I had just put in my mouth. "Excuse me?"

"Like what do you do? Hold that thought. I'm going to go grab a banana and you can give me a play-by-play."

I put my hand on her shoulder to prevent her from standing up. "Liza, I'm not going to show you how to give a blowjob."

"Please? If it gets physical with V I have to know what to do. I don't want him to think that I'm a loser."

"You're not a loser. And it doesn't matter what some stupid boy thinks anyway. Believe in yourself."

She nodded. "You're right. I don't need a man to validate my self-worth. Oh let's watch this part, I'm really excited about how much Ben vibes Kelly right now." She gestured to the screen.

Vibes? I didn't know Liza very well at all. I certainly never thought she'd use the term vibes. My eyes gravitated to the screen.

CHAPTER 22
Sunday

I was trying to think of the perfect lead in. Liza clearly didn't want to talk about work. And the extent of what she wanted to share about Eli had already been divulged. Even though I had a million more questions.

She shoved another Mike's Hard Lemonade into my hand. My stomach was full of booze and junk food already. But whenever she gave me something she'd give me a stern look until I started eating or drinking it.

I had drunk so much I couldn't even think straight anymore. Screw waiting for the perfect moment. We were on the third episode of The Bachelor, and in my opinion, Ben wasn't vibing anyone. And this horrible witch Jazmine needed to be sent home before I lost my shit.

"If he doesn't send Jazmine home at the end of this episode, I'm going to kill everyone," Liza said. "I swear I'll do it, and I won't regret it for a second."

I slapped her arm. "I was literally thinking the same thing!"

"Yeah?"

"Um…yes. She's the freaking worst. How can Ben not see that he's being played by a she-devil?"

"I know! And she doesn't get along well with anyone else in the house. How does he expect she's going to be when the shows over? Suddenly nice?"

We both laughed.

For the first time all night I actually realized that I was having a good time. A great time really. This was fun.

We stared at the TV and screamed at the end when Jazmine got the last rose of the night.

"He's going to regret his choice as soon as he sees this train wreck in these episodes."

I nodded. "And I don't see how whoever he chooses will forgive him either."

"Word." She tapped her bottle against mine.

I realized that it didn't even matter if I brought up something that Liza didn't want to talk about. She'd talk about it anyway because clearly we were best friends. I wasn't sure why I hadn't realized it before. We even both hated Jazmine. And I was having the best time. If this night didn't turn out to be a little progressive though, I'd wake up feeling bad. *I need answers, damn it.* "So I know you said that you liked V's mask..."

"Oh, I really do. I love it. It's so sexy, right?"

"Yeah."

Liza laughed. "I knew you still had feelings for him."

"What? No, I absolutely do not." I didn't say that. Had I just said that? God, how many of these stupid bottles had she made me drink?

"You just admitted that he's sexy," Liza said.

"Fine. Whatever. But who knows what he's hiding under that mask. Let's find out."

"I'm sure he'll reveal himself eventually."

I kicked her under the blanket we were sharing.

"Ow! You're such a slut!"

This time I did laugh at her not so nice nickname for me. "Liza, I'm serious. I don't want to wait. Let's unmask him tonight. It'll be so much fun."

She took a huge sip of her drink and her eyes grew round. "Like…tonight, tonight?"

I nodded.

"Oh my God, you're right. Let's do it!"

"Yeah?" I didn't think she'd be that easy to convince. "Great. Well…do you have a plan?"

"Let's drug him and then take off all his clothes. Including his mask of course. We can tie him up and everything."

I laughed. "That's a bad plan."

"No, it's a flawless plan. What could go wrong? We can use those little darts he uses to knock people out." She stood up and stumbled slightly toward the faux wall. She lifted up the painting that covered the keypad and typed the code in. The wall slowly lifted and disappeared into the ceiling. "It's a brilliant plan. We can use his own technology against him. And then I can finally kiss him!"

"When he's passed out?"

"Mhm." She lifted up a dart off one of the glass tables and came back over to the couch.

"Liza, you seem super devoted to this date rape plan, but there's probably a better way."

She laughed. "Date rape?" She pushed her glasses up the bridge of her nose, nearly stabbing herself with the dart. "That's bad. You're right, we should try something else first."

I was a little concerned that date rape was still plan B. But that just meant we needed a really great plan A. *Hmm.*

"I got it!" Liza said way too loudly.

"Shh, be quiet, he'll hear us. All I know for sure is that we're going to need the element of surprise."

"Absolutely. Okay," she whispered, but it was much more like a speaking voice. "I have the perfect plan. We knock on his door and then we say that we'll take off one item of our clothing in exchange for one of his. Eventually he'll only have his mask left and he'll *have* to take it off. There won't be any other choice."

"That is literally the best plan I've ever heard. Especially because there's two of us and only one of him. There's no way that together we aren't wearing more clothes than him."

"It's foolproof." Liza clapped her hands together.

"Absolutely." I stood up, accidentally spilling the remnants of Lo Mein on the floor. "Oops."

Liza giggled.

"Oh, we can make it so that it's even more impossible to fail."

She stared at me, completely perplexed. "How is that even possible?"

"We can put on more layers of clothes. Like a lot of layers. All the layers."

"You're a genius," Liza said. She stood up, linked her arm through mine, and we skipped down the hall in drunken bliss.

We stopped at the coat rack and started pulling on gloves, hats, and winter coats. When we both looked like huge barefooted winter monsters, we stumbled toward V's door.

"Do you think he'll take my flower when he gets me naked?" Liza didn't whisper it, she practically yelled the words.

"How could he not? You'll be naked. It's the logical next step." I was about to knock on the door, but stopped. "And I promise I'll back away as soon as I see his face. He's all yours, I promise."

She nodded. "I'm nervous."

"Don't be nervous."

That didn't seem to help at all. I grabbed her arm and turned her toward me. "Liza, I've had so much fun with you tonight."

"Best night ever!" she screamed.

"Shh!" But I started laughing hysterically too.

"We need to do this every week," she said. "Or every night for the rest of our lives."

"That one. Definitely that one."

"Best friends forever!" Liza screamed at the top of her lungs and started laughing even harder.

Our laughter died when V's door opened.

Liza made a small peeping noise.

"What are you ladies up to?" V asked and put his hand on the doorjamb to block our view of his room.

"Girls' night," Liza said. "Now get naked or else."

I laughed.

But V did not laugh. He just stared at us. "Excuse me?"

I elbowed Liza in the side and she laughed. "What Liza meant to say was that we want to play a game."

He smiled. "What kind of game did you have in mind?"

"This is how it works," I said. "For every article of clothing you take off, one of us will take off an article of clothing too."

"It's going to be so much fun," Liza added.

"But you're dressed like Eskimos." There was a twinkle in his eye. "That hardly seems fair."

I looked back and forth between Liza and me. We were wearing a lot of clothes. Plenty, really. "Okay, for every one article of clothing you take off, we'll each take one off. So we'll go twice as fast as you. It's your lucky night."

"Um…no you'll be going at the same pace as me."

"No, I think Summer has done the math correctly on this one," Liza said. "There's two of us. And only one of you."

"No, I get that…" his voice trailed off.

Clearly he had realized his blunder. Our math was flawless.

"Okay, I'll humor you. What's this game with very realistic rules called?"

"Strip," Liza said.

"Naked game," I said at the exact same time.

We both laughed.

"That definitely sounds legit," he said.

"Mhm. It's the strip naked game," Liza said with a very straight face. "And it's real. You first."

"You're both very drunk."

"How dare you, sir," Liza said. "We haven't had anything to drink tonight at all. Right, Summer?"

"Correct. We just had some lemonade." I winked at her.

"You're up first," Liza said. "Go."

"I think you should both sleep this off. After you take off the winter jackets so you don't sweat to death."

"Only after you take off some of your layers," I said. "The rules are…rules."

"I'm not playing this game with you," V said.

"Wrong answer," Liza said. She threw the dart that was in her hand as hard as she could. It missed him by a whole foot, hit the wall, bounced off, and fell directly onto her bare foot.

"Oh shit," Liza said. "Plan C! Initiate plan C!"

"I don't know what plan C is! Liza?"

She teetered to the side and V caught her.

"What the hell were you two trying to do?"

"See your face," Liza said and reach up and touched his mask. "Your beautiful, perfect face you lovely man, you." And then she immediately fell asleep and started snoring.

"Is she dead?" I asked. "Liza, wake up!"

V looked up at me. "No, she just passed out."

"Don't date rape her."

"I'm not going to," said V. "Seriously, are you high or something?"

"Lemonade." I pointed down the hall at the mess we had left in the family room.

"I see." He lifted Liza in his arms and carried her to her bedroom.

I followed close behind to make sure he didn't do anything unlawful. When he set her down on the bed, he pulled off her hat and gloves. He went to unzip her jacket and I caught his hand.

"You're breaking the rules. You owe me three articles of clothing."

He brushed my hand aside and pulled off Liza's coat. "I'm not playing your game." He pulled her blanket on top of her.

For a moment I remembered my father tucking me into bed. I tried to swallow down the lump in my throat. V was so caring and sweet. Just like Liza had said.

He went to leave the room, but I stayed where I was. I felt bad for trying to trick him into taking his mask off. And I didn't want to be alone with him. Because all these feelings were swirling around in my stomach and I made Liza a promise. A best friend promise. V was completely off limits. Besides, I loved Eli.

"She needs to sleep," he said and grabbed my arm, steering me back into the hall.

My body betrayed me. I melted into his side.

"You're burning up," he said and pulled the hat off my head.

I stood there in the hall as he took off each of my gloves. My heart fluttered as he unzipped my winter jacket. His fingers traced down my arms as he pushed my coat off.

"You owe me so many articles of clothing," I said.

He laughed.

I wanted to beg him to let me see his face. Instead, I said, "Are you sure she's okay? Maybe I should stay in there with her."

"You need sleep too."

I nodded. "Okay. Yeah, I'll go to sleep." But I didn't move.

His hands didn't leave my arms.

We both just stood there, staring at each other.

Until he stepped closer.

Until I lifted my face to his.

Until his lips were a fraction of an inch from mine.

I turned my cheek at the last moment and his lips brushed against my skin instead.

"Sadie." He inhaled deeply and it felt like he was inhaling all of me. "I meant what I said the other day. I do love you."

His words were a knife to my heart. "Stop." I stepped away from him. "Liza really likes you."

"I know."

"So…you should try and work things out with her." I took another step away from him.

"There's nothing to work out with her. We're just friends. It's you. It's always been you. I told you that."

"And you also told me that you didn't love me just a few months ago. Remember that?"

"I'm asking you to believe me now."

"Then take off your mask. Show me who you are."

"I need you to love me before I take off my mask. It's the only way to know if this is real. It's the only way."

He was hiding something big from me. Something monumental. And scary. I took another step away from him. *He's Don.* The realization slammed into me hard and it was suddenly hard to breathe. He had to be Don. Why else wouldn't he want me to see his face?

"Stay away from me," I said when he took a step closer.

"Can we please just talk for a few minutes? If you would just give me a chance to explain."

I ran into Eli's room.

"Sadie, don't…"

I slammed the door in his face and locked it. V had laid Liza down in bed like he truly cared. He treated her tenderly. He was kind and sweet.

It was the opposite of how Don would have behaved. He would never treat another human that way. He would have left her to sweat it out in the hall.

But not V.

So who was he? I couldn't deny the fact that my stomach had butterflies when he'd leaned in to kiss me. But I hated that it did. I felt gross. I looked around Eli's room. I didn't deserve to sleep in here tonight.

I pressed my ear against the door. There wasn't any noise. Hopefully V was gone. I slowly opened it. The coast was clear. I tiptoed down the hall to my room and quietly opened the door and walked in.

I saw the form in my bed. Before I screamed, I realized that I knew who it was. The shape of his broad shoulders. The familiar hood. It was V. He was facing away from the door, but it was definitely him.

The room hadn't felt stale earlier. My bed had magically been made. Had V been sleeping in here for a while?

I slept in Eli's room because I missed him and I loved him. Was that why V slept in my bed?

It felt like my heart was shattered in a million different pieces, just like V had said. I wasn't sure if that was what made me close the door and walk to the bed. Or if it was how alone I felt. Or guilty. Or lost.

I pushed back the covers and climbed in beside him.

He immediately rolled over, wrapping his arms around me. It was like he knew I would come. Like he had been waiting for me. How many nights had he hoped I would come?

Neither one of us said anything because there was nothing to say. This wasn't some momentous occasion. *Right?*

I was just drunk. And I wasn't thinking straight. But God, it really felt like home in his arms.

CHAPTER 23
Monday

I slept soundlessly. It was like I was transported back in time to when I had first slept over at V's place. I had never felt so safe.

I didn't want to open my eyes. It was too soon for the moment to end, but I could feel the sunlight streaming through the window, hitting my face. I needed to sneak out of the room before he woke up. Maybe he'd forget about the whole thing. Hopefully I would too.

But when my eyes opened, I couldn't move. For the first time, it seemed like there was something familiar about him. Something about the small crinkles around his eyes.

My train of thought quickly derailed. What had I done? Hadn't I learned anything from my past mistakes? I could still picture Kins' face when she saw me almost kiss Miles. Apparently I had no girl code. This was going to make Liza hate me. And I was not about to lose my only friend. I had to go.

But were those freckles under his eyes? And those long eyelashes really did seem familiar. Or was it just because it had been awhile since I was so close to him? If I could just get a little closer…

Stop.

In the grand scheme of things, V's identity didn't matter. At all. Our paths were only aligned until I got vengeance against Don. That was it. Yet, I still leaned forward.

It was like V could sense my proximity. His eyes opened and I froze.

Oh God, it probably looks like I was leaning in to kiss him.

A smile spread across his lips.

I needed to do something that would change the mood in the room. Because right now it felt like electricity was running through my veins. Like something amazing was about to happen. Which it absolutely could not.

"What were the 80s like?" I asked. It was the first thing I could remember from my research about Dr. Miller. He was born in 1981, which meant he'd remember that decade.

V propped himself up on his elbow. "How would I know?"

I stayed where I was. "Didn't you grow up during the 80's?"

He stared at me, a smile playing at the corner of his lips. "You know that I didn't."

Liar. And what did he even mean by that? I didn't know who he was. My best guess was that he was Dr. Miller. "Well, what did you think of Seattle?" It's where Dr. Miller had gotten his PhD. *Slip up, V.*

He reached his hand out toward me. I should have moved, but I was still frozen in place. He tucked a loose strand of hair behind my ear. His hands were so cold.

"What are you talking about?" he asked. "I've never been to Seattle. Is that somewhere you want to go one day? After all this is over?"

"No." I sat up and climbed out of bed. I was not going to talk about the future with him. He was the one that had said we were living on borrowed time.

"Sadie…"

"Please just pretend like last night didn't happen."

"I can't do that." He climbed out of bed and grabbed my arm before I could run out of the bedroom.

"Please, V. Don't make this into something that it wasn't."

He shook his head. "You came to me, not the other way around."

"I was drunk. I wasn't thinking straight. It was a mistake."

"No, it wasn't. I know you feel it too. And I'm sorry that I pushed you away before, but I'm not pushing you away now. I realized my mistake. I'm here and I'm not going anywhere."

"You realized your mistake because I moved on? That's not fair, V. And you can't keep changing your mind for no reason other than jealousy."

"I never changed my mind. I told you I regretted saying that I loved you, but you didn't give me a chance to explain."

"A chance to explain? You never asked for one. You let the window close and put an end to the conversation. One which I begged you to have by the way. You were never going to bring it up. As far as I'm concerned, there's nothing else to say." I tried to wiggle out of his grip, but his fingers tightened on my forearm. He was trying to get me to stay, but he still wasn't explaining himself. This was ridiculous. "I'm not going to stand here all day and expect anything from you. I've learned my lesson." I opened up the door with my other hand, but he reached above me and slammed it closed.

I wanted to run, but I knew it would be useless. I couldn't outrun him. That much was obvious from our training sessions. I couldn't outfight him either. And when he was this close to me, I didn't want to. I hated myself for that.

Still he said nothing. He shook his head back and forth like he was at a war with himself.

"I'm no longer asking for an explanation," I said. "I don't need one and I don't want to hear it. All I'm asking is for you to get out of my way." I tried to duck under his arm, but he moved forward, pressing my back against the door, caging me in.

It sounded like a growl escaped from his throat. "I wanted to say those words for the first time without my mask. Because I thought that was the only way that we could make sense. It's certainly the only way I deserved to hear it back. But I'm more me behind this mask than I am without it. And I'm having a hard time coming to terms with that. And I was just scared that you wouldn't want me this way."

"What way?"

He shook his head. "All the goodness in me is gone."

It didn't matter how angry I was at him. I didn't want him to be in pain. "You tucked Liza in last night. You didn't take advantage of me in my drunken state." I left off the fact that I might have actually let him do it. "You're not a bad person, V. You're not. I know what you do with all the money you get from criminals. You've helped so many people. There's so much goodness in you."

He shook his head. "Then why can't you love me back?"

I didn't know where this was coming from. Why he suddenly realized he wanted me. But no matter how drawn to him I was, I didn't love him. I didn't want a life like this. It was toxic and dark. The small bouts of goodness weren't enough. I needed so much light because my soul was dark too. Darker than his. "Because I'm in love with Eli."

He recoiled from me, like my skin burned him. He turned away from me and this time I knew I heard the growl. It sounded like a wounded animal. It sounded like his soul was dying.

And I did the weakest thing possible. I slipped out of the room and left him alone with his demons. It wasn't like I knew how to piece him back together. I was broken too.

***

I was even more of a coward when I had a hangover. For most of the day I had locked myself in Eli's room. His scent was no longer lingering on his sheets and I missed him terribly. Enough was enough. I needed to go see him.

The only problem was that I still had no idea how. I finished scrubbing the last burner on the stove and wrung out the washcloth. The stovetop sparkled back at me. I knew how much V liked everything spotless. It wasn't my turn to clean, so I was hoping this could help persuade V to give me some type of reward for good inmate behavior. Like a free pass to the outdoors. I rolled my eyes at myself. There was no chance this would actually work. At least I had gotten some of my pent-up frustration out on the burners.

I was tempted to go bother Liza. I had knocked on her door earlier and it sounded like she had thrown a shoe at it. She probably had a worse hangover than me. Combining alcohol with a heavy sedative wasn't a great idea. I laughed, remembering how the dart hit her foot. She had terrible aim.

I looked up at the camera mounted in the corner. "Truce, Athena?"

She didn't respond.

"I'll dust your hard drive if you let me out of here."

Nothing.

"She's no longer programmed to respond to your voice."

I turned to see V standing by the kitchen counter, his hands tucked into his pockets. The casual air about him contrasted so powerfully from how I had last seen him. Now it looked like he wanted to laugh, when hours ago, I was pretty sure he was about to cry.

His hoodie wasn't zipped up as high as usual, and I got a glimpse of his tan neck. Which was odd because it was the middle of winter. And he never took off the damn hoodie to get any sun on his skin. He must have been naturally tan. My eyes wandered back up to his mask.

The expensive cologne he wore invaded my air supply. Maybe he had just taken a shower. *Why the hell am I thinking about him taking a shower?* I sat down at the kitchen counter and lifted up one of the doughnuts leftover from last night. "Awesome," I said and took a bite. I took my time to swallow, trying to figure out what to say to him to gain my freedom back. "So if there's a fire and I'm the only one in here, I'll burn to death?"

"Voice activation doesn't trump safety protocols."

I wanted to strangle him. "Eli needs me."

"He needs rest."

"Why did you go see him the other day when you wouldn't let me?"

"He's my friend."

"That's not...you know what I meant. I'm just as stealthy as you. You trained me yourself. I'm not going to get caught."

"You're not as good as me."

Arrogant prick. "And you two aren't friends. You hate each other."

"That's not true. I respect Eli. That's what our friendship is built on."

"Well it's certainly not mutual respect for boundaries with his girlfriend."

V ignored me and pulled something out of his pocket. He placed my Sagitta pendant down on the counter. "You told me this meant everything to you. You said it made you feel like you weren't alone. That it reminded you of your parents, your grandparents, and what it was like to be happy."

I stared down at the necklace. I was surprised he remembered that. It seemed like ages ago that I cared about that pendant. I had been so obsessed when I had lost it.

When in truth it was a worthless trinket. V had been right the whole time.

"But that was a lie, right?" he asked.

I shook my head and looked back up at him. "No." It wasn't a lie. I just felt more content now carrying around a gun than some stupid necklace from a boy that had cast me aside. I hated that necklace and I hated what it stood for. My past needed to stay in the past. A constant reminder wasn't helping me.

"You lied to me then and you're lying to me now. It reminds you of Miles."

Hearing his name made me want to cry. I wasn't even sure why I still had such a strong reaction to him. I should have felt nothing. I wanted to feel nothing. "You don't know what you're talking about."

"Why else would you have stopped wearing it? It meant everything to you, remember? Your words, not mine. If it means everything then why was it stuck in a drawer in your desk instead of hanging from your fucking neck?"

I stared at him. Why was he so worked up about this? "Despite what you might think, it felt like a link to my past. And I'm done with my past."

"If you had seriously moved on from your past, then you wouldn't still be hell-bent on killing Don."

"I'm allowed to want justice for what he took from me without wanting to hold on to a stupid trinket from my past." I could feel my heart rate accelerating. It was like he was purposely trying to push my buttons. What was his problem?

"Just admit that you don't want to wear it anymore because Miles has moved on with his life and doesn't want you back anymore."

"He stopped wanting me back when he stopped writing to me!" I took a deep breath. I knew that Miles never stopped writing, but it still felt like he had. V was making the memories swirl to the surface. This conversation was suffocating me. I wanted to leave it in the past. I needed to leave it in the past. "It has nothing to do with him."

"He's the one that gave it to you."

"When I thought he loved me!" I wasn't sure why I was yelling. And I wasn't sure why there were tears forming in my eyes.

"Just admit that I never had a chance. And neither did Eli."

"Yes, okay? It reminded me of Miles. But I'm over him. That was so long ago. I was just a stupid kid."

He pulled an envelope out of his pocket. "Don't pretend for a second that what you just said is true. And stop lying to me and saying that you love Eli. Because you don't. You're still in love with your childhood sweetheart. And the saddest part is that you don't even know if he's the same person anymore. You know nothing about him besides for the fact that you used to like him. It's pathetic." He placed the envelope down on the counter next to the pendant. His hand was on top of it so that I couldn't see who it was addressed to. "Yet, your heart beats for one person and one person only. Miles Young."

This again? "You know what? We've already had this conversation. I'm not going to rehash this with you right now."

"All I'm saying is that it's not me. And it's certainly not Eli." He lifted his hand off the envelope.

Miles' name was scrawled across the front of the envelope. In my handwriting. And it was opened. I grabbed the envelope and pulled out the letter I had written Miles when I thought I was going to die. The one I had slipped under his door and told him to read. How did V have this? Unless...I looked up at V. *Miles?*

It was like he could sense my question. "I followed you that night. I got the letter back before Miles ever saw it. You had just confessed to loving me and Eli and I knew you were about to do something idiotic. Which you did."

I swallowed hard. "Miles never saw it?"

V shook his head.

For months I'd thought he knew and didn't care. "You're saying that he doesn't know that I'm Summer?"

V shrugged.

Miles didn't know? *Miles had no idea who I was!* He just thought Sadie disappeared. And why would he care about Sadie? I had always acted like a complete lunatic around him. He didn't know who I even was. Which meant he hadn't necessarily given up on me. The only thing that mattered was that he didn't stop looking for Summer.

It felt like my heart started beating again. And then it cracked a little more when I thought about Eli. And then it exploded into fire when I looked at V. "If Miles never saw this letter, then why was it opened?"

"Because I read it. I needed to know why you'd never love me back."

"It wasn't addressed to you."

He took step toward me. "And you promised all of us that you'd stop seeing him. And you definitely promised to keep your identity a secret."

"When did you read it?" I asked, ignoring him.

"As soon as I found it. While you were busy on the roof."

I thought about how cold V had been to me the past few months. He had read my letter to Miles. He knew I had slept with Miles. He knew everything. Yet he still said he loved me before he thought we were going to die. Because his feelings were that strong. And when reality came crashing down? He realized that loving me was a waste of time. Because my heart belonged to Miles.

"You knew about this for months and didn't tell me?" It was like he was trying to rob me of my happiness. I looked around the apartment. Like he was trying to keep me locked up so I couldn't go to anyone else. "You're insane."

"I needed more time with you."

"Time? You've been so cold to me. If you wanted more time you should have utilized it a little better."

He put one of his elbows on the counter. It bothered me how casual he looked.

"Like how you've been utilizing your time with Eli?" he asked. "I never wanted to lie to you. I was waiting for you to realize that it was us written in the stars, not you and Miles. Because you're not Summer Brooks anymore. You're not. You were supposed to forget about him."

"And you thought that it would help if I thought he had forgotten about me?"

"I thought it wouldn't hurt. But clearly I was wrong because you love leaving a trail of broken hearts in your wake."

"That's a little dramatic…"

"Is it? I've only ever loved you. And I'll only ever love you. Even when you're completely blind to your own feelings."

"What?" Liza croaked from the entrance to the kitchen.

Shit. "It's nothing, Liza. V's just completely lost his mind."

She looked so hurt. It was like reliving the moment when Kins saw me almost kiss Miles. And I hated that I was just on an unending loop of hurting people. *Leaving a trail of broken hearts in my wake.*

"I'm going to go visit Eli," Liza said and backed out of the kitchen before I could say anything else.

"You just broke her heart," I said to V. "So don't you dare pretend that you haven't hurt anyone." I grabbed the letter and necklace off the counter and followed Liza.

"At least I never pretended to reciprocate her feelings like you did with me," he said to my back. "And you're free to leave the apartment now. But don't come crawling back to me when nothing is as it seems."

I ignored his haunting words. He was manipulative. He was insane. And I hated that maybe he was just a tiny bit right about me.

CHAPTER 24
Monday

I leaned against the wall outside my old dorm building. I didn't know why I was here. The first thing I should have done with my new freedom was go to Eli. Yet, here I was. I wasn't worried about anyone recognizing me. I hadn't exactly made a bunch of friends on my floor. But I still kept my knit hat pulled low. My face was plastered on news stations. And V was right, my hair wasn't fooling anyone.

It was late. I'd be lucky if someone came in or out so I could slip in. And I wasn't even entirely sure that I wanted to talk to Miles. He had been laughing and flirting with that blonde girl on move-in day. I hadn't imagined that. Just because he didn't read my letter didn't mean he didn't know the truth. I mean, I literally just thought about my hair not fooling anyone. Miles still could have known and he still could have moved on. Showing up here was insane. *Right?*

I pulled out the letter from my pocket and unfolded it. I barely remembered what I had even written. Some days I even wished that I had died that night. That everything had ended. That my whole body was no longer filled with pain. I closed my eyes for a moment and took a deep breath. I felt like my whole body was worn to the bone. Like I was approaching 80 instead of 19. Like I was frail. I opened my eyes and read the letter.

Miles,

I fell in love with you the first time I ever saw you. It didn't even feel like a choice. I honestly couldn't help falling in love with you. And a part of me has always believed it was because we were written in the stars.

That night in your tree house when you took my hand, I thought it was the best night of my life. But life is such a fleeting thing. You can have your whole life in front of you one second, and then it can be taken away in a flash. But I always had you. I needed you after my parents died and you were my one constant.

Until suddenly you weren't. For years, I felt so alone. You hurt me. So I know I hurt you too. And for that, I'm so sorry. I'm sorry I disappeared. I'm sorry you couldn't find me. But it wasn't my choice. I never wanted to disappear. I never stopped wanting to be found. I never stopped needing you, Miles. That was the whole problem. I needed you more than ever and it felt like you didn't need me.

My love for you mixed with hate. I still loved you, but I fucking hated you too. I hated you for abandoning me. I hated you for forgetting about what we were. But I understand now. I'm sorry about the years apart. I'm sorry if you ever felt cut as deep as I did. And I'm sorry if your life stopped like mine.

I lived with a monster. And I became one too. I was torn between wanting you to find me and wanting you to never see what I had become. The truth is, I'm not the girl you remember. The years changed me more than you could ever know. And I don't want you to know what happened. I don't want you to dig. I don't want you to get hurt more than I've already hurt you. Summer Brooks is dead. It's important that you understand that.

But you've always seen me. You saw through my disguise right away at the diner. I had never heard anything as sweet as my name on your lips. And I'm sorry I couldn't tell you. I got mixed up in something bigger than you and me.

I just need you to know that I don't forgive you. Because you never did anything wrong, so you don't need my forgiveness. And you deserve everything I could never give you. Live your life for me. Just because I don't get any more heartbeats doesn't mean your heart has to stop beating too. Live the life I couldn't.

And if a part of you still remembers me when you look at the stars, let it be the smallest part. Let it be the smallest constellation in the sky on a late night in September. And let it slowly fade away as the seasons change.

I wiped away my tears and looked up at the sky. It was a clear night, but there were no stars in the sky. New York City at its finest. I folded the letter back up and slipped it in my pocket. My situation hadn't changed. I had wanted Miles to forget about me. He had his whole life to live. If I got what I wanted, I'd end up behind bars. I didn't want him to be part of that.

Besides, he was moving on. I needed to stay lost. I was just about to walk away when someone stepped out of the dorm building.

I grabbed the handle before it closed and slipped inside. *What am I doing?* My mind was saying one thing, but my feet were guiding me on the familiar path. I had walked up these stairs so many times, but tonight felt different. It felt like I was actually saying goodbye.

I just needed to see if he was okay. *Hear* if he was okay. I'd put my ear to the door, hear him laughing or something, and walk away forever. Easy peasy.

I opened up the door to my old floor. It was deserted. I stopped outside of Miles' door and was about to press my ear against it when I heard laughter. But it wasn't Miles. It was female laughter.

"Shut up!" She laughed again. "Tell me you're not serious?"

And it was like my hand had a mind of its own. I needed to see who Miles replaced me with so easily. I just needed to know. The sound of my knock echoed in the empty hall.

The door flung open and the same blonde I had seen him with at the beginning of the semester was standing in front of me. Her hair was in a messy bun and she was wearing workout clothes. She was tan and fit and beautiful. And I felt ridiculous all bundled up with my hat pulled low. With my dyed blonde hair. I freaking hated my hair this color.

"Um…I'll call you back in a sec," she said into her cell phone and then pulled it away from her ear. "Can I help you?"

"No. I mean…" I looked past her into the room. It was decorated with all her crap. Posters of pop stars and a pink rug. Not only had Miles moved on but he had removed his posters of the constellations. *Just like I stopped wearing the Sagitta pendant.* I was wearing it again now and it felt like it weighed a hundred pounds. "Is Miles here?" I blurted out before my brain could kick into flight mode.

"Miles?" She looked confused for a second. "Oh, Miles Young? The old R.A.? No, he doesn't live here anymore."

I wasn't expecting that response. So they weren't dating? The necklace felt a little lighter. "Did he move out or something?"

"I really have no idea. We didn't really talk, he just trained me on the position. I think maybe he took the semester off or something."

"For what?"

"I don't know. Personal reasons probably. But yeah…he's not here. Is there something I can help you with though?" She gave me a once over.

"You have no idea where he went?"

"None." She placed her hand on her hip. "Do I know you? You look so familiar."

"I just have one of those faces. Thanks for your help." I glanced down the hall. All I wanted to do was go talk to Kins. But I had already made enough mistakes. Blowing my cover with her wasn't a good idea.

"Are you sure we don't know each other?" the blonde asked.

"Positive. Have a nice night!" I walked in the opposite direction of the stairwell. Going to my old room wouldn't blow my cover. Kins wouldn't be there. She was always with Patrick. And I just needed a second to calm down. I needed to process everything before I went to visit Eli.

He'd know something was bothering me, and I didn't need him to worry about anything but getting better.

My sensor pass hadn't worked outside. But that was an easy change for them to make. A key though? I doubted they changed the locks on the doors whenever a student dropped out. There was no reason to.

Although, I was wanted for murder. I slid my key into the lock and it clicked open. Apparently campus safety wasn't a top priority at Eastern University.

CHAPTER 25
Monday

When I turned on the lights, I froze. All my stuff was exactly as I had left it. My comforter was still on my bed. My books still stacked on my desk. One of them was even opened to the last page I had read. Nothing had moved at all.

I hadn't been expecting that. Part of me thought Kins would have a new roommate. Or that maybe she would have switched dorms to move in with someone else. But all her stuff was still here too.

I walked over to her nightstand. There was a framed picture of her and Patrick. They were both smiling hard for the camera. I always wondered how the two of them were doing. I had watched them from a distance a few times and it seemed like they fought more than anything else.

I turned around and breathed in slowly. The room smelled like home. Which was odd. I hadn't lived there for very long. But I was comfortable here. Happy even. For a while anyway. Before the bloody slippers had shown up. I peered under my bed just to check.

Nothing.

As I looked around the room, I felt sad. The room reminded me of everything I didn't have growing up. Moving from foster home to foster home. There was no way those beds weren't filled after I left. Another kid to ignore. Or another child to love instead of me. I was easily forgotten. But here? Kins didn't want to forget. And something about that gave me hope. That maybe she hadn't given up on me. That maybe Miles hadn't either.

There were hushed voices outside the door. And then the sound of a key entering the lock.

Shit.

I glanced around before jumping into the opened closet. *Ow.* I grabbed my side after it collided with a vacuum cleaner. I was just able to scramble into the dark corner and crouch down out of sight when the dorm room door opened.

"You didn't have to walk me back," Kins said. "I can take care of myself."

It was a dismissal if I'd ever heard one.

"Babe, I'm sorry I brought it up. I just think it's important for us to talk about if it's still an issue."

I recognized Patrick's voice. I slowly moved some of the hanging dresses to the side so I could peer out at them.

"It's not an issue," Kins said. "God, can't we just have one normal night where you don't try to psychoanalyze me?"

Patrick sighed. "All I want is a normal night. But look around you. Clearly it *is* still an issue."

"Patrick, there's no point in talking about this. You never listen to me. What's the point in rehashing it right now?"

"The point is that I don't want you sneaking around behind my back."

"Seriously?" Kins opened up her dresser and pulled out a pair of pajamas. "I should have known. You're jealous that I went to visit Eli? I only went because I was looking for Sadie. And for the record, he didn't know where she was. Apparently they broke up months ago."

Broke up? I shook the thought away. I knew Eli was just trying to protect me. I stared at Kins. Apparently everyone had been to visit him but me. I bit the inside of my lip.

"Isn't that proof enough that she…"

"No. It's not. Eli didn't break up with her because she killed someone. He said he broke up with her because she always seemed distant. If you ask me, by the way he looked when we talked about her, I think she cheated on him. But that's beside the point."

I thought about V's arms around me. When had Kins visited Eli? I shook away the thought. Eli was just covering for me. That was all. I wasn't distant. I had been so present. Until he got injured. I hadn't visited him. And now that I was finally able to, I was here spying on Kins for no reason at all. What the hell was I doing?

"Distant?" Patrick asked. "Maybe she was distant because she was plotting how to murder her next victim."

"She's not a criminal!" Kins yelled.

"She killed that woman. She…"

"You didn't know her like I did. She wanted to be a psychologist. She wanted to help people. She wasn't going around making bombs and blowing people up. She's a good person."

"The cops…"

"They're wrong."

"It doesn't matter whether I'm right or wrong. This obsession you have is unhealthy. She's not coming back. You have to let it go."

Kins slammed a drawer shut. "I'm exhausted, Patrick. And I have an 8 a.m. tomorrow."

There was an awkward silence in the air. I could feel the tension between them, beyond just their words. I thought by me leaving, Kins would be safe and happy. But she wasn't. I was ruining her relationship without even being around. I pushed the dress aside even more and stared at her face. She looked like she was about to cry. That was my fault. Everything was my fucking fault.

"Let me spend the night," Patrick said and stepped toward her.

She put up her hands to stop his embrace. "Not tonight. I'll see you tomorrow at lunch, okay?"

He kissed her forehead and then glanced toward the closet. I held my breath. Had he seen me? But then he immediately left, leaving Kins standing there alone. I slowly exhaled. As soon as the door closed, Kins wiped tears away from underneath her eyes. She lifted up the opened book on my desk and threw it.

Tears pooled in my own eyes as I watched her.

"No." Kins ran over to the book. "No, no, no." She picked it up and thumbed through it, looking for the page it used to be on as she set it back down exactly where it had been.

I watched her fall apart until I couldn't take it anymore. She needed me. She needed to know the truth. Or maybe I just missed her. Maybe I wanted a tiny piece of normalcy back in my life.

The hangers screeched as I pushed them aside.

Kins screamed and reached into her purse. When I stepped out of the closet I half expected to see her holding a gun, but she was just aiming a canister of mace at my eyes.

"Stay back!" she yelled.

"Kins, it's me."

Her eyes scanned my face. There didn't seem to be any recognition. "I swear to God I'll make you go blind," she said.

I stepped forward.

"Someone help me!" she screamed at the top of her lungs.

"It's me! Sadie."

She shook her head. "Intruder! Help!" Her finger moved to the trigger on the mace.

Damn it. I grabbed her arm and twisted it as a stream of mace went over my shoulder. I lifted my knee and slammed it against her wrist. The mace fell out of her hand and skidded across the floor. "Kins, would you stop yelling? I'm not trying to end up in jail tonight."

"You're not my friend, you're a freaking ninja." She tried to pull her arm away.

I let go of her and pulled off my hat.

She looked at my dyed blonde hair and then back at my face. Finally she seemed to recognize me. "Sadie?"

I nodded.

"Oh my God, Sadie!" She threw her arms around me. "I knew you'd come back."

I didn't cringe. I just hugged her back. "I'm so sorry," I said. "I'm so sorry about everything."

She pulled away from me. "You just mean about abandoning me, right? Not about murdering that woman? You didn't kill her? You couldn't have…"

"I didn't kill anyone." I kept off the fact that I desperately wanted to kill Don. That I dreamed of vengeance. That I wasn't the same person she had met.

"I knew it. I told everyone you were innocent. Did you know that they made me start seeing a therapist after what happened? They tried to make me take the rest of the year off. But I told them that I needed to be here. That you'd come back." She started to blink fast like she was about to cry again. "Everyone thinks I'm crazy, Sadie."

"You're not crazy. Trust me, I know how it feels when you think you're losing your mind."

She laughed.

For a moment I didn't care about what Liza, Eli, or V wanted. Kins was on our side. And we were close. I knew we were close to solving everything. Bringing Kins into the loop wouldn't put her in danger. Would it?

"Well maybe you can tell my therapist that," Kins said and dropped her purse on her desk. "She thinks I'm a loon. You should come to my next session."

I was barely listening to her. There was a row of prescription bottles on her desk that I'd never seen before. I remembered she used to take a multi-vitamin with breakfast, but that was it. "What are all those prescriptions for?" I asked.

"Anxiety mostly. And paranoia." She shrugged. "After you left, I kept thinking some guy was following me."

"Who?" It felt like my heart was about to beat out of my chest. "Did you recognize him?"

"This guy in a suit. But I didn't recognize him." She shivered. "Actually, I told my therapist that he looked like the mayor. You should have seen the look on her face when I said that. She doubled my doses. And I think it was the right call. Clearly I didn't actually recognize him. Why would the mayor be following me?" She laughed and scratched the back of her neck.

I stared at her. For the first time, I noticed the dark bags under her eyes. Her normally tanned skin looked pale. She was thinner than I remembered, and not in a healthy looking way. The worst part is that she was in danger and no one was even listening to her.

"Pack up some things for the next few days. You need to come with me."

She glanced at the pills on her desk.

"And you don't need those, Kins. You're not crazy."

"Where are we going?" she asked as she looked back up at me.

I told her the one thing I knew would get her to follow me. "I've been staying with the NYC vigilante. I think it's about time you met him."

CHAPTER 26
Monday

"Can we backtrack for one second?" Kins asked as we climbed the emergency escape ladder toward my apartment.

I had caught her up on all the important things. The fake witness protection program. The fact that my name was actually Summer. And that the mayor wasn't who he said he was. I'd tell her everything else soon. I needed to talk to Eli, V, and Liza first so we could figure out what else Kins should know. I was already looping her in on enough information without their permission.

My stomach churned. I had been allowed out of the apartment for hours now and I still hadn't gone to see Eli. I needed to visit him. I'd just fill V in and leave him and Kins to get to know each other.

"Are you even listening to me?" Kins asked.

"What?" I stopped outside my apartment window and turned toward her.

"I don't understand what the mayor has to do with any of this. You said I wasn't crazy but you didn't tell me why I wasn't. Was it really him following me?"

"I'm going to fill you in on everything soon, I promise." I typed in the code on the keypad and there was a whirring noise. The window slowly rose.

"But the mayor has to be who he says he is. He's literally the mayor…" her voice trailed off. "Holy shit," Kins said from behind me.

And I knew she didn't say it because the apartment was amazing. We had made the entranceway look as normal as possible. Not that entering your home through a window was normal. But we tried. She had said it because V was standing there with his arms folded across his strong chest. And he was staring at me like I was the plague.

"Come in," I said, trying my best to ignore him.

"Sadie, can I talk to you in private?" V said. He had formed it like a question, but there wasn't a hint of a question in his tone. And he didn't even acknowledge Kins.

"I thought you said your name was Summer," Kins whispered.

V disappeared into his bedroom.

"Long story. Just wait right here," I said. The window automatically shut behind her as soon as she stepped into the apartment. "I'll only be a minute." I followed V into his bedroom.

He immediately slammed the door behind me. "I thought you'd go see Miles! Or Eli. Not…*Kins*." He said her name like she disgusted him more than I did. And the rumble in his voice terrified me.

It was like I was standing in front of Don. Like I was transported back in time. The blinds in his room were drawn closed and we were bathed in darkness. He morphed into Don. His leering smile. His haunting gaze. I winced and turned my face away from him. I was waiting for the fury. For the pain.

"What are you doing?"

I closed my eyes. I wanted to tell him that Kins was in trouble. That she needed to stay here. But my throat constricted. I took a huge gulp of air and my throat squeaked.

"Sadie." The anger had thawed from his voice. "You're alright. It's just me."

Just me. I opened my eyes.

"It kills me that he hurt you." He put his hand on the side of my face.

I wasn't going to have this conversation with him right now. He was manipulating my life. He made me believe that Miles had given up on me. He twisted everything I thought I knew. I had absorbed whatever anger he had just released. But for some reason, I didn't push his hand away. "She's in trouble, V. Don's been following her."

"Why would he follow her?"

"To get to me? I don't know. But she's not safe in that dorm. I wasn't safe there. She should have been here with us this whole time."

He sighed. "Fine. She'll sleep in your room. You'll stay with me." His hand dropped from my cheek.

Before I could protest he had walked out of the room. "Where the hell did she go?" he said from the hall.

I followed him out of the room. Kins' boots had been kicked off by the window, but she was nowhere in sight.

"Kins?" I called as I followed V toward the kitchen. When I turned the corner Kins was standing in our headquarters staring at the target on the wall. She reached out and ran her finger along one of the arrow tips.

"Don't touch those," V said.

She jumped and turned around. "So...so all this is real? Everything? You're really the mysterious vigilante that's been terrorizing the city streets?"

"I'm not terrorizing the city."

"That's not what the news says." She looked over at me. "But I know they lied about you. So I don't exactly trust them anymore."

"V is saving this city, not tormenting its citizens," I said.

Kins nodded. "I won't tell anyone who you are. You can take off your mask."

V didn't move.

"Even if I did tattle, no one would believe me." Kins walked over to the couch and sat down. "No one believes anything I say." She stared at V. "What, you don't trust me?"

"No."

"It's nothing personal," I said. "He doesn't trust me enough to take it off either."

She looked back and forth between us. "So you two live together and he never takes off his mask? Doesn't that get uncomfortable? And I don't just mean the awkwardness of lack of trust. I mean literally that material doesn't look comfortable."

"It's fine," V said. "It's a proprietary blend of Turkish cotton, Pakistani cashmere, and Peruvian llama wool." He smiled.

What the hell was that?

Kins laughed. "If you say so. You look really familiar by the way."

Are they flirting? My stomach churned. *Why does my stomach hurt at the thought of them flirting?*

"We've never met." He cleared his throat and his smile disappeared. "I'm going to let you two talk. And you can stay in Sadie's room…temporarily." V started to walk back toward the hall.

"Why don't you call her Summer?"

He froze.

"That's her name, right?"

V turned around. "No, not anymore."

"But you know the truth about the witness protection program. Sadie isn't her real name. She's going to legally change it back to Summer as soon as she can."

He glanced at me and then turned his attention back to Kins. "That's not what I meant."

"Then what did you mean?"

"That Summer Brooks died as soon as Don Roberts laid his hands on her."

The way he said it sent a chill down my spine.

"Don Roberts?" Kins asked. "You mean the mayor? Mayor Roberts?"

"We hadn't gotten to that yet, V," I said.

"You have a lot to talk about then. I'll leave you to it." He walked away, leaving me with the lingering questions. Apparently visiting Eli would have to wait.

I sat down next to Kins. "It's a long story."

"I have time." She smiled.

I watched her smile vanish as I told her about my parents' deaths. I watched the way her expression changed when I talked about what happened in the years that followed. It was the same way Mr. Crawford looked at me. Like I was damaged. As if I needed their emotions to know it was true.

Kins shook her head. "Why is he doing all of this? Do you think it's because you look like your mom?"

"That's our working theory."

"How quickly love can turn to hate," she said.

"Yeah." The awkward silence was almost palpable.

"I'm really sorry…"

"We don't have to talk any more about that," I said at the exact same time.

We both laughed.

"Really, just ask me a normal question. Something that people our age are supposed to be talking about. I've missed you."

"I've missed you too. And I am dying to know…are you and V like an item?"

I shook my head. "No. I'm dating Eli."

"I hate to break it to you, Summer, but Eli is not aware of your relationship status."

"He was just acting. He doesn't want me to end up behind bars. He barely got out of this mess himself."

"He's a really good actor then."

I remembered her conversation with Patrick. "What do you mean?"

"He was laughing and holding some other girl's hand when I visited him. They looked smitten if you ask me."

I frowned. "What did she look like?"

"Short. Frizzy brown hair and glasses. I actually kinda thought they were dating."

Phew. "No, that's just Liza."

"The other girl that lives here? You're sure they're not hooking up?"

"No, she's my friend. She wouldn't do that." *Right?* "Besides, she's madly in love with V."

Kins laughed. "Oh, yeah, I get that. Geez, he really does look familiar though. Not his face obviously, but his build. I know I've seen him before without the mask. I just can't place it. That thing that messes with his voice doesn't help either."

"Tell me about it. I've been trying to solve the mystery of V for months."

"So that's it? You've been together with Eli this whole time? That's great. We can still go on double dates."

"Actually I'm not really supposed to leave the apartment. And we haven't been together this whole time. We recently decided to give it another go."

"So…"

"So…nothing."

"You told me you kissed V once. Back when we were still roomies. Remember that?"

"Yeah." I shrugged. "We had a short tryst."

Kins laughed. "Doesn't that make things awkward?"

"A little. Speaking of relationships, how are you and Patrick doing?"

"We fight a lot. About you mostly." She smiled. "Not that I'm blaming you. I blame him. He wouldn't believe me when I insisted that you weren't guilty. He's been so annoying. All he ever wants to do is talk about it. And I didn't want to talk about it, I was upset."

"I'm really sorry that I left. I thought the note would…"

She laughed. "Oh, your very informative note that kept me completely in the dark but with just enough intrigue to make it impossible to forget about you? Thanks for that."

"Intrigue? I just said goodbye and that you were my friend."

"*Best* friend. You called me your best friend and asked me to forget about you. Best friends don't forget about each other."

I smiled. "I guess not. I noticed that Miles moved out." The words just came out of me like vomit. I couldn't even swallow them back down if I tried. I had been dying to ask her about it ever since she showed up in her dorm.

"He did, unfortunately."

I was just about to tell her that Miles was the childhood friend I had talked about, but she kept going.

"The whole thing was really weird. He stopped by our room before he left actually. He wanted me to tell you something if I ever saw you again. Hold on, I wrote it down because it was so strange." She pulled out her phone and scrolled through some notes. "Here it is. He said, 'Seasons change but they always return.' What on earth do you think he meant by that?"

Seasons change but they always return. Summer. Summer was a season. He was talking about me. I thought about how V always said I wasn't Summer anymore and that I never could be. Miles was saying the exact opposite. He knew who I was. And he believed a part of Summer still existed inside of me. That had to be what he meant. "Did he say anything else?"

"Nope that was it. Like I said, it was really odd."

"But why did he leave?"

"He said he needed time to figure out what he wanted. I guess he was having a crisis over what to major in." She shrugged. "I miss his sexiness in the halls. Our floor isn't the same without him. And the new R.A. is such a bitch."

I laughed. "Why do you say that?" Miles needed to figure out what he wanted. Did that mean me? He needed time to figure out if he still wanted me? I shook my head. That didn't make sense. He had wanted me on the roof that night. And judging what he said to Kins, he knew who I was. Had he known the whole time? Had he figured it out after we had been together?

"Because she always hits on Patrick whenever he visits. She's a jerk."

I remembered the new R.A. flirting with Miles. It was nice to know that he hadn't been trying to get in her pants. But Kins should take a look in the mirror. She flirted with everyone too.

She yawned. "Is it okay if I get some sleep? Although, I'm a little worried that I'm going to wake up and this is all going to be a dream."

"Kins, I promise you're not crazy. But yeah, my room is the third door on the right. Make yourself at home."

"It's really good to have you back," she said as she stood up and stretched. "And I'm glad you're not a murderer."

I laughed, knowing perfectly well that I would be eventually. "I promise that I'm not. I'll be in soon."

"Okay. Goodnight, Sadie. I mean Summer. That's going to take some getting used to."

"Night, Kins." I should have gone with her. I should have put the thoughts stirring in my head to rest. And I certainly shouldn't have given V any reason to think I was actually going to share his bed with him. But as soon as Kins went into my room, I walked toward his. We had a lot to discuss. Mainly why he was trying so desperately to control my life.

CHAPTER 27
Monday

I tried to turn V's doorknob, but it didn't budge. Catching him unaware would have made this conversation easier to control. But he seemed to think of everything to keep the scales tipped in his favor. Before I even lifted my hand to knock, the door opened.

He was pulling his mask down and I got the smallest glimpse of stubble underneath his chin before it disappeared from view. *Stop focusing on him.* I looked past his shoulder. I had never been in his room when the lights were on. But there wasn't much to see. The room was completely empty. Nothing on the walls. No pictures of any kind. And everything was black. A black comforter on his bed. Black pillowcases. A black chair and desk. It was so unemotional that it made me feel sad. No wonder he had been sleeping in my room. This felt like a prison.

The only odd thing was that there was a stack of posters on his desk, facing down. Had he taken them off the walls so I wouldn't know what he was interested in?

V cleared his throat. "I thought you'd be stubborn and sleep in your room with Kins."

I turned my attention back to him. "I am going to sleep in my own room. I just needed to talk to you."

"We'll see about that."

I rolled my eyes. I didn't even try to hide it.

"How was your visit with Eli?" he asked.

I stared at him. He knew perfectly well that I didn't go to Eli. He knew it and was just trying to push my buttons. Because I should have gone to Eli. Yet, all I had done was try to see Miles and now I was here with him. I was the worst girlfriend in the history of girlfriends. "Did you follow me?"

"There was no need. I know exactly who your heart belongs to."

"If that's true, and I'm not saying it is, then why would you steal that letter? Why would you prevent Miles from knowing the truth? And if you know everything, then you knew he left. You knew he was gone. So why the hell did you let me go to him in the first place?"

"So you admit that you were going to him?"

"Of course I went to see him. I had just found out that you interfered with…"

"Do you love him?"

I pressed my lips together.

"Just say it."

I didn't know what he wanted me to say. There were no words.

"You love him. It's always been him."

I shook my head.

"You two were written in the stars, right? You were destined to be together. He's your one great love."

"He broke my heart."

"And didn't you do the same to him?"

I wasn't even sure why he was asking me these questions. He had read the letter I wrote to Miles. He knew the answers. He knew everything.

"Just admit that you're still in love with him."

"Why? Why does it matter to you?"

"Because I want to know the truth."

A tear rolled down my cheek and I quickly wiped it away. "I think you've already made up your mind."

"And I'm sick of waiting for you to make up yours."

I wanted to tell him that I had. That I was in love with Eli. That I wanted nothing more than to be with Eli and only Eli. But why had I gone to Miles? Why the hell was I with V now? "Do you know where he went?"

"Miles?"

"Who the hell else would I be talking about?"

V smiled. "He's still in the city if that's what you're wondering."

"Where?"

"I thought you didn't want me to interfere…"

"Would you just tell me one single thing I want to know?"

"You'll find him when you're ready. But don't be surprised if he's not who you remember. I'm pretty sure he's changed as much as you."

"That's the thing, V. I don't think he has. Because he still believes I can be Summer."

"And we both know that you can't be."

Fuck you. I opened up his door.

"Where are you going?"

"Anywhere but here. You can hang your posters back up. I'm never stepping foot in your room again."

"I'll see you in a few hours."

I turned and looked at him before closing his door. And for just a moment, I thought I saw the night sky in his eyes. A darkness with no light from the stars. Did my eyes reflect his? I didn't want the darkness in my soul. But I was scared that he was right about me. No matter how much I still wanted to be Summer, I hadn't been her in so long. I didn't even remember what it was like to be happy. To be truly, madly, deeply in love. To look at the world with hope instead of dread. I had lost sight of the stars.

CHAPTER 28
Monday

It was as easy as I thought it would be to sneak into the hospital. I could have been coming every day if V hadn't locked me in the apartment. I scanned the list of names. Room 454. I ducked down as a nurse came around the corner.

There was a beeping noise and I heard her sigh. I lifted my head to see the nurse walking back in the direction she had come from. *Close call.* I slid the clipboard back in place and hurried down the hall until I reached room 454.

I was expecting it to be locked or something. But like the rest of the hospital, the security was severely lacking. I walked into his room and froze. Liza was lying in his hospital bed with him. Her head resting on his shoulder. His arm around her. They looked so content. They looked so happy.

Kins had said that he was doing a great job acting. Maybe her initial assumption was correct, though. What if he wasn't acting? Because it certainly seemed like I was intruding. I didn't belong here. It felt like my heart was beating in my throat. I stepped back and ran into something. A metal tray clanged as it fell to the ground.

Liza sat up with a start. "Summer?" She shifted away from Eli. "What are you doing here?"

Eli groaned.

Interfering. I swallowed hard. "V let me out."

"That's great." Her voice sounded squeakier than usual. She slid off the bed and Eli groaned again. His hand moved like he was reaching out for her.

I recognized that noise. I recognized that movement. He did the same thing whenever I left his arms. That groan was the smallest noise. But it meant everything. I was just wrong about the meaning. Because I thought it meant he loved me.

I blinked away the tears forming in my eyes. "I should leave you two alone."

"Don't be ridiculous. I…"

"No," I said. "Really, it's okay. I'm just going to go. I'll come back when he's awake."

"Summer." Her voice had lost the squeakiness. She just sounded sad and tired. "This isn't how it looks. I was upset when V said he loved you, but I wouldn't…it's not what you think."

I shook my head. How could she possibly know what I was thinking? I didn't even know what I was thinking. My stomach was twisted in knots. I felt nauseous. I stepped back again, this time stepping on the metal tray. It screeched as it slid on the floor.

"Summer?" Eli's voice was groggy. His eyes focused on me. "You came."

Liza grabbed her jacket and rushed past me without another word.

I wanted to go over to his bed. I wanted to kiss him. I wanted to tell him everything was going to be okay. But I couldn't move. And the longer I stood there, I realized none of it was true. I wanted to *want* to go to him. I didn't actually want to. Honestly, I'd rather retreat with Liza. I cleared my throat. "Of course I came."

He didn't tell me to come closer either. He didn't say anything at all. It was like a light switched on and whatever we had was left back in the darkness.

"I wanted to come sooner," I said. "But V locked me in the apartment."

Eli didn't say anything. His eyelids drooped like he was about to fall asleep again.

"He wouldn't let me leave. You can even ask Liza. I came as soon as I could." The lie came out before I could stop it. I had gone to Miles. I deserved to be looked at the way he was staring at me.

"V's been here," Eli said with a yawn. "A few times actually."

So? "I know."

"He was trying to protect you. I get that." Eli shrugged his shoulders like it was nothing, but his eyes narrowed at me.

"Do you? Because you look mad at me."

"Mad that you didn't come sooner? Why would I be mad about that?" He didn't let me respond. "I almost died, Summer."

"I wanted to be here."

"Did you? Because it doesn't really seem like you did."

"I…"

"Did you know that I got an infection after the operation? Did you even care enough to ask V or Liza about how I was doing?" He laughed even though it was the opposite of funny.

Was he on painkillers? I looked at the IV in his hand. *Probably.* "I kept trying to get to you. I…"

"I needed you, Summer. And obviously you didn't feel the same."

A lump had formed in my throat that wouldn't go away.

"You know how it feels to be abandoned. Why would you do that to me?"

Abandonment was the only feeling I knew. And he was completely right. Why the hell would I leave him when he needed me most?

"I've always been there when you needed me," he said as he looked down at his hands.

"I know. I…"

"If you loved me you would have found a way to come." He had laughed just a minute ago and now it looked like he was about to cry.

My feet finally moved. I grabbed his hand and crouched down next to his bed. "I do love you. I tried everything."

"Can we just be honest with each other for one minute?" He still didn't look at me.

"I am being honest, Eli. When you got hurt, I couldn't eat or sleep. I cried until I was dehydrated. And I did ask Liza about you all the time, but it was hard for me to hear the specifics knowing that I couldn't be here with you. I just kept asking if you were okay. And as soon as I could be here I was." I squeezed his hand. "I'm here now and I'm not going anywhere."

He pulled his hand away. "V called me four hours ago saying you were coming."

Shit.

"Or was it three?" He stared at the clock on the wall. "I don't remember. It was a long time ago. So where did you go? What was so important that you couldn't come here first?"

"Nothing." I exhaled slowly when he looked at the ceiling, still avoiding my gaze. "Eli, I was just upset. You have to believe me. V showed me this letter that I had left for Miles before the explosion and it just messed with my head."

"He finally told you?" He turned back toward me and he was smiling again. "I didn't think he had the balls. Well, I guess that's the end of that."

The end of what? I laughed because I didn't know how else to respond. Eli was acting so strange. "You knew about the letter?"

"I'm a detective." He laughed too. "Of course I knew. I knew all of it."

I wasn't going to ask him why he didn't tell me. This conversation was already strained. But he was smiling now. I looked up at the bags attached to his IV. There was morphine in one of them. I turned back to him. There was no reason to press him about the letter to Miles. It was V's secret to tell me, not Eli's. He was just being a good friend. And I loved him for that. "So that was why it took me so long to come tonight. V dropped a bomb on me and I just needed time to process the information."

"And?"

"And…now I've processed it."

He searched my face.

"I was mad of course. I think he thought it would bring us closer together or something. But he's a complete lunatic. How could he keep something like that from me for months? And here I thought that Miles had left me again. He made me feel so…" I let my voice trail off. *Abandoned.* The same way that I had made Eli feel.

"And now that you know the truth, you two can finally be happy."

"What? I'm here. I don't want to be with Miles. I just want you."

"You don't, Summer. We both know that you don't. Or else it wouldn't have taken you so long to come here tonight. I think a part of me did die when I got shot. Because I knew he was close to telling you. I knew that being apart would give him time to weasel his way back into your life. I knew and…there was nothing I could do about it. It's okay really. We had a good run." He reached out with his hand and lightly tapped my chin with his fist. Like I was a child that just needed to cheer up. What was wrong with him tonight?

"Why are you giving up on us? You said you wanted it all with me. You said you could picture raising a family. That you didn't care that I couldn't have children of my own. That…"

"That was a dream. *My* dream. But it was never yours. Go be with Miles. It was always him. Get." He shooed me away.

"I can't. I don't know even where he is."

"See. You didn't say you didn't want to. I always knew when he finally told you who he was that you'd run back to him. You love me but you were never in love with me. Not the way you are with him."

Running back to who? What was he talking about? "Are you talking about V now? He didn't tell me who he was."

"But you just said that he…" his voice trailed off. He immediately cleared his throat and then started laughing. "Oh shit. He's going to kill me. Oh well. The cat is out of the bag. Or I guess…the man is out of the mask? I don't know. Do you think you could get a nurse to get me some Jell-O? I'm hungry."

"Eli, do you know who V is?"

His laughter picked back up. "I'm a detective, Summer. We just talked about this. Of course I know. It's my job to know."

"You've known this whole time and didn't tell me?"

"No, no, not the whole time. It took me a few weeks to put it together. Besides, he wasn't trying to hide it from me."

He was just trying to hide it from me. "How could you?" I stood up. My mind felt like it was spinning, piecing our conversation back together. Yes, Eli was on painkillers, but the pieces had to fit together. Something had to make sense in our conversation. "How could you keep this from me?"

"It wasn't my secret to tell. And honestly, I understood why he did it."

My mind had stopped spinning. Everything was pointing in one direction. It always had been. "Why did he do it?"

"You broke each other. You both needed a fresh start. And I think a part of him wanted to prove that he could save you after all these years that he failed. A part of you knew all along right? But you were mad at him and didn't want to see it. He was just as angry with you. Kind of like I am with you right now." He put his hand on the side of my face. He didn't look angry. There was a smile plastered to his face. "But it's okay, Summer. I've always just wanted you to be happy. And it's a hell of a lot better for one heart to be broken instead of two."

"I have to go," I whispered.

"I know."

CHAPTER 29
7 Years Old
Flashback

I hopped from one rock to the next, humming The Colors of The Wind from Pocahontas. It was my new favorite movie. There was nothing I loved more than running around outside with the wind in my hair. And playing in the water was even more fun. Especially when it was so hot that the pavement burnt the bottoms of my feet.

I had invited Miles down to the creek with me. He responded by telling me that my dress made me look like a troll and that he didn't play with trolls. Last month he had insisted that I was a girly girl and didn't like to do anything fun. This month he said I looked like a troll. How could I be both a girly girl and a troll? It wasn't possible. Boys didn't make any sense.

And I knew Miles liked the creek. I knew it because he played in it all the time with his friends. So I wasn't a girly girl and I wasn't a troll for asking him to play in the stream. He was just a meany mean face for pretending he didn't want to come.

I didn't stay mad at him for very long though. Because Miles had come to the stream despite the fact that he thought I was a troll. I saw him follow me. Or maybe he was just playing by himself. But I knew he was there in the woods somewhere. Otherwise I wouldn't be at the creek at all. My parents said I wasn't allowed to come alone. And I always followed their rules. *Mostly.* I mostly followed their rules. Besides, technically I wasn't alone today. Miles was here. Watching me. I smiled to myself.

"If the savage one is me, how can there be so much that you don't know," I sang as loud as I could. I hoped he was listening. I sang that line specifically for his stupid boy ears. I had come to the conclusion that all boys that weren't grownups were dumb. But Miles was the stupidest of the stupid boys. Because he was the only boy I wanted to play with and he was the only boy I knew that refused to play with me. Plus his reasoning didn't make any sense. Trolls were really fun to play with. I loved my trolls.

I jumped to the next rock in the creek. "Can you paint with all the colors of the wind?" I sang. I spun around in a circle, letting my dress twirl up around me. If he was looking now, he'd probably think my dress looked pretty and not troll-like at all. I smiled to myself and jumped to the next rock. Then the next. I started humming the song from the beginning again.

A tiny fish swam by and I crouched to look at it. "But I know every rock and tree and creature." I put my hand in the water next to the fish. It immediately swam away from me. I stood back up and jumped to the next rock, trying to follow it. "Has a life, has a spirit, has a brain," I sang.

But I wasn't paying attention to the rock I was jumping to. I was focused on the fish swimming away and the lyrics going through my head. I had no idea that the rock was mossy. My foot slipped on the moss and I fell forward. The water splashed underneath my hands as I tried to catch myself. My knee collided with the rock and I slid forward. The water splashed again as the rest of my body ended up in the water too. *Ow.*

I tried to blink away the tears in my eyes. I didn't want Miles to see me cry. If he was even still out there. The thought of him no longer being in the woods made me even more upset though. I should have listened to my parents. I shouldn't have been here alone.

My tears started to fall faster. I wanted my daddy. When I pushed myself up out of the water, my knee stung. I looked down and tried not to panic. Blood streaked down my leg from the cut. *Oh God.* I was going to die. I started to bawl my eyes out in the middle of the creek.

"Summer!" Miles appeared out of nowhere. He ran through the water, not even bothering to jump the rocks. "Are you okay?" He stopped a few feet away from me and stared at my leg.

I tried to blink away the tears in my eyes. "Yes, I'm fine." My voice was shaky. "I'm fine," I tried to say again, but it still came out weird. I didn't want Miles to finally pay attention to me today. Not when I was crying and my dress was all wet. But there was no point in hiding my pain. I was clearly dying anyway. "I want my daddy."

"I'm going to go get him, okay? Just stay right here."

"Don't leave me! I don't want to die alone!"

"You're not dying, Summer…" he stopped talking when he looked down at my knee again. "Nothing bad is going to happen. Come on, let's get you home."

"My leg is probably going to fall off." I sniffed, trying to stop the tears.

He grabbed my elbow and helped me out of the creek. "It's not going to fall off. I promise. We're only like 2 minutes from home."

My bottom lip trembled. "But it hurts."

"I know." He kept his hand on my elbow as we wove through the trees.

I sniffed again. I wasn't sure how much longer I could possibly resist collapsing on the ground and accepting my fate.

He lightly squeezed my elbow. "You know, those aren't the lyrics of The Colors of the Wind."

I frowned at him. "How would you know? You said Pocahontas was only for girls."

"Well, either way, rocks don't have brains."

"What?"

"You said, 'But I know every rock and tree and creature has a life, has a spirit, has a brain.' Those aren't the lyrics."

"Yes they are, Miles. I've listened to it a hundred times. I think I'd know the words."

"Brains? Really?"

I thought about the rock I had fallen on. It seemed pretty smart to me. It had tricked me after all. "How do you know that rocks don't have brains? They might. Pocahontas would know. She loved being outside just like me."

He laughed. "Every rock and tree and creature has a life, has a spirit, has a name. A name, not brains."

"You watched the movie?"

He shrugged. "You promised it was good. Just like I promised we'd make it back to your house before you died."

We had just stepped onto my driveway.

My dad opened the door, like he could sense that I was in pain. He always knew when I needed him.

"Summer, what happened?" He was running over to me before I could even answer.

"She fell in the creek, Mr. Brooks," Miles said.

My dad scooped me up in his arms and carried me the rest of the way to our house. I buried my face in his shirt so Miles wouldn't see me cry anymore.

"Can I come in Mr. Brooks?" Miles called from behind us.

My dad left the door open for him. He carried me to the bathroom and grabbed a towel to wipe away the blood from my knee. "Were you playing in the creek by yourself again?"

Again? How did he know everything? "No, Miles was there."

"A good thing he was." He stood up to grab the Band-Aids out of the medicine cabinet. He crouched back down next to me. "You need to turn that frown upside down," he said with a smile. "Besides, isn't Miles getting along with you what you've been nagging your mother and I about ever since we moved here?"

"I never nag you."

He pitty-patted my shoulder. "Why won't Miles swing with me?" He pitty-patted my shoulder again. "Why won't Miles play catch with me?" He pitty-patted my side sending me into a fit of giggles. "Why won't Miles let me in his tree house?"

"Stop!" I somehow managed to say through my laughter.

He finally ceased from tickling me and pulled out a Band-Aid.

I caught my breath just as I heard the front door close. Miles had never ever not once asked to come into my house. Maybe I had died and gone to heaven. *I hope I remembered to organize all my stuffed animals on my bed.*

My dad placed the Band-Aid on my knee. "So turn that frown upside down and enjoy your victory." He winked at me and stood up just as Miles appeared in the doorway. My dad patted Miles' head as he left us alone in the bathroom.

"Are you okay?" Miles asked.

I nodded.

"So…" he looked around the bathroom. "What do you want to do the rest of the day?"

He was going to stay *all* day? I didn't know where to start. I had been dreaming of this moment forever. I wanted to tell him that I loved him with my whole entire heart. That I dreamed of us getting married. That I wanted to have a million babies with him and that I already had some of the names picked out. But I didn't want to scare him away. I'd tell him all those things after he admitted he wanted it first. After we were married. That made the most sense.

"Um…we could watch a movie?" I said.

"We should probably watch Pocahontas so that you can learn that rocks don't have brains."

"Admit that you just like the movie." I stood up, completely forgetting the fact that a few minutes ago I was knocking on death's door.

"I don't like it," he mumbled.

But I was pretty sure he loved the movie as much as I did. Especially when we laughed at all the same times. And when he pretended to be John Smith when it was over and chased me around with a paper towel roll he was pretending was a sword.

And in one afternoon Miles became my best friend. I couldn't wait till we were married and I could finally tell him that I loved him.

CHAPTER 30
Present Day – Monday

The past ten years of my life had been a series of bad luck. But I had always held out for one thing. One hope. That Miles Young would come back to me.

My feet skidded in the slush. I grabbed on to the railing and continued to climb as fast as I could. Who had I been kidding? I couldn't love anyone else. It was him. It had always been him.

I thought about what Dr. Miller had said. That V's heart was frozen. That wasn't true. V's heart could never be frozen. Because Miles' heart could never be frozen. He was the kindest person I knew. The sweetest. The most compassionate and understanding. Someone like him couldn't stop loving. It wasn't in his blood to become cold.

I pressed in the code to our apartment. There were a million things I needed to say to him. A million things I had never gotten to say the first time around. The window started to rise. I ducked down and climbed in when I could barely fit, leaving a trail of wet boot prints behind me as I ran to V's room.

"V?" I pounded my fist against his door.

No answer. I tried to open the door but it was locked.

"V!" I yelled again and knocked even louder. "It's important!"

Liza came out of her room and stared at me. "What's going on?" She wiped beneath her eyes. She had clearly been crying a moment ago. The tears on her cheeks were a good clue. But her eyes were also red beneath her glasses. And her posture was all wrong.

"Liza, is everything okay?" I kept knocking on V's door while I looked at her. I wanted her to say yes even though she was clearly upset. I didn't have time to comfort her right now.

"Summer, I'm so so sorry. I…" her voice trailed off. "I've been spending a lot of time with Eli and I swear I never crossed any line or anything. But I'd be lying if I said I didn't have feelings for him. And I…"

"That's fine." I breathed a sigh of relief. That was easier than I thought it would be. "He's all yours." I turned back to V's door and tried to turn the handle again. "V, let me in!"

"What do you mean he's all mine? You two are dating." She stepped forward and grabbed my arm so that I'd stop knocking. "You're supposed to be upset with me."

"We broke up. Really, it's fine." I tried to lift my hand to knock again, but she was stronger than I thought.

"It's not fine!" she hissed. She pulled my arm so that I'd look at her. "It's not fine," she whispered this time. "I swear we didn't kiss or anything. If you broke up with him because of me I'd never be able to forgive myself. I broke all sorts of girl code. We're best friends and I…"

"Liza, I promise it's not a big deal. I hope you two make each other happy. You both deserve that."

She released her grip on my arm. "That should have been sarcastic, but it didn't sound sarcastic." She paused.

"No, this is not how this conversation is supposed to go. I've done research. You're supposed to yell at me and call me a slut."

"You just said you didn't even kiss him yet. And it really doesn't matter. I'm in love with someone else."

"Who?" Her eyes narrowed on my hand as I started knocking on V's door again. "Not V."

I ignored her.

"You can't love someone that you don't even know."

"You were in love with him just a few days ago, remember? Besides, I *do* know him."

"Nobody *knows* him. He wears a mask for God's sake."

I continued knocking.

She grabbed my arm again to stop me. "Do you know who he is?" Her eyes bulged. "Summer, you have to tell me if you know."

"It's Miles. *He's* Miles."

"Miles your friend from when you were little?" She shook her head. "That doesn't make any sense."

"Yes, what other Miles is there?"

"There's approximately 25,000 in the US alone…"

"Liza, can you please just tell me where he is?"

"And if you factor in his last name too, that narrows it down, but it's still…"

"Liza! Please just tell me where he is."

She pushed her glasses up the bridge of her nose. "It's his night on surveillance."

I turned toward our command center.

"But he's been going on the roof to do it lately."

I smiled and walked past her toward the window. "To look at the stars."

"What?"

"He's looking at the stars." *He's waiting for me.* My whole body felt warm, and it wasn't because I was wearing a winter coat indoors. I felt alive. I felt whole again.

"There's something else I need to tell you, Summer. We got a better angle of the people that have been hanging out with Mr. Crawford. At least one of them. And you were right. They're not new recruits. I..." her voice trailed off. "I'm trying to talk to you, where are you going?"

"Liza, I'll be back soon. You can fill me in then." I climbed out the window before she had a chance to reply. I ran up the emergency escape ladder. How was I going to do this? Tell him I knew everything? Attack him in a bear hug? I smiled. I'd tell him he was right. That rocks don't have brains. That hot chocolate is better with whipped cream. That mint chocolate chip is the best ice cream. And that my life isn't complete without him.

I stepped onto the roof of our building, but he wasn't there. I pulled out my phone and clicked on V's name. Each ring made my heart race. I had been waiting my whole life to tell him how I felt. I wasn't sure how much longer I could wait. I was about to burst.

The ringing stopped but all I heard was silence. "Hello? V?"

More silence.

"Are you there?"

"I've been here the whole time," he finally said. And then the line was dead.

I've been here the whole time? Did he know that I knew? I looked up at the sky. The snow had stopped and the clouds had parted. There were two places I would go on a clear night to be closer to the stars. The observatory or the roof of our old dorm building. And he'd be dressed like V if he was on surveillance. Which ruled the observatory out.

He knew. He absolutely knew. And he was waiting for me. I had told Miles that I loved him when I was Sadie. He wanted to go back to that moment. He wanted us to do it right this time.

I took a deep breath, ran as fast as I could, and leapt off the edge of the building.

CHAPTER 31
Monday

I landed softly on the other side of the roof as Miles. He was leaning against the ledge, staring down at the city below. I slowly stood up. Eli's words tumbled through my head. About how Miles and I broke each other. How we both needed a fresh start. And how badly Miles wanted to save me after all these years.

I wiped away a tear that had trailed down my cheek. I had stopped watching Disney movies after my parents died. I completely stopped believing in fairy tales and happily ever afters when I was sent to live with Don.

But in my heart I knew that wasn't true. All along I knew that Miles was my knight in shining armor. My prince. My happily ever after. I touched the center of my chest. Even though there was a winter coat in the way, my Sagitta pendant was there. It was like I could feel my heart beating against it. It had always been Miles and me. We were written in the stars. And it was finally time for me to tell him how I truly felt. How I'd always felt.

Yes, I felt broken when I thought he stopped writing. When I thought he had abandoned me. And I know he felt the same. But it was all a lie. Our hearts had never stopped beating for each other. I wiped away another tear. We broke each other, but now we had our whole lives to put the pieces back together.

I took a deep breath. "You were right, you know. Rocks don't have brains."

I thought he'd turn, but he didn't.

"And hot chocolate is better with whipped cream. And mint chocolate chip ice cream has always been my favorite ever since I started sharing it with you." I laughed, remembering tackling him in his family room in order to get my bowl back.

But he didn't laugh. He didn't say anything at all.

"I know it's you, Miles. Who else would try so hard to keep me safe? Who else in this whole world cares about me but you?"

He just continued to look down at the street. What was he doing? The stars were what was worth looking at. Not the city streets. "Miles?" I started walking toward him.

"I've been here the whole time," he said.

No. No, it wasn't him. I froze. It was his voice, but it was louder than it should have been from this distance. It sounded like a recording. And it was the same thing he had said on the phone.

"I've been here the whole time," the recording said again.

I started to run toward him, but skidded to a stop when lights flooded the rooftop. For the first time I realized that Miles' body was hunched forward at an awkward angle. But the snow at his feet was all I could look at. It was dyed a deep crimson, stained with his blood.

"Miles?" My voice came out as a croak.

A shadowy figure emerged from behind an air-conditioning unit beside Miles. I knew who it was before he even stepped into the light. Before his laughter broke through the frigid air like a knife.

"Hello, doll," Don said. The light hit his face, revealing the burns I had given him.

Fear gripped my heart and I stepped back. I wanted to run. My whole life all I had done was run. My eyes focused on Miles. If there was anything in this life worth fighting for, it was him. I held my ground and swallowed hard.

"You're not going to say hello?" Don stopped right beside Miles. "Your friend wasn't very welcoming either."

I put my fake face on. The one I always wore around him to try and prove he didn't bother me. And I hoped to God he couldn't see through my mask tonight. "What did you do to him?"

"The notorious V?" Don laughed. "What does it look like? He fell right into my trap. Just like you did."

There were some muffled sounds and then a recording of my voice started. "In trouble, V." My voice echoed around me. "Don's been following…" the recording cut out.

It sounded like I was panicking. "How did you get a recording of my voice?" I touched my throat. I didn't remember saying those words. Parts of it had definitely been cut away. It felt like Don was worming his way into my soul. Owning every part of me again. Controlling my voice.

Don tilted his head to the side like he was examining me. "I don't like what you've done with your hair. Why would you dye it?"

"Are you joking? I've been hiding from you." I knew he was violent. But with everything that had happened, it was getting clearer that he was also insane. All of this was complete madness.

"Hiding from me?" He laughed. "I've had tabs on you as soon as I stepped foot in this city. I had to keep you away from prying eyes."

Whose prying eyes? I shook my head.

"No, you were hiding from him. Right?" He pointed to Miles. "And why I wonder? All those notes you wrote him." A smile spread across his face, stretching the scars on his cheek until they shimmered in the light. "Why on earth would you hide from him after all these years?" He grabbed the back of V's hood and lowered it.

If I had any doubts about who V was, they disappeared. I'd recognize that color brown anywhere. The curve of his neck. "Don't touch him!"

"Because you can't hide from me, Summer," he said, ignoring me. "I own this city. The good." He straightened his tie. "The bad. And every inch in between. You can't possibly do better than me."

Was he trying to win me over? That couldn't be what this was about. I couldn't be the reason why the streets were filled with crime. Why he became mayor. He had never wanted to win me over before. He just took me. He took me without asking. Again and again and again. I felt the tears falling down my cheeks.

"This can all end tonight. Just come home, Summer."

His words echoed around me, swirling with my memories. How many times had V told me to go home? I stared at his back. V had been telling me to go to Miles. Miles had always been home to me. And he wanted me to go home where I belonged, right next to his side. He was waiting for me to choose him. And now I was worried I was too late.

"Home isn't a place, Don. It's a feeling."

"You've always been naïve. Just like your mother."

There were pieces of my mother's story that I didn't understand. I had held her on a pedestal my whole life. But she may have cheated on my father. She may not have been the woman I thought I knew. That didn't mean he could judge her though. He ruined her life just like he ruined mine. And he may have taken her life too. "I know what you did."

"Which thing?"

The way he said it made the little hairs on the back of my neck rise. I was done playing his games. I grabbed my gun as fast as I could and held it out in front of me. "Step away from him."

Don didn't move. "Or what? You'll shoot me?" He laughed and placed his hand on Miles' shoulder.

"I swear to God, Don." My hands were shaking. I wasn't sure if it was because of the cold or my own fear. But I knew if I took the shot I might miss. It was like all my training evaporated as soon as I saw Don. And I couldn't afford to miss when Miles was so close. "Get the fuck away from him!"

"That's enough, doll. You're coming with me." He nodded and someone grabbed me from behind. My gun skidded away from me. I kicked and screamed, but whoever it was just held me tighter.

Don patted Miles' shoulder. "Come morning, the whole city will know the identity of the New York City vigilante. And that their beloved mayor made sure that V would no longer be terrorizing this city." He pushed Miles forward and his body toppled over the ledge.

CHAPTER 32
Monday

An ear piercing scream made my eardrums feel like they might burst. It sounded like something was dying a brutal death. I didn't even realize that the sound was coming from me until I needed to take a breath. I screamed again as soon as I could. The agony needed to escape from me and screaming was the only way I knew how.

The man holding me in place loosened his grip, probably trying to get away from the awful noise I was making.

I pulled my arm back fast and elbowed him straight in his Adam's apple. Twice.

He wheezed and grunted, but didn't let go of me. So I lifted my foot and slammed my heel between the man's legs. He immediately dropped me.

I landed in the slush on my hands and knees. But I didn't feel the coldness against my palms. All I could feel were flames. There was no time to think. I held my breath and ran as fast as I could. For one second.

If I leapt off the side of the building could I reach Miles before he hit the sidewalk below?

For two seconds. How high up were we?

For three seconds. Could I break his fall?

For four seconds. None of it mattered. I had to try.

For five seconds.

But before I could jump, Don caught me around my waist. I screamed again, the sound piercing the quiet night.

And for just a moment, it felt like I was back in time. After Don had cut me with a knife. After he killed my baby. I could feel all the hope draining out of me again. And then my mind turned, taking me back further. When I realized my parents were never coming home. My body felt numb.

But this? It was the third time in my life that I let Don take everything away from me. And this time I had no fight left. No hope of a better tomorrow. He had officially taken everything from me now. Every. Single. Fucking. thing.

"There, there." His voice oozed with insincere sweetness.

His cologne filled my lungs. I let my body fold in half, limp in his arms. I was broken. My heart shattered into a million tiny pieces on the sidewalk with Miles' body. What was the point in fighting when I had nothing left to fight for?

The haunting scream tried to escape my throat again but it came out as only a whisper.

CHAPTER 33
Tuesday

My eyes flew open and I took a huge gulp of air. I took a deep breath to slow my rapid heart rate. *It was just a bad dream.* I blinked, trying to get the dark room to come into focus. *It was just a bad dream.*

But the room was all wrong as my eyes slowly adjusted to the darkness. It was empty and emotionless. The air was stale. I pushed the covers off of me and stared down at the white plush robe I was wrapped in. Was I in a hotel?

God, it wasn't a dream. It felt like I was choking as I scrambled out of bed. I ran my fingers around on the nightstand until I found a light switch. As soon as the light came on I found the room's phone and lifted it to my ear. But there was no dial tone. I looked down at the cord. It was dangling beside me, unattached to the phone's base. *Damn it!*

I looked around for my clothes. My cell phone had to be here somewhere. I turned around in a circle. But the room was empty besides for me. I ran into the bathroom and switched on the light.

When I saw my reflection in the mirror, I backed up and almost tripped into the tub. I put my hand over my mouth as I stared at myself. My hair was red again.

I closed my eyes and took a deep breath. *This isn't happening.* But when I opened my eyes, my hair was still red.

That sick bastard dyed my hair? I barely recognized myself. Maybe I really wasn't Summer anymore. Just like V said. *Miles.* I turned away from the mirror.

I had to get fucking out of here. I ran out of the bathroom and over to the window. It was sealed shut. I lifted up the broken phone and slammed it against the glass. *Nothing.* I hit it again.

"We're on the 20th floor, doll," Don said from behind me.

My hand froze and the phone fell to the ground.

"What, do you think you can fly? You're not a superhero like your boyfriend." He chuckled. "Like he *was* I mean."

Like he was. His words echoed around me. I turned around to face the devil himself.

He was smiling at me. That smug look on his face that I loathed so much.

"You look better now," he said.

I felt like throwing up.

He stepped toward me

I'm going to kill you. I knew it wasn't the right time to threaten him. Not when I was caged in here like an animal. So I bit my tongue. But it had been a long time since I was this close to him. I could easily picture blood gushing from his throat. Dripping from his mouth. Seeping into his chest. I smiled.

"There's my girl," he said and touched the bottom of my chin.

The smile vanished from my face. "I don't belong to you or anyone else."

"That's where you're wrong. You've always been mine."

I stepped back so that his fingers fell from my face. "Don, you need to let me go. The cops are looking for me. You made me a wanted criminal. They'll find me and they'll see that we're connected. You'll go down for everything you did. You…"

"I'm not scared of the cops," he said and laughed. "Every time we moved, the first thing I always did was get the cops in my pocket. Haven't you been paying attention to anything around you? I fucking own everything in this city. Every single thing." His eyes raked over my body.

I used to think I'd never get away from him. That I'd be trapped in his clutches for my whole life. But now that I'd gotten a taste of freedom? I couldn't go back. And I knew I never would. He couldn't possibly control all of me. "You can do whatever you want to me. But you'll never have my heart."

He shook his head and walked over to the mini bar. "Are you thirsty, Summer?"

I didn't answer him.

He twisted off the cap to one of the bottles. "I tried to keep you away from that little shit. All those letters." He shook his head.

I didn't doubt what Miles said about the letters was true. It was different hearing the truth from Don though. How had I not figured that out when I was little? Of course Don had taken my letters. Of course he had. He had taken the one thing I had left in my life and tainted it.

"Young love is such a complicated thing."

He tipped his head back and drained the bottle. He set it down and lifted up another.

"I was just trying to save you from the pain of rejection."

"You mean like how my mother rejected you?"

Anger flashed across his face. He licked his lips as he stared at me. "Your mother didn't reject me. She was just scared of taking a chance. She loved me and I loved her."

I shook my head. "That woman you sent to do your dirty work. My aunt. She told me the truth about what happened in the woods that day."

"The truth? You can't believe everything you hear, doll. It was *her* truth. And everyone's truths are bathed in lies."

"Which is why I don't believe a word that comes out of your mouth."

"But why would I lie like her? I'm not about to die. She was scared and troubled."

That was true. She had been terrified. But I knew lies when I heard them. After all, I had grown up with him. And my aunt hadn't been lying. Filled with resentment, yes. But lies, no.

"You hated her for choosing Mr. Crawford. And you're taking it out on me because I look like her? You're insane."

He lifted up another bottle. "Ah, William Crawford. Good old Will." He shook his head. "He's in the next room, you know."

I swallowed hard. "Why?"

"Because I'm going to kill him. I spent years trying to keep you away from that Miles boy and he dumps you in the one city that he shouldn't. There's no forgiving him this time."

I still didn't know all of Mr. Crawford's story. But I knew he didn't deserve to die. "You're wrong. He told me to stay away from anyone I recognized from my past. He made me promise that I would."

"And what would you tell a vulnerable girl? I'd fucking tell her she had to stay away from her childhood sweetheart. He basically insured that you'd run to Miles. He put you in the same city. The same school. The same fucking floor as him. Coincidence only goes so far."

It was too much of a coincidence. I had taken it as fate. But maybe Don was right. Maybe Mr. Crawford wanted me to run to Miles. To tell him everything. "But why?"

"Because he loved your mother too."

I knew that. My mom chose him over Don. But then she had to go into hiding because she was scared Don would come for her. My grandmother and mother changed their names. They moved. I wanted to believe that she left Mr. Crawford in the past, but I knew that wasn't true. I knew it was even possible that he was my father.

I thought about how all of Mr. Crawford's addresses had been close to mine growing up. But that had even been before Don took me. He had been nearby when my parents were alive. I sat down on the edge of the bed. "I don't understand."

He walked over to the bed. "He's been trying to save you, doll. From me." He put his knee between my legs, pushing my thighs apart.

I couldn't breathe.

"Like you'd want to be saved from me." He grabbed the cord around my robe and pulled.

Stop. I tried to close my thighs, but he leaned forward and put his hand on the center of my chest, pushing me backward on the bed.

Fire. His touch felt like flames. The feeling spread through my chest. *I can't breathe.*

I felt my robe slip open.

Don ran his fingers down my torso and over the scar on my stomach. Tears pricked my eyes. I wasn't strong enough when I was 16. But now? I had been training for this exact moment. I wasn't some weak girl anymore. I balled my hands into fists. No more pain. No more hurt. He was never going to touch me again.

The expression on his face morphed before my eyes. His smile turned more sinister than I had ever seen as his fingers left my skin. He put them up to his ear like he was listening to something. He turned away from me.

I took a huge gulp of air. The feeling of fire left my skin. My head cleared. I gripped my robe closed and I eyed the phone on the ground. If I grabbed it, I could knock him over the head.

"Fuck!" Don yelled before I had even started to inch away. He lifted up a vase from the coffee table and threw it against the wall. It shattered into a million tiny pieces.

"We'll continue this later." He walked out of the room and slammed the door closed.

It felt like the walls shook with his fury.

CHAPTER 34
Tuesday

I slammed my fist against the glass one last time. It wouldn't budge. There was no use. What would I do if I broke it anyway? I was too high up.

The sun was starting to rise, but the city was eerily still. There were barely any taxis zooming by below. Barely any noise. It was almost peaceful. Everyone would be waking up soon and no one was going to care that my life was over. That I had just lost everything.

I turned away from the window. My eyes followed the light streaming into the room and landed on the vent. *The vent.* I ran over and knelt down on the carpet. *Please.* It wasn't a way out. But it was a way to get answers.

"Mr. Crawford?" I whispered into the vent.

I stared at it. The morning sun was lighting it up in an odd way. Like I was meant to be speaking into it. Like maybe this was where I was meant to be. I shook the thought away. *Meant to be?* I was meant to be in Miles' arms. No one deserved this.

I cleared my throat. "Mr. Crawford?" I said a little louder.

I looked behind me. There was another vent across the room. Maybe he was on the other side. I ran over and knelt down, putting my lips close to the vent. "Mr. Crawford?"

Nothing.

"William?" I tried.

Nothing.

I pressed my forehead against the wall. It was no use. I'd never get my answers. I'd never get a chance to live. The game was over. Don had won.

"Summer?" The voice was a whisper.

I lifted my head. "Mr. Crawford, is that you?" I pressed my ear against the vent.

"It's me."

I had a million questions to ask him. "Are you okay?" The words tumbled out of my mouth. All the answers I needed and that was what I asked him. What if he was my father? What if he was the only family I had left?

He sighed. "No. No, not really. Has he..." his voice trailed off. "Has he hurt you?"

Almost. "No."

"Thank God." He sounded truly relieved.

"You're not part of the witness protection program, are you?"

"I'm sorry, Summer. I didn't want to lie to you. I was just trying to keep you safe."

I closed my eyes. "Why?"

"Because I was friends with your parents."

Both of them? I opened my eyes back up. "What?"

"You really didn't remember me, did you? I hoped you wouldn't. It was easier that way."

"Remember you? Remember you from where?"

He cleared his throat. "You used to call me Uncle Billy."

Uncle Billy. The memory came flooding back. I remembered him giving me a stuffed animal for my birthday. Forever ago. Before I even moved in next to Miles. I couldn't have been more than 5. I didn't remember him, but I did now. Barely. He looked so different. The years had changed him. "You're my uncle?"

"No, no, just a family friend." He laughed. "You moved in next to Miles when Don was closing in on your parents. And I started to stay away. It was safer that way."

But he hadn't stayed that far away. "You and my mother…were you…" I let my voice trail away. I needed to rip the Band-Aid off. "Are you my dad?"

"What?" He laughed and then started to cough. "No." It sounded like he was in pain. "Why on earth would you think that?"

"You always lived near my parents. My aunt said…"

"She lost her mind a long time ago. Yes, I loved your mother once. But that was over twenty years ago. We were just friends when she met your father. And I was fast friends with him too. He was a good man."

I exhaled a breath I didn't know I had been holding. "So why are you a part of this then?"

"It was my fault that Don was trying to find your mother. She chose me over him all those years ago. I was trying to protect her ever since." He paused. "And then there was you. You were just a kid." Another long pause. "Summer, it took me forever to find you after Don adopted you. Every time I was close he'd disappear. It took me so long to finally get to you."

"Why didn't you adopt me after my grandmother died?"

"I would have. I wanted to. I filed the paperwork but you disappeared. You always just…disappeared. He had ties everywhere. You were in his clutches as soon as you entered foster care. Why do you think you moved around so much even before you met him?"

I wiped the tears away from beneath my eyes. "Because no one wanted me."

"That wasn't true."

"The agency said I had my head in my books too much. I was sad all the time. I tried to get the families to like me. But there was always something wrong with me. Always."

"Summer, there was nothing wrong with you. There *is* nothing wrong with you. You've always been wanted."

Even those years before Don, I felt so alone. Moving from one foster family to the next. It seemed like everyone around me was adopted. But Don was just keeping me away from Mr. Crawford. Keeping me away from happiness. "What does he want from me?" I wiped my tears away again.

"At first I thought it was revenge. But I think it's more than that now. He wants what your mother never gave him."

I was trying so hard to keep it together. Love. He wanted love. "I can't." My voice broke.

"Summer, I'm going to get you out of here. He's not going to hurt you anymore."

"You did get me out. But he just found me again. He'll always find me."

"Take a deep breath, okay?"

"I don't understand why you did this. Why you left me alone in New York. Why didn't you just tell me everything? Why didn't you just let me stay with you?"

"I thought you'd be safer without me. Don wants me dead. I wanted you to know the truth. I knew you'd figure it out when you dug deeper about your new name. And with Miles so close by, you'd have someone if you needed them."

"Miles is dead. Don killed him right in front of me." I couldn't stop the tears now.

"Summer, I'm so so sorry, I…"

"Did he kill my parents too?" That was the question I had been dying to ask. I had to know.

"It was reported as an accident. But he had the cops in his pocket. I don't know how…" his voice trailed off. "I know he killed your grandmother though."

"So why hasn't he killed me yet?"

"Like I said, that's not what he wants from you."

Right. He wants me to love him. I stared at the empty hotel room. "I don't have anything left to live for."

"Don't say that."

Miles' love lifted me up. My whole life it had. It helped me out of this hell. But now? There was nothing to lift me back up. I wasn't stronger now. I was pretending to be tough this whole time. I had always been good at make-believe. Really, I was weak. And stupid. And worthless. Just like Don always said. Don already took my body. He was seared into my brain. What did it matter if I gave him my soul? It was rotten anyway. "I'll give him what he wants," I whispered. "And then I'll be able to get my revenge."

"Revenge? Summer, that's not you."

I stood up.

"Summer? Summer there's more we need to discuss!"

I walked away from the vent. I didn't have any more questions for Mr. Crawford.

CHAPTER 35
Tuesday

Every time I closed my eyes I saw V falling. I gripped the edge of the sink. Part of me didn't believe it. Couldn't believe it. How could I still be breathing if he wasn't?

I opened my eyes and stared at the ghost of Summer Brooks. I understood why V always called me Sadie instead of Summer. We had both changed. But we were still written in the stars. We always had been. The stars couldn't be rewritten. Miles was dead. And I was about to be.

I finished the small bottle of vodka, ignoring the burn in my throat. Liquid courage. I shook my head. That wasn't it. I was trying to numb the ache in my chest. But I knew it would never go away.

I cracked the small bottle against the side of the sink. The glass shattered and I was left with several piercing shards sticking off the bottle's neck. The next time I saw Don, I was going to sink it into his throat.

Now I just had to wait. I walked over to the window and looked out at the city street below. The cars and taxis sped by just like on any other day. The whole city kept going like nothing had happened. The fact that no one else's life had stopped made me feel even more alone. Each beat of my heart hurt. *It should have been me.*

I used to have so many dreams. But the feeling of home had been ripped out of my chest. It no longer felt like I was living. There was only one thing keeping me breathing. The fact that Don still drew breath.

I wasn't sure how long I stood there before the door to the room opened. My cheeks were stiff from my dried tears. I wasn't scared of what I was about to do. The world was going to be a better place without Don in it. I watched the people walking on the sidewalk below. And not a single person was going to miss someone like me.

I plastered a fake smile on my face, took a deep breath, and turned around. "Don." I ran over to him and threw my arms around him. I swallowed down the bile rising in my throat. We had never hugged like this before. I had never pretended to want anything he gave me. I had just become used to it. Numb to it.

His arms wrapped around me. "Feeling better, doll?"

"So much better. I've been so scared without you. I…" I let my voice trail off. I couldn't force anything else out like that. "When you sent those hitmen after me…"

He pulled back and grabbed my shoulders. "I was angry with you." He stared into my eyes. "I wasn't thinking clearly after you left. That was a long time ago. I never meant it."

But didn't you? Or else you wouldn't have tried to have me killed. I swallowed hard. "I know."

"Please forgive me."

Please? I had never heard him use that word before. Hearing it made me even more uncomfortable. He was up to something. "I forgive you." *Never.* "Can I please have my clothes back now?" It was worth a try if we were suddenly using the word please.

He smiled. "I don't think you'll be needing them. Are you hungry?" He nodded to the table. There were two covered trays sitting on it.

Eating wasn't on my list of things to do this morning. "I'm not hungry."

"You need to eat," Don said.

I tied my robe a little tighter even though it would be coming off soon enough.

His eyes followed my movement. "Sit. Down." The anger I was all too familiar with was back.

I wished I could forget what the edge in his voice meant. I wished I could forget everything.

"Summer."

I looked back up at him and all I saw was death. He killed Miles. He killed him. My parents. My grandmother. How could I pretend everything was okay? "V is dead. You got what you wanted." My plan was flying out the window. I was losing control. My fingers itched to reach into my pocket and grab the broken bottle.

"I don't have everything I want." His eyes traveled down my neck and stopped at where my robe crisscrossed. "Not everything."

Me. All I had to do was play make-believe for a little longer. Until he used my body. Until he was relaxed and happy. Until I had the perfect moment to stab him in the throat. I smiled. "And what is it that you want?" Before he could respond, I added, "because before Joan knocked me out in her diner, she said that the only person you wanted dead more than me was V. You got that. What else could you possibly want?"

He smiled. "Did you love that boy? Is that what this is about?"

With all my heart. He was my everything. "No." I shook my head. "No, I didn't love him." It hurt to say the lie. It didn't just hurt, it made me angry too. My heart started to race. And for the first time I realized it wasn't beating against something. Where was my necklace? It was the last thing I had left of Miles. "He was a childhood friend, nothing more." I tried to pause between my thoughts, hoping it was long enough so that he wasn't suspicious. "Do you know where my necklace is?"

He pulled the chain out of his pocket. "You mean this?"

I reached for it but he held it away from me. "I always wondered why this trinket was so important to you."

"It reminds me of my parents, that's all."

"You don't need to remember them." He tossed the necklace onto the table.

I kept my eyes glued to him and shrugged my shoulders. If he didn't think it was that important, he wouldn't keep it from me. The silence stretched between us.

"Your mom was a slut."

It felt like he had slapped me. But I kept looking at him. His words weren't true. There was no reason why they should affect me. It was impossible not to think about my plan, though. That would be one of the last things he ever said. That was justice enough. *Just wait. Wait till the right moment.*

"And your father was weak."

I put my hand in my pocket, wrapping it around the bottle. "Did you kill my parents?" The words tumbled out of my mouth before I could stop them. He didn't even have to reply. I could see it in his eyes.

"Weak until his dying breath."

I thought the bottle might snap in my hand.

"Like you were when we first met. But I knew I could make you strong. You're welcome, doll."

He didn't make me strong. Yes, Miles had trained me. But the strength I had was my own. It came from within me. I was made of fucking steel.

I lunged at him, pulled the bottle out of my pocket, and aimed for the side of his neck.

He knocked it out of my hand before I even reached him, like it was nothing but a nuisance.

I hadn't waited for the right moment. What the hell had I been thinking? I took a step back from him.

He slapped my face with the back of his hand.

My body fell toward the table. I was able to put my hands out just in time to catch myself.

"Not as strong as I thought then," he said with a laugh.

I grabbed one of the metal covers for our food, turned around, and slammed it as hard as I could against his face.

The noise it made was satisfying, but he barely stumbled back.

He ran his hand down the side of his scarred face. "You're going to regret that." He stepped forward and wrapped one of his hands around my neck.

I took a strained breath before he cut off all my oxygen.

He lifted me up until my feet were dangling off the ground. I gripped his wrist and pulled as hard as I could. *I can't breathe.* It was like I was transported in time to the last time he had done this. *But I'm stronger now.* I dug my nails into his skin.

He slammed my back down against the table. "Do you think you can fool me? Do you think you can try to run from me and suddenly I'll believe that you missed me this whole time?"

I tried to shake my head, but his hand was holding me in place. I never thought he was stupid. I had always just thought he was a monster.

He tightened his grip.

I had learned one very important thing in my training with Miles. When in doubt, kick your assailant where it hurts. I lifted my knee but Don's legs were closed.

He smiled. "When in doubt, go for my nuts, huh?"

My eyes bulged. How did he know?

"I've been keeping you away from prying eyes this whole time. Did you ever think about why it was so easy to rent your new place? Why the cops haven't caught you yet? Did you ever think about any of it? You've never left my sight. I've been listening to you. Watching you."

I was starting to feel light headed.

"I own you. And you're not getting away from me this time, doll."

CHAPTER 36
Tuesday

The sound of wood splitting made me think the table was about to collapse beneath me. Don was finally going to do it. I'd never be able to pretend to love him. This was how it was always meant to end, with one of our hands wrapped around the other's throat. I had just hoped it was me.

There was distant shouting. Screaming. But I couldn't look away from Don. *It was supposed to be you struggling to breathe. It should have been you.*

We just stared at each other. Maybe he was thinking this was finally the end too. As soon as I was dead, the past that haunted him would be obliterated. My mother's bloodline would be completely gone. I thought that I couldn't live until his heart stopped beating. Had it been the same for him?

The splintering of wood sounded in my ears again. The noise pulsed with the blood trying to pump to my head. Everything was muffled, but it sounded like the door had swung open.

Don's gaze finally left mine, but his fingers didn't loosen around my neck.

"Get away from her!" someone yelled.

A loud bang echoed in the room. It sounded like a gunshot. I started to close my eyes. I had never been so sleepy before. The room started to blur and tilt in front of me.

"You've got to be kidding me," Don growled as his hand finally fell from my neck.

I slid off the table, landing on my knees. My fingers clutched my neck as I took in huge gulps of air. The spinning started to subside and I saw Liza and Kins standing in the doorway. There were two men in suits writhing on the ground behind them.

"Walk away and no one has to get hurt," Don said. He lifted his hands.

No one moved.

"You have to get closer to tase me."

Still no one moved.

"Why don't you just drop it?" He sounded so calm. "We can work something out." He started to walk toward them.

This time I knew it was a gunshot that rang out. Kins was standing there with the gun shaking in her hands and a shocked look on her face.

"Fucking bitch!" Don yelled as his knee buckled and he fell to the ground. Blood seeped into his pant leg. A second later Liza tased him and his body started to convulse like the guards outside.

"Take that you dirty…pig!" Liza said and kicked Don's stomach.

"Oh my God, I just shot someone," Kins said. Her hand was shaking even more as she lowered the gun by her side.

"We have to go," Liza said and helped me to my feet. She let go of the trigger of her taser and Don's body slowly started to stop shaking.

"I shot the freaking mayor!" Kins yelled. "I'm going to go to jail!" Her gun accidentally fired again, a bullet slicing through the carpet. She shrieked and dropped the gun on the ground. It fired again and plaster went flying from the wall.

"Stop firing that thing, you psycho." Liza grabbed the gun from the floor. "Where did you even get this?"

Kins pointed to one of the guards behind her.

"Jesus, your fingerprints are all over it now." Liza shoved the gun into her coat pocket. "I taught you how to use this," she said and picked up a taser off the ground. "Not a freaking gun! What were you thinking? You could have killed us!"

"I'm sorry!" Kins said. "Oh God, what have I done?" She stared at Don's body on the floor.

"It doesn't matter, it was just his thigh. But we have to go. Now." Liza grabbed my arm and pulled me to my feet.

"Wait," I said.

"Wait? They're going to get up any second. And surely everyone on this floor heard the gunshots because *someone who shall remain unnamed* is trigger happy." She glared at Kins.

Kins put her hands over her mouth. "I'm going to go to prison," she mumbled into them. She dropped her hands. "We have to get out of here!" She ran out the door.

"Kins, we have to stay together!" Liza yelled and ran after her into the hall.

I didn't move even though I knew Liza was right. The guards at the door were starting to stir. The police would surely be coming any minute.

I stared down at Don's body. I wanted to kill him. I needed to kill him. My eyes scanned the room for the broken bottle. Where had it gone?

"I'm going to spend the rest of my life in jail!" Kins sobbed from the hall.

What the hell was I doing? I wasn't going to put my friends' lives in jeopardy. They had come to save me. Not to kill Don. I grabbed my necklace off the table and ran after them.

We burst out of the stairwell into the hotel lobby.

The man at the front desk looked up at us as we ran by. "Ladies are you okay?" He looked down at my bare feet and then at the doors we were running toward. "It's freezing out there."

"We're great! We're going to leave you a raving review!" Liza said as she ran past him.

"Excuse me!" he yelled after us. "You can't…that robe is hotel property!"

We pushed through the doors and ran down the front steps of the hotel. I didn't feel the icy concrete on my feet or the wind against my bare legs. All I could feel was fire. Everywhere Don touched me was aflame. I stood there, gripping my robe shut as Liza hailed down a taxi.

She pushed me and Kins in before climbing in after us. Kins started crying hysterically as soon as the door shut. I sat there frozen. Liza calmly gave the taxi driver directions to somewhere near our apartment.

He eyed us from the rearview mirror. "Look, I don't know what kind of party you girls were at, but I'm not…"

"We'll double the fare. Please just go," Liza said. "Now!"

He stared at us for another moment before he finally pulled out onto the street.

Liza clapped her hands together and squealed. "Girl power!" She lifted her hand for a high five.

When Kins didn't offer her hand, Liza reached across her, lifted mine and proceeded to slap it.

"Oh my God, I can't believe we just pulled that off! Can you believe it?" She nudged Kins with her shoulder.

Kins lifted her face out of her hands. "We're going to go to prison for life, right?"

"Sh!" Liza hissed.

"Longer? Oh God, what if it's longer?"

"It can't be longer than life, drama queen. Besides it's not like we killed someone."

The driver scrunched down in his seat a little, but kept driving.

"I said we didn't do that," Liza said and tapped the cab driver's seat. "We definitely didn't do that. Don't tell anyone we did that."

"I'm not going to say a word," he said. "I swear."

"Good." She laughed and clapped her hands together. "I wish there was a sunroof in this thing. I'd stick my head out and scream at the top of my lungs. That was so exhilarating! I can't wait to do that again!"

I didn't feel exhilarated. I touched my neck where Don's hands had been. I was still breathing. My heart was still beating. I was alive. And I desperately wished that I wasn't.

How could I go back to our apartment without Miles there? This wasn't right. None of it. One of the last things I had said to him was that I wanted to be with Eli. Because Eli was filled with light.

Yet, I was the one that had pulled Miles into the darkness. He became V for me. It was my fault that he was dead. And all I wanted was to take his place. I'd give up my breaths, my heartbeats, my life in a second and give it all to him.

"I'm too young to die," Kins said. "Are shivs a real thing? Am I going to need to learn how to make one? I barely know how to sharpen a pencil. I always use mechanical ones. Or pens. Can you make a shiv out of a pen?"

"Snap out of it," Liza said. "Tell your friend to get a grip," she said to me.

I barely even heard them.

"Summer?"

"Summer, are you okay?" Kins asked.

I looked up. They were both staring at me with concern etched across their face. I shook my head. "No." Tears started streaming down my face. "I'm not okay."

Kins pulled my head down on her shoulder and patted my hair.

Liza reached over and squeezed my knee. "Everything's going to be fine. We'll be home soon."

But she was wrong. I'd never be home again. Because Miles had always been home to me.

CHAPTER 37
Tuesday

"Drink this," Liza said and handed me a glass filled with an amber liquid. "It'll make you feel better."

Nothing was going to make me feel better. But I drank it anyway. I immediately coughed. For some reason I thought it was some magic elixir to take away my heart-ache. But it was just whiskey.

She smiled and sat down next to me. "Now tell us what happened in that room."

I shook my head and handed her the glass back. There was nothing to say. I had squandered the best opportunity I had ever had.

Liza snapped her fingers. "Refill!" She tossed the glass at Kins.

The glass almost fell as Kins struggled to catch it. "A heads up would have been nice." She grabbed the bottle off the coffee table and handed me the whole thing instead of a glass. "Careful with that, a little goes a long way."

Nothing would ever be enough to numb the ache.

Liza tilted the bottle up to my mouth.

I just wanted to die. I wanted to be with my parents again. With Miles. *Miles.* I lifted the bottle up to my mouth and took a huge sip. And another. And another.

"Okay, that's enough liquid painkillers." Kins snatched the bottle back. "Summer, you have to tell us what happened."

"Did he…" Liza's voice trailed off. She pushed her glasses up the bridge of her nose and looked away from me. "I was looking up rape kits online and if we could get a sample of his…"

I shook my head. "No, he didn't have time. You guys…you…you saved me." The only problem was that I didn't want to be saved. I wanted revenge. I wanted justice. *Damn it.* My chest ached. What if I never got another chance to kill him? I should have taken more time to find the broken bottle. Why had I run after my friends? What the hell was I thinking? I was so close.

"That's what best friends are for," Kins said and squeezed my hand.

Liza glared at her. "Excuse me?"

"I said that's what best friends are for."

"Oh, no, I heard you. But *I'm* her best friend. Not you."

Kins laughed. "I'm pretty sure that I'm her best friend."

"Keep dreaming."

"I met her first!"

"Well she shared all her secrets with me," Liza said and folded her arms across her chest. "Tell her, Summer."

I hadn't shared my secrets with Liza. She had just done a ton of research on me behind my back. That was completely different. But it was true, she did know more about me than Kins did. I had purposefully kept Kins in the dark.

My mind was foggy. What was I even thinking about? Was I seriously debating who was my best friend right now? It didn't matter. Nothing mattered. I laughed. My life was over. I started laughing harder.

"Great, you just got her drunk," Kins said. "Now she'll never tell us what happened. All we'll know is that she stole a bathrobe and dyed her hair red for some reason."

"As her best friend, I know that her natural hair color is red. Ha! I win."

"Oh my God, you're relentless, Liza! There was no way I could have known that. When I first met her she was a brunette."

"Same. But as her bestie I knew that she was originally a redhead. Therefore I win. You lose."

"You're insane, you do realize that, right?"

I laughed again. "It doesn't matter. None of it matters."

"She's right," Kins said. "Just drop it, Liza. It's not important."

"It's important to me," she mumbled.

Ignoring them, I slowly stood up and walked into our command center.

"What are you doing?" Liza asked. "We're trying to talk to you."

I grabbed a gun off the wall.

"Whoa, calm down there, killer," Kins said and ran over to me. "You'll regret shooting that. Trust me." She tried to take it from me but I pulled it away.

"Mr. Crawford isn't my father," I said. "At least there's that. One positive on a list of a million awful things."

"How do you know?" Liza asked

"Who's Mr. Crawford?" Kins asked as she tried to grab the gun away from me again.

"An old family friend. He was being held in the hotel room next to mine. I finally got some answers." I cocked the gun. "I'm going to go get him out. And then I'm going to end this."

Kins grabbed my arm. "That hotel will be swarming with cops now. You're not going anywhere."

"Plus you're still wearing a bathrobe," Liza said. "I'm sure they have a warrant out for your arrest. You won't make it 5 blocks."

"I have to try. Don's down right now. I need to get him while he's down. It's my only chance."

"It's not your only chance. We can come up with a plan."

"I don't need a plan! I don't need to do this by the book!"

"You'll go to jail for homicide!"

"He killed my parents!" I was gasping for air. "He killed everyone I ever loved!"

"We don't know that for sure…"

"He told me! He told me." My voice cracked.

Tears appeared beneath Liza's glasses. "Summer."

"He called my mother a slut. He said my dad was weak. Weak until his dying breath. Like me."

Liza shook her head.

"I was too weak to save him."

"You were just a kid. It wasn't your fault."

Kins sniffed. I looked over at her. Her hands were pressed against her chest like hearing this was hurting her. If only she knew how much pain I was in. She'd let me go. She was more compassionate than Liza.

"I have to do this," I said. "I have to. It feels like my heart is in a million pieces. I can't breathe. I need to do this. You have to let me go. Please."

Kins' lips parted, but she didn't say anything.

"You have nothing to prove," Liza said. "You were a child. There was nothing you could have done to save your parents. Nothing."

No. I wasn't talking about my parents anymore. I was talking about Miles. "No, Don's right. I've always been weak."

"You're not weak, Summer," a deep voice said from behind us. It rumbled in the most perfect way. In a way that had always made me want to hear the real voice beneath.

I looked over at the ghost standing in the living room. The dark blue hoodie pulled low over his eyes. The sweatpants. The converses. A fragment of everything that was gone.

"You're made of steel, remember?" Miles said.

And as soon as he said the words, he disappeared. I blinked and stared at the empty living room.

CHAPTER 38
Tuesday

I had lost my mind. I was officially crazy. Liza's words had floated right over my head. But Miles' memory? It hit me like a punch in the gut. I remembered the first time he had said that I was made of steel. It was empowering. I was better when I was with him. I was whole. And I was strong. It was easy to believe when he was by my side.

I stared at the spot where I had envisioned him.

"Summer." He reappeared, a little closer to me. "You're okay." His voice sounded strained, like he couldn't believe it.

I was definitely hallucinating. V never called me Summer. He refused to. But he looked so real. I tilted my head to the side as I stared at him.

"Is she having some kind of nervous breakdown?" Liza whispered from behind me.

"You just let her drink too much," Kins said. "And she's still in shock. Maybe we should give them a minute or something?"

I looked back at them. "Wait. You see him?"

"Um…yes? He's standing right there," Liza said. "Why wouldn't we be able to see him? I wear glasses but I'm not blind." She folded her arms across her chest.

"Come on. Let's give them some privacy." Kins pulled her out of the command center.

I just stared at him, expecting him to disappear. "I saw you die."

He stepped closer to me and I saw him wince. "I wanted to come help get you out, but I…" he grabbed the side of his stomach. "I was giving myself stitches and I must have passed out. They left without me."

I shook my head. "You're not real. I saw you die." I wanted to reach out and touch his face, but I kept my hands to myself. I didn't want him to disappear.

"I landed on the emergency escape ladder. Well, I woke up on it anyway. I'm not exactly sure how I got there but I must have fallen. The last thing I remember was being on the roof of our old dorm looking for you. I got pretty banged up, but I'm still breathing. I'm sorry I wasn't there for you today." His eyes dropped to my neck, which was surely bruising already. "I'm so fucking sorry, Summer."

We both just stared at each other.

"I swear I'm not dead," he finally said.

"You're not?"

He lifted his hand from his side and put it on my cheek. "I told you I'd never go anywhere."

There were so many things I wanted to say. So many years of unspoken thoughts. But one thing outweighed the rest. "I love you."

"That's probably the bottle of whiskey talking. Last time we spoke…"

"I love you. I…" for some reason it didn't seem like the right time to tell him I knew his real identity. It felt important to let him know that I liked this part of him. Wasn't that the whole point? That I loved what he had become? "I love you exactly the way you are. I love you, V."

"What about Eli?"

"We broke up."

He rubbed his thumb beneath my eye, removing a tear I didn't know I had shed. "What about Miles?"

I reached into my pocket and grabbed my necklace. "It's true, a part of me will always love Miles. But when I said that this meant everything to me, I was wrong. You mean more to me than some old pendant." I placed it in his hand. "Maybe Miles was perfect for me when I was a kid. But I'm not a kid anymore. It's like you said, I'm more Sadie than Summer." *Just like you're more V than Miles.* He had been right the whole time. I needed time to accept that. Time to understand that the Miles I knew didn't really exist anymore.

"I was wrong to say that. I just wanted you to accept the fact that you had changed. I needed you to be able to forgive me for all the things I've done."

I nodded. "Of course I forgive you."

He shook his head. "I need to tell you something. And I need you to promise me that you'll forgive me for this too."

I wanted this conversation to be perfect. It needed to fix all the hurt I had. It needed to fix years of me thinking he had abandoned me. This wasn't the right moment. I wasn't thinking clearly. A part of me still thought I was imagining him. "I've had a lot of days that I would have classified as the worst in my life. But then things keep happening to take the cake. I thought I lost you last night and a piece of me died." I put my hand against his chest.

His heart was definitely beating. "I need to wash it off. I need to wash *him* off."

He placed his forehead against mine. "Did he…"

"No." I cut him off before he could even finish the thought. "But I can still feel his fingers on my skin. I feel like I'm on fire."

He grabbed my hand and pulled me toward the bathroom. He flicked on the lights and locked the door behind us. I watched him turn on the water. Steam slowly filled the room.

I wasn't even sure why, but I felt like I was about to cry. "Thank you." I stepped in without shedding my robe and closed the door. As soon as I was under the water, I put my hand over my mouth and started to sob. Miles had just said I wasn't weak, yet here I was falling apart. It felt like my knees were going to stop holding me up. I put my hand on the wall. I didn't want him to see me like this.

As soon as I had the thought, the shower door opened. He stepped in beside me, fully clothed. Without a word, he put his hands on the sides of my face. He opened his mouth like he was going to say something, but I cut him off.

"Your hands are so cold," I said.

"I'm sorry." He pulled his hands away.

"No, I meant…I meant it feels like you can erase him." Like he could erase the years of pain.

He wrapped his arms around me and pulled me against his chest. "You didn't give me a chance to tell you that I love you back," he whispered into my hair. "Exactly as you are. I love you, Summer Brooks. I always have and I always will."

I didn't have to be strong all by myself. After all these years of feeling alone, I finally had him back. I let my tears mix with the water cascading down on us. And I let him hold me up. I let him support me. And I tried to let go of all the pain.

CHAPTER 39
Wednesday

I woke up tangled up in him. And I couldn't imagine a more perfect way to start the day. I breathed in his familiar scent and smiled. My head was pressed against his chest and his arms were wrapped tightly around me. I had never felt more secure.

I didn't remember changing out of my wet robe. Or how I wound up in his bed. I was just happy to be there. He had held me all night. He had been there when I needed him. And it did erase some of the pain. It made my heart feel whole again.

But then I realized something startling. The side of my face wasn't just pressed against his chest. It was pressed against his *bare* chest. He wasn't wearing his hoodie. And the familiar smell wasn't his expensive cologne. He smelled like grass and sunshine. He smelled like Miles. My eyes flew open but they were greeted by darkness. I reached up and felt fabric covering my eyes.

"Wait," his voice rumbled as he pulled my hand away from the fabric. "Just…I need to explain. Everything."

"Did you blindfold me?"

He laughed. "I didn't want you to wake up in the middle of the night and see me. Not until I told you the truth."

Last night wasn't the right moment. But apparently this was. And I had a few things I needed to say too. I sat up in the bed and felt a soft material clinging to me. "Did you change me into…" I ran my hand down what I was wearing. "Into a t-shirt last night?"

"You passed out in the shower. I didn't want you to catch a cold in that wet robe. But I need to apologize for something a little bigger than seeing you naked."

"I forgive you." As soon as I said it, I realized that he'd have no idea what I was talking about. "Not just for the changing my clothes and blindfolding me thing. That's all fine. I mean I forgive you for *all* of it. For whatever you're about to say. And I'm sorry too. God, I'm so so sorry." I reached for my blindfold again, but he grabbed my hand to stop me.

"You don't even know what I'm apologizing for yet."

"I have a feeling that whatever it is, you did it for a good reason."

"You don't understand." His voice sounded strained. The bed dipped slightly as he sat up beside me. "I just want you to hear me out. I'm worried that you're going to hate me."

"I don't hate you."

"I'm pretty sure you've actually said 'I hate you' to me on multiple occasions and absolutely meant it. And I've been waiting for you to come around. I've been waiting for you to…accept me I guess? I don't know. It sounds stupid when I say it out loud. And I should have just been honest with you from the beginning. But I was so angry with you. I couldn't just turn off that feeling when I saw you. It was there. And I needed time to forgive you too. Because I thought…" his voice trailed off. "I had this whole speech planned and as soon as I started talking I forgot what I was going to say. And it's probably better if I just…"

"I know. I'm sorry too."

"You still don't know what I'm apologizing for."

"Keeping your identity a secret. Lying to me. And for giving up on me all those years ago. But I did the same to you. All of it. And I wish I could take it all back. I never should have stopped believing in you." I reached out and placed my hand on his chest. I finally felt like I was exactly where I was meant to be. "But you never really gave up on me right?" I ran my fingers along the spot where I remembered his tattoo of an arrow was. "You kept me right by your heart. Where I belong."

He lowered the blindfold from my face.

I wasn't sure I had ever seen anything so perfect. His hair was mussed up from sleeping. There was stubble along his jaw line. His deep brown eyes were staring right at me. And he was smiling out of the corner of his mouth.

How many nights had I lain in bed dreaming of that smile? How many nights had I dreamed that he was out there thinking of me too?

He tossed something onto his nightstand and then ran his hand down the side of my face. "You already knew?" He sounded just like Miles again instead of V. He must have removed the voice-altering device.

"I already knew." I leaned into his touch. "I thought I hated you too. But God, how could I? I've always loved you so freaking much. It doesn't matter if you're wearing a mask or not. I love you, Miles. And I've missed you." I threw my arms around him.

He groaned and I immediately pulled back.

For the first time I saw the bandage on the side of his stomach. It was tinged in red. He had held me all night, but he was the one in actual pain. "Your stitches. Miles, I'm so sorry. We should probably change the bandage." I reached out, but he caught my hand.

"It's okay." He winced but pulled me back into his chest. "I feel like I've waited a lifetime for this moment. And I'm not going to wait another second."

I smiled against his chest. "Did you know I was Summer before the letter I left you?" I felt foolish for thinking V had snuck into Miles' dorm room and taken the letter. Of course it had just been Miles the whole time. Of course it had.

"I knew who you were as soon as I bumped into you in that diner. But I knew you weren't ready. You looked so scared. And sad. It killed me."

He was right, I wasn't ready. I was still so mad at him. I needed time to understand what had happened to us. "You knew the whole time?"

"Didn't you know who I was right away?"

I pulled back. "Yeah, but you weren't wearing a disguise."

"Your eye color and hair don't define you. It's this…" he moved his hand between our chests. "It's an indefinable pull I have to you. It's this feeling of…"

"Of home."

He nodded. "Yeah. Of home. Of love."

Of love. For ten years I had no love in my life. Just fleeting memories of what it was like to feel loved. My parents. My grandmother. Him. Knowing he had loved me this whole time made me want to cry for my childhood self. "Of love."

He reached into the pocket of his sweatpants and pulled out my necklace. "Speaking of which, I believe this belongs to you."

I pulled my hair up as he fastened it back around my neck.

His eyes locked with mine as his fingers trailed down the necklace, stopping at the Sagitta pendant. "Next to your heart. Where I belong. I still can't believe that you kept this all these years."

I shrugged. I didn't want to ruin the moment and cry, but I felt the tears pricking the corners of my eyes. So I said the first thing that came to my mind that wasn't sad. "This really cute boy gave it to me."

He smiled his perfect smile. "There are so many things I've been dying to tell you." His gaze dropped to my lips. "But I can't seem to focus." He leaned forward and buried his fingers in my hair. "I'm going to kiss you now. And I never plan on stopping." He drew a fraction of an inch closer. "So if you don't want this, you should tell me."

I didn't say a word. I had never wanted anything more.

"Tell me I've been dreaming all these years and that this isn't real. Tell me I'm insane. Tell me I have to move on. Tell me what everyone has been telling me for years."

I felt like he had just made me whole again. But those words shattered me. He had been as broken as me. And he had held on to the same hope that I had all these years. "Miles, I've loved you since the first moment I ever saw you. I remember it like it was yesterday. You were riding a bicycle without a helmet and it was the sexiest thing I had ever seen."

He smiled.

"It's true, though. You have been dreaming all these years. But that's the thing...I've had the same dreams. And now we get to live them."

A knock sounded on his door.

Neither one of us moved or said a word. This was the moment we had both been dreaming about. We didn't want to ruin it.

"V!" Liza said from the other side of the door. "There's something important we need to discuss."

His eyes stayed locked on mine.

"V!" She pounded on the door again.

Miles sighed. He let go of my waist, leaned over, and grabbed a small cylinder off his nightstand. He pressed it against the side of his neck. "I'll be there in a minute." His voice rumbled.

It was weird seeing him like Miles yet hearing him like V.

"Just hurry!" she said. "And bring Summer too, it's important."

He pulled the cylinder away from his neck.

I could tell he didn't want to move. I didn't want to either. But if there was something to discuss that she deemed important, it probably was. And if I didn't move right this second there was a pretty good chance I never would. I slowly pulled away from him.

He watched me as I climbed off the bed and looked around for something else to put on. "Your robe is probably still a little wet."

"You can burn it. I never want to see it again."

He still didn't move.

"Aren't you coming?"

He cleared his throat. "I need to change."

"Actually, you don't. Liza knows who you are too. When I figured it out last night, I told her."

"And how did you find out? You didn't say."

This was a little awkward. "I visited Eli and he kind of let it slip. But he was on painkillers. He didn't mean to."

Miles laughed.

For some reason that wasn't the reaction I was expecting. "What's so funny?"

"He's been keeping us apart for long enough. It's about time he helped push us back together again."

No hard feelings. I was relieved. But really, why should there have been? Miles had been with other women. He had already told me as much. Kins had even warned me of his reputation around campus. But then I had a sinking feeling in my stomach. I had told Eli I loved him. We had talked about a future. That was a lot different than what Miles had been doing.

We talked about it before. Actually, we fought about it. I had sworn I loved Eli and he had sworn I couldn't possibly. He said I couldn't because I was harboring feelings for Miles. How had I not put it together before?

But even though I had told V the truth, it felt different than telling Miles.

"You can go ahead," he said as he looked down. "I just need a second…"

"I can help you with the bandage if you want."

He looked back up at me.

And I realized I needed to rip the Band-Aid off. I needed to tell him before we went any further. I was so sick of secrets. "I told Eli I loved him. And I did mean it. I was mad at you. Both of you. I mean...you you and V you. If that makes any sense?"

"Summer, we've already talked about this."

"I know. But that was when I didn't know who you were. And I thought maybe we should talk about it too. I was just so tired of all the lies. I needed something..." I let my voice trail off. I couldn't find the right words. "Eli seemed so..."

"Easy?" Miles looked back down at his lap. "That worked. Thanks." But he didn't sound thankful. He slid out of bed.

I realized that he wasn't stalling getting up because he was going to transform back into V or change his bandage. He was stalling because he had been desiring me. My eyes traveled down his body.

He turned away from me.

Why had I chosen that moment to tell him I had loved Eli? God, what was wrong with me?

He ran his fingers through his hair as he stared out the window. I knew he wanted me to leave. But I couldn't leave like this.

"Miles..."

"It's fine." He cleared his throat and walked toward the door.

"It's not fine. Clearly you're upset with me."

He stopped with his hand on the doorknob. "You could have slept with a hundred men and I wouldn't love you any less."

"Is that how many women you've slept with?"

"No." He lowered his eyebrows slightly. This was just getting worse. "And I can promise you that I never told a single one of the women I've slept with that I loved them."

"I'm sorry, Miles. You broke my heart and I…"

"You broke mine too, Summer." His Adam's apple rose and then fell. "I can't even imagine what you've been through. I can't. But these years have been hell for me too."

I never meant to diminish his pain. That wasn't the point of this conversation.

He opened the door and stepped out into the hall.

"Miles," I hissed as I followed him. "I never said that they weren't. Of all people I understand your pain. I thought you had abandoned me. You thought that I had abandoned you. I understand…"

He stopped in his tracks. "It was more than that. I thought you were dead."

I swallowed hard.

"Don't you get that? For years I thought you might be dead."

I shook my head. "I didn't know." My words hung in the air. "Some days I wished that I was." As soon as the words came out, I wished they hadn't.

"This isn't a competition to see who suffered more." He started walking again. "It kills me that I couldn't find you. It kills me that you went through…"

"I know." I grabbed his arm to stop him from moving. "I'm sorry. I'm sorry about everything. You asked me to forgive you. Can't you forgive me too?"

"That's what I've been struggling with this whole time. I know it's better to leave the past in the past. I know that. But everything we've had is in the past. And I can't let go of that. I'm not sure we can have it both ways."

I let my hand fall from his arm. What did he mean by that? We either forgave each other and moved on with our lives apart? Or stayed together and lived with these demons? Those weren't the only two options. Didn't he see that? We could hold on to the good memories and stay together.

"Miles, wait!" I ran after him.

CHAPTER 40
Wednesday

When I caught up to Miles in the kitchen, the sound of metal clanging made me draw my eyes away from him.

Kins was sitting at the kitchen island eating a bowl of cereal. Her eyes were glued to Miles. Or they were at least glued to his abs.

"Um, hey, Miles." She tucked a loose strand of hair behind her ear. "What are you doing here?"

"He's V," Liza said as she came into the kitchen from the command center. "Nice to officially meet you by the way, Mr. Miles Young. It's nice to put a face to the name. Or a name to the face. Or well…I knew what Miles looked like, but I didn't know what V looked liked…you get it." She stuck her hand out for Miles to shake.

He laughed and shook her hand.

"Although you do owe me an apology. I'm pretty sure I guessed you were Miles and you legit lied to my face. Not cool, buddy."

"I…"

"And I really don't know why you lied about it to me anyway. I can keep a secret. Even from my bestie." She winked at me. "Don't do it again." She pointed at him.

"You're V?" Kins asked.

"Yeah." He shoved his hands into his pockets. "I'm sorry if I lied to you too. It was never my intention to have to mislead anyone but Summer."

"You're really V?" Kins looked at me and then back at him. "Oh. Oh!" she said a little louder. "Oh." The last oh sounded disappointed.

This was awkward. I remembered Kins calling dibs on Miles. What could I say to make it better?

"There is one thing I don't get," Liza said, breaking the tension in the air. "Why did you refuse to call her Summer? I mean, you knew her best. Yet you kept calling her Sadie."

Miles looked over at me. "Because I'm not the same person she remembers and she's not the same either. Not to mention it felt wrong to call her Summer. It made my lies feel worse."

"That sounds…heavy," Liza said.

"Wait, you *knew* him?" Kins asked me. "Why didn't you tell me?"

"I wasn't supposed to tell anyone," I said. "I was part of the witness protection program. At least, I thought I was." I looked back at Miles. I knew we had both changed. But I wanted to hold on to a piece of who I was. Didn't he?

"Another question," Liza said. "Did you two have fun reuniting last night?" She wiggled her eyebrows, causing her glasses to slide down her nose.

"Didn't you say you had something important to discuss?" Miles asked.

Liza slid her glasses back up. "Right. I do." She held up her finger and ran back toward her computers. She came back with a file folder and paged through it. "Remember when we thought Mr. Crawford was bringing in new recruits? Well, he wasn't." She pulled out a picture.

I leaned forward to get a better view. It wasn't the clearest image, but it was unmistakable. My old babysitter's face was staring back at me, smiling. "Julie?"

"Yup. Julie Harris is alive and well. And I'm guessing that's Jacob, although I couldn't get a good visual on his face." Liza pointed to the man beside her.

"Right, her fiancé." I put my hand on my chest. I had been hoping it was them. God, it felt like a miracle. "She's okay?" For months I had been worried about what had happened to her. She had just disappeared. I thought she was dead. I was almost certain of it.

"She's definitely okay. But actually, it turns out that Julie isn't who you said she was. Your glowing comments of her led me on a wild goose chase."

"What?"

"Julie Harris isn't on our side. She's the daughter of Deidra Harris. Maiden name Deidra Roberts.

Roberts?

"Julie is Don's niece."

"She…" my heart felt like it stopped. "She babysat me all the time. My parents trusted her. She…" my voice trailed off. "How could she?"

"You were meant to see that article about how she went missing. You were meant to feel bad for all these months. All of this was planned. For years maybe. First to trap Mr. Crawford, who surely saw the same articles. And then to trap you."

"What do you mean to trap her?" Miles asked.

"I got audio of the whole plan," Liza said. "I left a bug in the hotel room that we rescued you from and listened to them scheming. We can finally end all of this. Tomorrow night at 9 p.m. you're going to get a phone call. Julie is going to sound distressed. And she's going to beg you to come save her." She put air quotes around the word save. "But really you're gonna get payback, bitch!"

I didn't care that she had just called me a bitch. I didn't care that Julie was a traitor. All I cared about was that this could finally end.

"So we already know that Julie was in his pocket. What if the cops were in his pocket back then too? If where you grew up was anything like what power he has here..." She clapped her hands together and smiled. It was like she was waiting for me to guess what she was about to say.

I didn't know what she was getting at. "It probably was. It was like that everywhere I lived with him."

"Exactly." She squealed.

I looked over at Miles to see if he had any idea what Liza was trying to say. There was a frown on his face that I didn't quite understand.

"Summer, did you actually see your parents' bodies?" Liza asked.

I could picture them clearly. A bloody, mangled mess. The death in their gazes. It was a vivid image in my memory. But I had never actually seen it. I had just imagined it. I had been haunted by the pictures in my head for years. "No. I didn't."

"What if they're alive?"

I shook my head. "That's not possible. I went to their funerals."

"But what if they're alive?" she said again.

CHAPTER 41
Wednesday

What if my parents are alive? The thought swirled around in my mind. I thought Miles had abandoned me. He hadn't. I thought Don was an abusive foster father. But he was tied to my mother's past. Everything I thought was real ended up being misconstrued.

What if my parents are alive? I kept repeating it over and over again. *What if? What if? What if?*

"I think they just got some model to pose as Julie's fiancé in that newspaper article," Liza said. "That whole thing was fabricated. She's probably not even engaged. Which means the guy in this picture most likely isn't Jacob." She handed it back to me. "And it was probably someone else that Mr. Crawford would trust. Could that be your dad?"

I stared at the image. *What if?*

My father was always smiling. But I couldn't see the man's face in the image, mostly just the back of his head. Even his hair was covered by a knit hat. It could have been anyone.

But what if?

"I went to the funeral too," Miles said. "There were two coffins. There…"

"But was it open casket?" Liza asked.

"No," he admitted.

I continued to stare at the image. *Turn that frown upside down.* Don had left me a note saying that. But the only person who had ever said that to me before was my dad. Could Don have been keeping my father away from me? *What if?*

"And that original image I captured before." Liza pulled it out of the folder she was holding. "We couldn't see either of their faces in this one." She handed it to me. "That might not be Julie here. It could have been your mom, Summer."

I stared at the two people walking next to Mr. Crawford. And stared. And stared. *What if?*

"Does it look like them?" she asked.

Would I even recognize them if I saw them? It had been so long. *What if?*

"If they are alive, we have to assume that Don has them if he has Mr. Crawford. We need an extraction plan for all three of them just in case. We have a lot to do." She started shuffling through more papers.

"No," I finally said.

Liza looked up at me. "No? It's better to be safe than sorry…"

I shook my head. "They would have found me already if they were alive," I said. "They're dead. I know they're dead."

"But what if they were being held against their will?"

I clenched my jaw. My memories were so vivid. My dad always seemed to sense my pain. I remembered him running out into the yard when I cut my knee at the creek. He was always there. Always. "My dad would have done anything to get to me. Anything."

"Summer…"

"He would have found me already." He would have saved me before Don had ever hurt me. He would have. I know he would have.

"Mr. Crawford couldn't find you…"

"Mr. Crawford isn't my father!" I felt Miles' hand land on my shoulder. I turned to look at him. "Miles was just a kid and he kept looking for me. He found me here." I locked eyes with him. "If my dad was alive, he would have already found me." I knew it in my bones.

It was more than that, though. I considered Miles to be my best friend growing up. But looking back on it, it wasn't entirely true. My dad was my best friend. No one had ever been there for me more than him. I had never loved anyone more than I loved him. I knew it because even though I had Miles back, it still felt like there was a hole in my heart. It still felt like I was bleeding.

I turned back to Liza. "Besides, I talked to Mr. Crawford about my parents dying." I tried to recall the exact words. "He referred to my father in the past tense. If he had just seen him, why would he have referred to him that way?"

"Well, what did he say exactly?" Liza asked.

"He said he *was* a good man."

"Maybe he's not a good man anymore."

How dare you.

It was like Miles knew her words stung me. His fingers tightened on my shoulder. "Liza, drop it," he said. "We need to focus on our plan for tomorrow night."

"Great. Well, Eli will be here soon. He's getting discharged today. And I called Patrick. He's meeting us here in about an hour."

"My Patrick?" Kins asked.

"What other Patrick?"

"But he doesn't know about any of this. He never believed me when I said Summer was good. He…"

"I explained it all to him. He's all caught up. We need as much help as we can get tomorrow night. We're bringing in everyone we have. Including Dr. Miller." She almost whispered the last sentence as she avoided eye contact with me.

"My therapist?" I asked.

"Apparently Miles' too," Liza said. "Besides, I think it would be good if you two both chatted with him at the same time. Sorted out all your inner demons and all that so we can go into our planning with clear heads. Dr. Miller will be here any second."

"We don't need therapy," Miles said. "We're fine."

I didn't say anything.

"Right?" he asked me.

I didn't get a chance to respond because there was a knock on our entrance window.

Miles looked up. "Why isn't Athena alerting us that he's here?"

"Oh, I had a fun night too," she said and winked at me. "Our whole place was bugged and I had to do a sweep."

I had completely forgotten that Don had said he had been watching me.

"Our apartment was basically infested." Liza laughed at her own joke. "Athena's been compromised so I shut her down."

"When the hell did that happen?" Miles asked.

"I think it's been going on for awhile. Your glamorous system has been selling us out. She was the leak that let Don know we were onto his plans in that theater. This time, there won't be a leak. We're finally going to get him. I'll go let Dr. Miller in. And don't freak out, he's not actually staying for the meeting later. He's a doctor after all. I know that he knows that Miles is V. But the less he knows about what we actually do here, the better. Agreed? Agreed." She walked out into the hall.

"Why did Patrick believe her when he wouldn't believe me?" Kins said. "Maybe we're the couple that needs therapy. I need to go call him." She walked past us out of the kitchen.

"You don't think we're fine?" Miles asked once she disappeared.

"I think that I want to remember the past but still be happy with you now."

"That sounds like a splendid idea," Dr. Miller said as he appeared in the kitchen. "It's nice to see that you're both not wearing any disguises." He smiled and sat down at the kitchen table. "I was told we had some time to talk if you don't mind taking a seat."

Neither Miles nor I moved.

Dr. Miller gestured to the seats in front of him. "Just for a few minutes."

I sat down and Miles slowly joined us.

"Do you mind if I speak candidly?" Dr. Miller asked. He didn't wait for us to respond, he just started talking. "Miles, you've been haunted by the memory of this woman for years." He nodded toward me. "And I know that there was a lot of pain. Clearly secrets and other hurts. It's easy to throw blame around. But as I understand it, you were both placed in a terrible situation. One that would have been hard for even adults to face. And as children, you both held on to hope. That's remarkable by itself.

"You both tried your best to cope in different ways. You both made mistakes. You both let each other down. Yet you somehow kept fighting for this." He gestured back and forth between us. "Find a way to let go of the pain. If you can somehow do that together, then I think you two will make it. Please just don't let your past hurts cause future ones. You love each other, that's all that matters." He tapped the table with his knuckles. "Is there anything that either one of you needs to say?"

"How do you recommend letting it go?" I asked.

"You could write down everything that hurt you, and then burn it or throw it out. Even exercise is a great way to release pent-up anger and aggression. Or you could just talk it out. Right here, right now."

I looked over at Miles.

"I don't know what you want me to say," he said.

"Miles, you made it seem like if we stay together you'll always be miserable. Or that you could let everything go including me. I don't want either of those options. I said I was sorry. And I said I forgave you. I don't know what else you need unless you tell me."

He ran his fingers through his hair. "You could do anything and I'd still love you. I told you that. It's not about what you did. It's what *I* did. I don't know how to forgive myself."

"For what?"

"For not finding you sooner. For not being able to stop Don from hurting you. For…"

"None of that was your fault."

"Well it was my fault that I hated you for shutting me out. I hated you for years, Summer. I was haunted by your memory."

"You think I didn't hate you for shutting *me* out? You think I just loved you for the last ten years? I hated you, Miles. I fucking hated you too! I was haunted by the memory of this boy that I thought loved me but then kicked me to the curb when I needed him the most!"

"I never stopped writing to you!" He stood up. The chair squeaked behind him.

I blinked back my tears.

"I never fell in love with someone else," he said. "I never saw my life with anyone else. You gave up on me, Summer."

A part of me did. He was right. I never stopped loving him, but I did give up on him. I stopped writing. I fell in love with Eli. I gave up on him. "I'm sorry that I let you down." I stood up and tried to walk away, but he grabbed my wrist.

"I'm sorry that I gave you a reason to," he said.

I stared into his eyes. They were different than I remembered. They weren't filled with warmth and laughter. My youth had been stolen by death and by Don. But I had stolen Miles'. "I froze your heart." That's what Dr. Miller had said before. That Miles' heart was frozen.

"I let you burn." His voice broke. "I can't forgive myself for that. Ever."

The way he said it made me feel cold. I talked about how Don's touch made me feel like I was on fire. He listened to me. He could feel my pain. He always had been able to.

"Tell me you don't want me, Miles. Tell me to walk away. Tell me you don't need me as much as I need you."

He shook his head. "I don't know how to breathe without you."

"I don't know how to breathe without you." I wanted him to kiss me. I wanted him to decide to move past this.

"I can't take away the things that Don did to you. And I can't undo the things I've done."

"I've already forgiven you." I leaned forward and touched the side of his face. "But you know that. You need to forgive yourself."

"I killed someone, Summer."

I didn't realize he was torn up about that. But of course he was. His heart wasn't as frozen as he seemed to think. He was full of love. He always had been. "You saved me. He would have killed me if you hadn't taken his life first." Miles leaned into my touch like I was the only one that could support him.

Dr. Miller cleared his throat. "Can we rewind for a second? Miles, did you say you killed someone? Summer touched base on that topic in our last session and I did have some questions about that."

"It's a figure of speech, doc!" Liza practically fell into the kitchen and Kins toppled in on top of her. "Like, man you killed that test," she groaned and shoved Kins off of her.

"That wasn't how he used it…" Dr. Miller's voice trailed off. "Were you two eavesdropping on our session?"

"It was her idea," Liza said and pointed at Kins.

Kins just shrugged. "Will you two kiss and make up already?"

I looked up at Miles. And suddenly it was like I was transported back in time when he first held my hand in his tree house. When he first kissed me on my grandmother's roof. There weren't any lies between us like when we danced in central park. Or when we made love under the stars. I was Summer Brooks again. And he was Miles Young.

My heart stammered as he moved a fraction of an inch closer.

"Don't give up on me this time," he whispered. "Promise me you won't give up on me."

"I will never give up on you, Miles." We weren't kids anymore. I could keep a promise. And I knew I'd keep this one until my dying breath. I would never let him go again.

His lips softly brushed against mine. It was like I could hear the summer cicadas and feel the hot breeze on my grandmother's roof again. But the memory disappeared when he pulled me closer. I parted my lips for him as he buried his fingers in my hair.

I stood up on my tiptoes, deepening our kiss. It was better than a memory. Better than a dream. Better than all the stars in the sky. It felt like he stole my soul in that kiss. Even though he already had it.

And I knew in that second that I had never loved Eli like this. Never like this. Not even close. How could I? Miles had always been the one for me.

"Ow, ow!" Kins yelled.

Miles pulled back far too soon, but I held him close and whispered in his ear.

"I've never loved anyone like I love you. I swear to you. My heart has always belonged to you, Miles. Always."

He pressed his forehead against mine and took a deep breath. It was like he was breathing me in. "I've missed you so damn much."

I knew exactly what he meant. Our time apart had almost killed me. He had said it right before. I didn't know how to breathe without him. And it felt so good to finally be living again.

CHAPTER 42
Wednesday

I grabbed another slice of pizza. There really wasn't much strategizing going on. Liza had gone over the plan several times already. We had it down. Now we were just suffering through an awkward group date. Or really, the interrogation of V. The rapid-fire questions seemed endless.

I glanced over at Eli and Liza. They seemed cozy. His arm was draped behind her chair. He wasn't touching her, but they were clearly an item now. I was happy for him. For both of them.

Patrick and Kins seemed happier than I had last seen them too. Although, they were fighting the last time I had seen them, so anything would have been better. His arm was wrapped tightly around Kins' shoulders and he kept giving Miles dirty looks. I guess he was probably aware of Kins' crush on Miles last semester.

And then there was Miles and me. *Miles and me.* I smiled to myself. I had waited a lifetime for us to be an us.

"So why did you go by V?" Patrick asked as he took another sip of his drink.

"A V looks like the point of an arrow," Miles said.

"Okay…"

"Like your tattoo?" Kins asked.

Patrick stared at her.

She nudged his shoulder. "He was walking around without a shirt earlier. I wasn't checking him out or anything."

"Yup, like my tattoo." Miles looked so uncomfortable. He had tried to dismiss himself from dinner a few times now. I understood why. The more questions they asked, the more uncomfortable I got too.

"Like an arrow and like your tattoo," Patrick said. "What significance does it have though?"

Miles looked over at me. "The arrow isn't the significance. It's the constellation it represents. Sagitta."

My heart melted.

"Summer used to wear an arrow pendant too," Eli said.

Used to. Miles smiled at me. There wasn't anger in his eyes. Our talk earlier had really helped. It was true, I had stopped wearing it when I was with Eli. I was wearing it again now though. It was back where it belonged, right next to my heart.

I pulled it out from underneath my shirt. There was no reason to hide it anymore. "When we were little, I used to sneak over to Miles' tree house at night to look at the stars. He taught me about all the constellations. Sagitta was my favorite. It was hard to find because it was so small. You had to search and search to really see it." I ran my fingers over the pendant. "The arrow reminded me of cupid's arrow too. I was madly in love with him and I always hoped he'd be struck by it." I let the necklace fall back into place.

"Is that true?" Miles asked.

I nodded.

"So sweet," Kins said. "God, you two are the most adorable couple ever. So all this time you still loved each other? Did you buy the necklace to remember him?"

"No, he gave it to me the first night we ever held hands." The memory was bittersweet. Bliss before utter destruction. My whole world had been flipped upside down in a matter of minutes. I could still see the sky lighting up blue and red from the police car.

Miles grabbed my hand under the table. It was like he could hear my unspoken thoughts. Just like when we were little. He squeezed my hand and tried to absorb my pain.

"There's nothing more romantic than childhood sweethearts," Kins said.

Patrick squeezed her shoulder. "What about college sweethearts?"

"Or secret vigilante team sweethearts?" Liza looked up at Eli.

Eli laughed. "By the way, I'm sorry I unmasked you, man. No hard feelings?" He stuck his hand out to Miles.

Miles narrowed his eyes slightly. "Nothing else you want to apologize for?"

"Miles," I said. "It doesn't matter."

"No, he's right," Eli said. "I'm sorry for trying to steal Summer away. Really. I knew who you were and honestly, I knew she was still in love with you and I still kept interfering. You two were meant to be together. I mean it." He stuck his hand back out.

Miles shook it.

"Besides, I finally opened up my eyes and realized that what I was missing was right in front of me." He looked down at Liza and her face turned bright red.

"I have another question," Liza said.

Miles sighed. "Haven't I answered enough questions for one night?"

She laughed. "It isn't anything bad. I was just wondering if you changed your bandages recently? They looked pretty…um…bloody earlier. We really need you tomorrow and…"

"I'm fine. But speaking of tomorrow, we need to get Patrick and Kins up to speed." He turned to them. "I heard there was a little bit of accidental firing in the hotel the other morning, Kins. I can teach you and Patrick…"

"Babe, you shot a gun?" Patrick asked.

She shrugged. "We kind of kicked ass yesterday. Didn't we, Liza?" She held her hand up for a high-five.

"Heck yeah we did, slut." Liza slapped her hand.

Kins just stared at her. "Why would you call me that? I've been dating Patrick for months. I…"

"Because we're friends. That's what friends do."

Eli whispered something into Liza's ear.

Liza nodded. "Okay so apparently some friends do when it's cool with everyone. We'll talk about that later. First we have some training to do." She rubbed her hands together.

"Miles, I can show them if you want," Eli said. "I heard you got pretty banged up yesterday."

Miles stared at him. "I'm fine. You just got out of the hospital. I got this."

"Really, I can…"

"I'll do it," I said and stood up. "You both need rest." I didn't tell them that the last time I had held a gun I froze. I had an opportunity to shoot Don, but I was worried I'd miss. At least, that's what I told myself. I was concerned that it was more than that though. What if I couldn't pull the trigger when it mattered?

I had another opportunity yesterday morning at the hotel. I couldn't find the bottle I had broken, but there were tons of things in the room. I could have even grabbed a lamp and hit him over the head. Or even strangled him. But I ran. I always seemed to run.

I picked up one of the guns and cocked it. I was done running. Tomorrow I was going to end this. I aimed at the target and pressed the trigger.

CHAPTER 43
Wednesday

I was expecting Miles to be asleep when I slipped into his room. But he was sitting at his desk reading a piece of paper. When he saw me, he slid the paper back into the envelope.

"What was that?" I asked.

"Nothing important." He tossed it on his desk and stood up.

It felt like I was dreaming as he walked over to me. And if I was dreaming, I never wanted to wake up.

He cupped my cheek in his hand. "Ever since you disappeared, I had this idea in my head that love was synonymous with pain. But we finally get to stop hurting now. We finally get to experience what it really is."

I used to think the same thing. That love was just some sick excuse to get hurt. "There are so many things I never got to say to you." I stared into his dark brown eyes and all my thoughts disappeared. "So many nights I stayed awake looking at the stars wishing you knew that I loved you."

"I knew." He smiled. "You wouldn't have been so annoying when we were little if you weren't in love with me."

I laughed. "You're so conceited…"

His lips crashed against mine, silencing me. I melted into him. I was addicted to all of him. Smell, sight, taste, touch, and sound.

"Annoying." His voice was low when his lips traveled down to my neck. "Kind." He kissed the side of my neck. "Frustrating."

I laughed.

"Intelligent." His kisses trailed down my collarbone. "Infuriating."

"Miles!"

"Funny." He pushed my sweater off my shoulder and kissed it. "And so fucking beautiful. So perfect."

"That was a list of good and bad things. Clearly I'm not perfect."

"No, they were all good things." His hand slid beneath the hem of my sweater and he traced the scar on my stomach with his thumb. "Every inch of you is perfect."

Yes, we got to say everything we never got to the first time around. But him saying that was all I needed to know. He accepted me, scars and all. No, not just accepted me. Loved me in spite of them. Loved me because of them.

"You're not just conceited," I said. "You were a terribly mean little boy."

He laughed.

"But sweet. Strong. Confident. Stubborn. And you're sexy as sin. I used to think that you were my prince. My knight in shining armor. I know you tear yourself up for not being there for me. But I don't think I was ever meant to be a princess. I was born to be a superhero too."

"You're a much better superhero than me. You'd actually look good in leather and spandex."

"Oh I don't know about that. You could pull off leather."

"We've been back together for less than 24 hours and you're already trying to change me?"

"No." I reached up and ran my fingers through his hair like he did so often. "I wouldn't want to change a thing about you." My hand paused on the back of his neck. "Except for how much I hurt you."

"I wish your heart had never been broken." His hand was still on my stomach. "I wish he'd never touched you. I wish I could take away your pain."

"You're the only person that makes me feel whole again." I used to think that his superpower was taking away my pain.

His hand slid farther up my shirt, pausing on my rib-cage. It was like he was waiting for permission to ravish me.

And I had the most heartwarming realization. He was the only person that had never pushed me farther than I wanted to go. Ever. I had grabbed his hand in his tree house first. I had kissed him first when we were little on the rooftop. I had kissed him first when he was V. It was always me that closed the gap between us. He respected me more than anyone else ever had. Him respecting me was one of the sexiest things about him.

I swallowed hard and looked up at him. "Remember when we were on the roof of our dorm building and I asked you to pretend for one night that you loved me? Because I wanted to know what it felt like to be loved?"

"And I told you I didn't have to pretend with you. I knew it was you, Summer. I've always known it was you."

I nodded. "But this time *I'll* know it's real."

"No masks." He grabbed my hips and lifted my legs around his waist. "No fake names." He lowered me onto his bed. "No lies. I promise you that this is real."

I grabbed the waistband of his sweatpants and pushed them and his underwear down. Maybe I always closed the gap, but he clearly always wanted me too. When I looked back up at him, he raised his eyebrow at me and it was probably the sexiest thing I had ever seen. I felt like I was going to internally combust if he wasn't inside of me in the next second. I pulled off my sweater and peeled off my leggings and underwear.

"And no foreplay apparently," he said.

I laughed. "I've waited so long for you. For us."

He climbed onto the bed on top of me, slowly pushing my thighs farther apart. "And the timing's finally fucking right."

I tried to say something, but my words blurred together in an incoherent mess as he thrust inside of me. *So fucking right.*

"I love you, Summer."

"God, Miles!" I pulled him closer to me. I hoped he knew that meant I loved him too.

He pulled me closer still until our bodies couldn't be any more perfectly aligned.

He took away the pain. He gave me every single thing I needed. I felt truly loved from my head to my toes.

Again.

And again.

And again until I passed out in his arms smiling harder than I ever had.

CHAPTER 44

Thursday

"It shouldn't take long at all for them to get here." Miles' voice sounded in my ear. "And the package is being delivered as soon as you initiate the distraction."

I didn't respond. I knew the plan. We had been over it a dozen times.

"I'll be watching the whole time, Summer. We all will. Nothing bad is going to happen."

His voice was calming, but my thoughts had been at war all day. Nothing bad was going to happen. But it could. I wasn't sure if I was going to stick to the plan. I wasn't sure if I could live with myself if I did. Don deserved to be in the ground, not behind bars. This wasn't justice.

"Just stick to the plan," Miles said, like he could hear my thoughts.

I touched the earpiece I was wearing. "I will." But there were two plans running through my mind, and I was thinking my plan was the better one. Miles knew I wanted Don dead. Eli knew it. Liza knew it. I was worried that they had a plan B too. Some safeguard to stop me from killing Don. If I was going to do it, I had to be quick.

But I had to get into his house either way. I was fine with this part of the plan. Don liked hurting me. He liked seeing me weak when he was the one that caused it. But he didn't like when other people hurt me.

I clutched Miles' hoodie in my hand and thought about the last time I saw my mother. I had said bye and gave her the shortest hug in the history of hugs. I should have said that I loved her. I thought about how my dad had ruffled my hair before stepping out the front door with her. When they closed the door I had thought "finally." *Finally*. Tears prickled my eyes.

I thought about standing at their funeral. I thought about my grandmother's face lined with sadness. I thought about losing her when I was finally feeling like her home was becoming mine too. A tear ran down my cheek.

I thought about the foster families I had lived with. I thought about Don putting his hands on me. And about Miles' letters stopping. How I'd never felt so alone. I thought about my baby's life slipping through my fingers. And how I'd never felt so weak. Tears streamed down my face.

A snowflake landed on the tip of my nose. I looked up at the sky. It felt like a sign. A kiss from the dead. When I was 16, my last reason for living had been taken from me in the snow. I remembered the blood in the snow. It haunted me. I touched my stomach. I was fucking going with plan B.

I walked up the steps of Don's mansion. We had lived in shitholes wherever he took me. But now he wasn't a criminal. He was New York City's savior. So many lies. So much blood on his hands.

Before I could even knock on the door, it swung open. Two of his minions stood there. I recognized one of them. He had been in our house before. He had ignored my cries. I clenched my hand into a fist. I was going to fucking kill him too.

"Where's Don? I…I need him." I tried to sound pathetic. It was easy. I had been pathetic my whole life. I pretended to wipe my tears away, when really I kept thinking about my unborn child so the tears would keep falling. And I thought about how he robbed me of the future I had wanted with Miles. I had always pictured children surrounding us. A family to replace the one that had been taken from me.

"Pat her down," the man that I recognized said.

I clenched my jaw when he ran his hands down my arms. My torso. My legs. *Fire.* I was burning alive. I remembered the way Don touched me. How he left a trail of bruises. My tears fell like the first time he laid his hands on me. I cried for my weakness.

"He wasn't expecting you yet," the man I recognized said.

That was the riskiest part of this plan. We could have waited for Julie's distress call. But that's what Don wanted. We thought it was better if we were the ones in control. The element of surprise was underrated. Besides, Julie had already led Mr. Crawford into a trap and I was done playing into Don's hand. And I couldn't wait until night fell. I couldn't wait another second.

"Can you please just go get him?" I pretended to wipe my tears away again. "Please."

He stepped outside, grabbed the collar of my jacket, and pulled me into the house. Such a grand foyer for such a rotten man. Gold trim. Mirrors and glass. It looked like an ostentatious hotel lobby. I took a deep breath. It was time for me to initiate the distraction.

"Don't touch me!" I screamed. I tried to push his hands away. "Don! Don!" I screamed at the top of my lungs. "He's touching me!" More of Don's minions appeared. They came through the archways, from the stairs, from the hall.

The man immediately let go of my jacket. He looked bewildered. "I didn't touch you," he hissed. "I escorted you inside."

You practically dragged me you prick. "Don!" I screamed. "Don!"

A few more minions showed up. That had to be most of them. But I kept screaming bloody murder.

Don appeared at the top of the stairs.

"Don." My voice cracked. I ran over to the bottom of the stairs to meet him. "Don, he put his hands on me." I pointed to the man that had sat there all those years ago and listened to Don rape me. *Fuck him.*

Don snapped his fingers and pointed at the man.

Two other men grabbed either one of his arms and started dragging him down the hall. "Don, I didn't touch her!" he yelled, but his voice died away.

I didn't have to kill him after all. Whatever they were about to do to him was probably worse.

"Are you okay?" Don asked as he stepped off the bottom stair.

I shook my head. "The vigilante. I...he tried..." I put my hand over my mouth and shook my head.

"What did he do?"

"He tried to kill me. You were right about him. He's been ruining this city just like you said. I…I finished the job." I shoved Miles' hoodie into Don's hands.

He looked down at it and a smile spread across his face. "You killed him?"

He seemed so surprised that I'd be able to do something like that. He was about to have the shock of his life.

"I'm so sorry about everything I've done. I never should have betrayed you. I'm so sorry." My tears started up again and I looked down, trying to get a glimpse of where his gun was. "Please forgive me." I didn't see his gun. His suit jacket was probably covering it.

"The package has been delivered," Miles said into my ear. "You're doing great, Summer. Just keep stalling. They'll be there any minute now."

"You came back, doll. That's all that matters. And this was quite the gift." He lifted up the hoodie.

I nodded. "Can we maybe…have some privacy?" I was running out of time.

Don tilted his head toward the stairs. But I didn't want to go anywhere with him. I just needed his stupid minions to leave so I could get this over with. Before he turned to go up the stairs, I threw my arms around him.

The smell of his cologne made me feel sick to my stomach. I tightened my arms around him, pulling him closer to me. I tried not to gag.

I heard footsteps. I pressed the side of my head against his chest and caught a glimpse of everyone leaving the room.

"I missed you." My words were barely a whisper as I slipped my hands under his suit jacket. The side of my wrist brushed against his gun. *Bingo.*

"I know. You'll be safe now."

Safe? Was he fucking kidding me? I had never been safe with him. I grabbed his gun and took a step back, holding it out in front of me.

He opened his mouth to say something, but I cut him off.

"Don't say a word, Don."

Instead of speaking, he smiled. Somehow that was worse. Like he was mocking me.

"I had a whole plan of what I wanted to say to you before I blew your head off. But really I just have a few questions."

"Summer, what are you doing?" Miles said into my earpiece.

I ignored him. "I want to know if you feel any remorse for tearing my family apart?" I clenched my jaw.

He kept smiling and shook his head.

"Summer, put the gun down!" Miles yelled.

I grabbed the earpiece out of my ear and threw it on the ground. This was between Don and me. No one else. I lifted the gun and took another step back from him.

"For raping me?" I asked Don.

"Doll, you wanted it." His smile grew. "Don't pretend for a second that you didn't."

He was the devil himself. I wasn't sure what I was expecting. I knew the blood in his veins was pure evil. My finger tightened on the trigger.

"We've done this dance already," he said. "You couldn't pull the trigger then, and you can't do it now. Drop the gun."

He was taunting me. But he was right, I could have already shot him. Why couldn't I pull the trigger? I was running out of time.

"Weak." He shook his head like he pitied me. "Your whole family was weak."

I lifted the gun higher and held my breath for one second.

Weak. For two seconds.

The word tumbled around in my head. For three seconds.

He couldn't have been more wrong. For four seconds.

And I knew that I needed to do the strongest thing I ever had to do. Because I refused to become him. For five seconds.

I exhaled and slowly lowered the gun. "You're wrong, Don. I'm the strongest person you'll ever meet. I lost my parents when I was eight years old. My grandmother a year later. I went from foster home to foster home and kept being told I wasn't wanted." I lifted my shoulders. "You kept my best friend away from me. You killed my unborn child." I tried to hide the crack in my voice. "And I'm still standing, asshole. I'm here despite everything you did to cut me down. And you think I'm weak?" I shook my head. "You don't know me at all."

I saw red and blue lights through the windows.

It's finally over. "Your game is done. The FBI is coming to arrest you. No one can ever pin you down for your crimes. So my team and I planted evidence on you." I looked at Miles' hoodie in his hand. "By the time the news comes on tonight, everyone will believe that you're the New York City vigilante. V was saving this city, not destroying it. You'll finally be put behind bars for good deeds. A little ironic huh?"

Something flashed across his face and he dropped the hoodie. For the first time, I believed there was fear in his eyes.

"Although, the rest of it will follow," I said. "The drugs, the murders. You'll go down for all of it in the end. You know, I thought I wanted vengeance. I thought I wanted to see your last breath. But I'm my parents' daughter, despite how you tried to raise me. I'm kind. And good. And fucking strong." I dropped the gun onto the ground. "I want justice for what you did to my family. For what you did to me. Not vengeance. Because I'm not the monster here. You are."

CHAPTER 45
Thursday

It was finally over. All of it. Men in tactical gear flooded into Don's foyer with their guns raised. I breathed a sigh of relief. But it didn't last long.

There was just one problem. All their guns were pointed at me. I held up my hands. "What are you doing? Arrest him," I said and pointed at Don. But no one moved.

Where was Eli? I swallowed hard. These were police officers, not the FBI. NYPD was written across the chests of their tactical gear. FBI agents were supposed to come, not these men. They were all on Don's payroll.

I had ditched my earpiece. Something must have gone wrong. And then I saw one familiar face in the sea of cops. Detective Lewis.

I had gone to the police after Don had kidnapped me and I had woken up back in my dorm. I couldn't get a hold of Mr. Crawford. I didn't know who I could trust. And Detective Lewis made me feel like I was crazy. Like I was just some dumb college kid that had too much to drink. I had doubted everything I thought was real.

"Good to see you again, Don," Detective Lewis said. He stepped forward and shook his hand. "We heard that the FBI thought the vigilante could be found here. Just wanted to make sure everything was okay. Looks like we came at a good time."

Any fear that had been in Don's eyes was gone. "She tried to frame me." He bent down and picked up the hoodie. "Not that having a hoodie the same color as the vigilante's would have been enough evidence to convict me."

"Want us to take a look around to see if there's anything else?" Detective Lewis asked.

Shit. I kept my hands raised and tried to look as innocent as possible. The hoodie wasn't the main evidence. Although, it would have looked nice if Don was holding it when the FBI showed up.

"Better to be safe than sorry," Don said.

"You heard him, boys. Check every inch of this place. I'll let the Feds know your house is clear so they don't need to bother coming." Before he put his cell phone to his ear, he winked at me. "Nice to see you again, Sadie. Or was it Summer?" He turned away and started talking into his phone.

Fuck you. I tried to swallow down my rage and focus. There had to be something I could do. I looked down and saw that the gun was only a foot away from me on the floor.

"Don't even think about it." Don grabbed it before I even had a chance to move. "What was it you were saying about winning the game? It looks like the tables have turned."

"Get off me!" Liza shrieked from upstairs. I looked up to see one of the cops pulling her down the stairs. He pushed her down beside me. The same cop shoved me to the ground too.

"We're going to die, we're going to die," Liza said over and over again. "I knew you'd end up getting me killed. I knew it. Oh God."

Gunshots fired upstairs. Shattering glass echoed around me. More shots. Kins screamed from somewhere in the house.

Liza grabbed my arm and started crying.

I didn't know what to say to calm her down. For all I knew, she was right. This was exactly what I hadn't wanted to happen. "Don, let them go," I said. "It's me you want. Please just let my friends go."

Don crouched down in front of me and pressed the gun to the side of my head. "He's here, isn't he? That pesky vigilante?"

A cop fell down the stairs and lay motionless on the floor. Don stood up. "Someone find him!" he yelled.

More shots fired from upstairs.

A cop appeared at the top of the stairs with Kins over his shoulder. She was screaming at the top of her lungs and reaching out for Patrick. One of Don's minions had Patrick's arms pinned behind his back and was leading him down the stairs. They were both shoved down onto the ground next to Liza.

Where was Miles? I didn't have to wonder for long. A cop was dragging his body down the stairs. Each step jarred Miles' head. But otherwise he wasn't moving.

No. I had just gotten him back. *No!*

The cop left Miles' body in a heap at the bottom of the steps.

"So that's the boy that you can't stay away from?" Don asked. "Him? Really?" He walked over to Miles' body. "You forgot your hoodie, you piece of shit." He tossed it on top of him. "If you think I'm going down for your crimes, you're dead wrong." He turned to look at me. "You're right, doll, it's time to end the game." He nodded and I felt a gun pressed to the back of my head.

Don walked back over to me. "I killed your mother because she didn't know her place. I guess it runs in the family." He crouched back down in front of me. "In looks and stupidity, you are most definitely your mother's daughter."

I pressed my lips together. His ignorant words didn't deserve a response. Besides, he was right. I was my mother's daughter. And I was damn proud of that. It was his own lack of awareness that he didn't know who either one of us was.

Don grabbed my chin in his hand. "What happened to the fight in you?" He looked utterly disappointed.

I was almost swallowed whole by my revenge. Almost. "I'd rather die as Summer than as some reflection of the monster you are."

He laughed and dropped his hand. "Take a good look, doll. I'm everything you'll never be."

"I fucking hope so."

He shook his head again, like he had never witnessed something so disappointing in this life.

I smiled. I finally felt free.

There was a cracking noise behind me. For a second I thought it was the sound of my own skull exploding. But I felt the gun slide down the back of my neck. There was another cracking noise and it sounded like wood splintering.

"Drop your weapons!" a deep voice yelled. "Everybody down on the ground!" The room flooded with more men in tactical vests. But this time FBI was written on their chests.

Don locked eyes with me. His smile was gone. He lowered his gun to his side.

The look of shock from him was even more satisfying than the look of disappointment.

"On the fucking ground!" one of the men yelled and kicked the back of Don's leg. He fell to his knees, still staring at me.

The gun on the base of my neck was removed. I didn't wait to see what happened next. I stood up and didn't stop when they told me to put my hands in the air. I ran over to Miles and dropped to my knees. "Miles?" I put my hand on the center of his chest. "Miles?" My eyes filled with tears. *No.* "Wake up. Please wake up."

Nothing.

"Miles," I choked. There were still so many things I didn't get to say. "You have to wake up. You have to." I cradled his head in my hands. "I was wrong before. You did save me." I placed my forehead against his. "You saved me, Miles."

"So I was your knight in shining armor after all?" His breath was hot against my cheek. He groaned as I threw my arms around him.

"Yes." I kissed the side of his neck and hugged him harder.

"You didn't kill him," he groaned.

I pulled back so I could see his face.

He smiled at me. "You didn't kill him."

I shook my head. "He ruined my life. But I don't feel ruined anymore."

He nodded like he understood. I hoped he did. He was the only reason I felt whole again. He reached out and touched the side of my face. "I knew Summer Brooks was still in there somewhere. It's good to have you back."

I nodded and let the tears fall freely. I took a deep breath and the air suddenly smelled sweeter, like a fresh spring breeze. "It's good to be back."

"That's not mine," Don said. "Check it for fingerprints. You won't find a single one of mine."

"You have $100,000 in stolen cash," the FBI agent said and lifted up the duffle bag that V had planted upstairs. "The first few bills we've checked match serial numbers belonging to the cash that was stolen in the North Union bank burglary last year. I bet there's a good chance that they all do." He rummaged around in the duffel bag. "Huh, and a gun." He lifted it up and inspected it. "What are the odds that it's unregistered?"

"How the fuck should I know?" Don seethed. "It's not mine."

"I bet the odds are just as high that the bullets will match the ones from the Gavin Moore homicide last year too."

Don just glared at him.

"Don Roberts, you are under arrest. You have the right to remain silent…"

I let the words fade away as I watched them handcuff Don. This had happened once before. But he was handcuffed by officers that were on his side. This time? I sighed. This time was for real. Maybe no one could tie him to the murder of my parents. But he'd end up on death row either way. And that? I exhaled slowly. That was justice.

Don stared at me just like he did last time he had been taken away. With a promise in his eyes that it wasn't over. That he'd find me and kill me. But this time I wasn't scared. His threats were empty now. Not only was he not going to get out of prison, but I was strong enough to take him if he did.

I watched Julie and her fiancé being pushed out of the house next. Even though I didn't believe that my father was still alive, it was still hard seeing Jacob. A part of me wanted to believe that my father was the man in the picture, not him.

"We need to check out how bad your wounds are okay?" An EMT had crouched down next to us.

I watched her remove Miles' shirt.

"You were lucky you were wearing one of these," she said when she saw his bulletproof vest. "Or else we wouldn't be talking right now."

"I'm fine, really," Miles said. "I just got knocked out. Someone hit the back of my head."

"Okay, let's see." She pulled out a small flashlight. "Follow the light for me." She watched his eyes. "You might have a concussion. We should get you to the hospital."

We both helped Miles to his feet. I glanced over at my friends. I hadn't even seen Eli come in, but he was standing there with his arm around Liza. He was wearing one of the FBI tactical vests. Everyone seemed okay. Kins looked horrified, but still healthy at least.

"I'll be right back okay?" I said.

Miles nodded.

I walked over to them and smiled at Eli. "I thought you weren't coming."

"I promised I'd help you get justice." He smiled. "Nothing could have stopped me from getting them here, especially a bunch of lying cops."

I laughed. "And all of you are okay?"

"We'll be fine," Liza said. "Go. He needs you." She nodded at Miles.

I looked over my shoulder. He was arguing with someone about getting on a stretcher.

"Was there any sign of Mr. Crawford?" I asked.

Eli shook his head.

I swallowed hard. "Keep me updated okay?" I ran after the EMT who was wheeling Miles away.

CHAPTER 46
Friday

I slowly opened my eyes and blinked at the light streaming into the hospital room. I was tucked in Miles' side. He did end up having a minor concussion and they insisted on monitoring him overnight. They also re-did the stitches in his side. They didn't even ask any questions about the injury which was a relief.

It felt like the FBI had questioned us all night. But I didn't mind telling my story. It seemed like it was the last time I would ever have to. And I was glad to let it all go. It was time to move on. My future was right beside me. I didn't want to bring any darkness into that.

I sat up and stretched. That's when I saw Mr. Crawford slumped forward in one of the chairs sleeping. One of his eyes was black and blue, but otherwise he looked okay. I carefully slid out of Miles' arms and sat down next to Mr. Crawford.

"Mr. Crawford," I whispered and lightly touched his arm. "I'm so glad you're okay."

When he opened his eyes, they looked wild for a moment. But then he focused on me and smiled.

"Thank you." I squeezed his arm. "Thank you for everything you did."

He shook his head. "If I could go back, I'd do a few things differently. Just know that I wanted you to know the truth, but I didn't think I'd be alive long enough to tell it to you when you were finally safe."

"Whenever we talked you always said if everything went right you'd never see me again," I said. He was willing to die to get justice for my parents. "I thought it was because you hated me."

He laughed. "No. I tried to end all this on my own. I didn't think I needed any help. It turns out that a team is a lot better than working solo."

"Yeah. It definitely is."

"Speaking of which, they're all in the waiting room. And I need to get going." He stood up.

"You're not going to stay?"

He smiled. "I've spent a lot of time trying to fix a wrong that I was a part of so many years ago."

"None of it was your fault."

"Your mom choosing me was the start of all of this."

I shook my head. "It wasn't your fault," I said again.

He patted my shoulder. "Regardless, I finally feel free. And so should you. Go live your life, Summer." He smiled. "I've been waiting to say those words to you for so long."

"Will I ever see you again?"

"The number I originally gave you is to my cell phone. It should be working again shortly. But there's still one last thing I need to do. After that, I don't think you're going to need me." He winked and walked out of the room before I could ask him what he meant. And I had the strangest sensation that he was my guardian angel.

Liza came running into the room before the door even closed. "We didn't make the evening news, but we did make the morning news." She grabbed the remote and turned on the TV. "How are you guys?" she asked, but her eyes were glued to the TV screen.

"We're good," Miles said.

I turned around and smiled at him. I didn't care about the news report. Mr. Crawford had put it exactly right. I was finally free.

Kins, Patrick, and Eli all came into the room with smiles on their faces.

"What now, Summer?" Kins asked and sat down on the edge of Miles' bed. "Are you going to re-enroll for classes next semester?" She looked so hopeful.

I wanted to tell her yes. That everything would go back to normal. But there were some things I needed to do first. I walked back over to Miles and grabbed his hand. "All I can think about is going home."

He squeezed my hand. "And we'll figure it out from there."

I wanted to see where so many of my favorite memories had evolved. And I had never been to the cemetery that my parents were buried in since the day of the funeral. My grandmother had always said it was too far of a trip. But really, I knew it was just too painful for her. It would be painful for me too, but I needed to do it. And I really wanted to see Miles' parents again. They had always felt like family to me. And I needed to thank them for trying to find me.

"Do you think you'll come back?" Liza asked.

I shrugged. "I don't know. Honestly, I kind of hate New York."

They all laughed.

Maybe I would come back eventually. Miles and I had a lot to talk about. I wanted us to make our decisions together from now on. But he was more than halfway through getting his bachelor's degree from Eastern University. Surely he'd want to come back in the fall. He'd be even closer to being done with school if he hadn't taken the semester off to help me.

"We're going to miss you," Kins said and threw her arms around me. "Both of you."

"We're all going to miss you," Liza said and joined in on the hug.

"I'm going to miss you guys too." And I would. So much of my life I had felt so alone. But now? My life was full of people that I loved.

Goodbyes were hard. But they were easier when I had the chance to say them. This didn't feel final. I wasn't losing them.

CHAPTER 47

Friday

"What if they don't remember me?" I asked as we stepped off the plane.

Miles squeezed my hand. "They'll remember you. I never stopped talking about you."

"What if they hate me? You hated me. I caused you so much pain. Surely they'll hate me for hurting you."

"I don't think my parents know how to hate anyone. Besides, they know how much I love you. And they've always loved you too."

"Maybe I should at least book a hotel room. They probably don't want me to stay at their house. God, we really should have told them I was coming. You should have at least told them you found me. You're going to give your mom a heart attack."

He laughed. "Summer, you're being ridiculous. This is going to be a great surprise."

"But what if…"

My words died away when I saw them. Mr. Young was standing there with a sign in his hands that read: "Welcome home, Miles."

Welcome home. Those two words made my heart swell. My name wasn't on the sign. They didn't know that I was coming. Hell, they didn't even know that I was alive. But it still felt like they were welcoming me.

Mrs. Young gasped and put her hand over her mouth. Tears started streaming down her cheeks.

"Summer?" Mr. Young's voice sounded far away, like he couldn't process that I was really here.

I felt tears falling down my face too as Mrs. Young ran over and threw her arms around me.

"Oh, sweetie. You're okay. You're okay, right?" She pulled back and grabbed my face in both her hands. "You're okay?" She kept crying.

"I'm okay, Mrs. Young."

She shook her head, keeping my face in her hands. "I never thought we'd see you again. Oh my, you're so grown up." She patted my cheeks. "You're a beautiful woman." It looked like she was about to cry even harder.

"We've missed you, Summer," Mr. Young said. He stole me away from Mrs. Young and hugged me so hard it almost hurt. But I wouldn't have changed a thing.

"I'm here too," Miles said with a laugh.

I stepped back and Miles wrapped his arm around my waist.

Mrs. Young's eyes lit up. She put her hand on her chest. "And you two are together? Yes?" She nodded like she didn't even need a reply.

I looked up at Miles. "I can't imagine my life without him."

Mrs. Young started bawling again.

"Mom, stop crying."

"I can't." She fanned her face. "You didn't tell us you found her. Why didn't you tell us you found her? Summer, he never stopped thinking about you. He's loved you since he was what…eight years old?"

Mr. Young laughed. "Now you're just trying to embarrass our son." He put his arm around his wife and squeezed her shoulders. "Let's get home, okay?"

Home. I was scared to see my old house. Scared of the memories it would bring to the surface.

"You've got this," Miles whispered in my ear.

I looked up at him. I didn't know how he always knew I needed him. But I felt so lucky.

Snow was falling when we stepped out of the airport. I breathed in the smell. It was different than snow in New York. It smelled like home here. I couldn't keep the grin off my face as I nestled into the backseat of the car next to Miles.

And somehow I kept smiling through a very short story about what I had been through. I was done telling it. I was done with the pain. I glanced at Miles as his phone buzzed yet again.

"Everything okay?" I asked.

He glanced at his phone for a second before sliding it back in his pocket. "Yeah, everything's great." He smiled at me. "Dad, could you take the next right?"

His dad hit his turn signal. "Are we stopping somewhere?"

Miles stared at me. "The graveyard is actually on the way home, Summer. I know you said you wanted to visit it."

Seeing his parents was so uplifting. I had planned on just visiting with them today and saving the hard stuff for tomorrow. But maybe it was better to do it now when I was smiling. Before I saw my old house. Before I had a chance for the memories to come to the surface.

I turned to the front seat. "If that's okay, Mr. Young?"

He looked into the rearview mirror to see me. "Of course." He made the right turn and in a few minutes he was pulling up to the graveyard.

I needed to do this, but it didn't stop my hand from shaking when I opened the car door.

"Do you want me to come with you?" Miles asked.

"No." I swallowed down the lump in my throat. "I need to do this on my own." I stepped out of the car before I could change my mind.

Even though I had only been here once, my feet remember the path. I left a trail of footprints in the soft snow as I wound my way through the gravestones.

I stopped and stared at their names. The last time I stood here, I had felt so numb. I didn't cry at their funeral. I think part of me didn't even believe it was happening. Because their memories seemed so close. But now? I struggled to hear my mom's laugh. I struggled to feel the joy from my dad's smile.

I wasn't numb anymore. My tears felt hot on my cold cheeks. "I'm sorry," I whispered. There were so many things I wished I could have said to them before they died. "I'm sorry I practically shoved you out the door that last night. But I know that you knew it. I know that." I shook my head. "I love you both so much."

I wiped my tears away. "And I'm sorry that I was mad at you for leaving me alone. I know you didn't want to. I know that. I know that you loved me back." They got caught up in something terrible. They tried to keep me safe. And I knew they tried their best. It felt like my heart was bleeding.

"I didn't let him win," I said. "I didn't let him turn me into someone you wouldn't be proud of. I'm still me. And I finally got justice for you."

I put my hand on my father's gravestone. It made me feel closer to him. Almost like he was here with me. I closed my eyes and tried to picture his laugh. But I couldn't remember. I started crying harder.

"You better turn that frown upside down."

The words he said to me so often swirled around me like the snow in the wind. But it wasn't a memory. And I was suddenly aware of the fact that I didn't feel close to him because I was touching his gravestone. I turned around and saw a ghost of a man.

His face was gaunt. His hair was gray and there were wrinkles creasing the corners of his eyes. He looked like he was starving. There was a scar down the left side of his cheek and neck that disappeared beneath his coat. He was so pale that his skin almost matched the color of the snow. He looked absolutely dreadful. Yet I had never seen such a perfect sight in my whole life.

"Dad?" The word came out of my mouth even though I knew it couldn't be possible. *This isn't real. This can't be real.*

He smiled and it was the one thing that was the same. There had always been so much warmth in his smile. It always made me smile too. And seeing it for the first time in ten years was the greatest gift I could ever ask for. He nodded, like he didn't believe the sight in front of him either.

I ran over to him. "Dad!" My voice cracked as I threw myself into his arms.

He caught me, despite how frail he looked. I felt his hot tears fall into my hair. "Baby, girl."

He smelled the same. He sounded the same, even though I had never heard him cry. And he was sobbing even louder than me.

"Summer." He held me even tighter. "I tried so hard to get to you. I tried." His voice broke.

I believed him. He had clearly been tortured. For years. He looked so much older than his age.

"I'm so sorry, Summer. I'm so sorry that I couldn't get to you."

"You have nothing to be sorry for. I just can't believe you're alive. You are, right? I'm not imagining this?"

"It's really me."

"What about mom?" I pulled away from our hug. "Is she…"

He put his hand on the side of my face. "She died instantly in the car crash." His eyes seemed to focus on the gravestone behind me. They were red from his tears. "Don was trying to kill me, not her. If I had died that night instead…"

"Then I'd still be alone." My heart ached. I knew how much he loved my mom. I thought I had lost Miles a few nights ago. I knew that feeling of loss. But at least she died in the car crash and never had to be tortured by Don. She got to die happy.

My dad's eyes focused back on me. "You were never alone, Summer. I was always thinking about you. And your friends are the only reason I'm standing here."

"What?"

"They thought that your mother and I might still be alive. They told William. You remember William...I guess you'd remember him as Uncle Billy?"

I smiled. "I remember."

"Don was keeping me in some storage facility in Colorado. William showed up this morning and found me." He looked up at the falling snow. "It feels so good to breathe fresh air."

His words broke my heart. "What did Don do to you?" I didn't want to start crying again, but there was so much pain in my Dad's face.

"Knowing you were out there without me was worse than anything he did to me."

"I can't believe you're alive. I feel like I'm dreaming."

He leaned down and hugged me again. "Is that Miles Young?" He released me from his embrace.

I looked behind me to see Miles walking toward us.

"Welcome home, Mr. Brooks." Miles held out his hand.

My dad shook it. "Thank you for bringing us back together, son. I knew you'd find her even if I couldn't."

Miles looked over at me and smiled.

"You helped find him?" I asked.

"Mr. Crawford did all the hard work."

I knew that wasn't true. I walked over and hugged him. "Thank you, Miles," I whispered in his ear. "Thank you for always believing in the impossible."

CHAPTER 48
Friday

I tossed and turned in one of the Youngs' guest beds. I was thankful that they let my father and me use their guest rooms. But I didn't know how to fall asleep without Miles' arms around me.

I slid out of bed and walked over to the window. I always found snow calming. Maybe watching it fall would help me sleep. But when I looked outside, I saw that the snow had stopped falling. The night sky was clear. I smiled to myself. Miles wouldn't be in his room anyway. He'd be in his tree house.

I pulled my winter coat on over my pajama top and shoved my bare feet into my boots. I felt silly slipping out the back door. We weren't kids anymore. It was possible that Miles was fast asleep in his bed. But I still climbed the rickety ladder up to his tree house. I knocked twice on the boards above my head.

"Secret password," he said.

I laughed. But it didn't stop me from trying to remember what the smallest constellation visible in the sky would be right now. "Caelum."

The floorboard door opened above me and I climbed up. "I can't believe you remembered," he said.

"I can't believe you're out here. It's freezing."

"The sky's clear. Where else would I be?" He patted the spot beside him. "Come here."

I curled into his side and looked up at the sky. "I never stopped looking at the stars. It made me feel close to you when you were so far away."

He kissed the side of my forehead. "Me too."

"Geez, this tree house is smaller than I remembered." If I stretched out I'd probably be able to touch all four walls at once.

"I think it's more so that we grew up. Speaking of which, I have something for you."

"Is it another pendant? Because I'm happy with the one I have."

"No, I promise I didn't buy you more jewelry from the quarter machine at the grocery store," he said with a laugh. "Close your eyes."

I stared at him. "You've already given me so much."

"Close your eyes, Summer."

I smiled and finally closed my eyes. I had no idea what he had gotten me. But I knew it couldn't top today. Getting my dad back. His parents accepting me. Finally coming home after all these years.

"Okay, open your eyes," he said.

I opened them and looked down at his two outstretched fists.

"Pick a hand."

I laughed. "Not this again." But really I was loving every second of him recreating that night that we first held hands. When we first admitted that we both wanted to be more than friends. I tapped his right fist.

He opened it. There was a piece of paper folded multiple times. "Read it."

I lifted it out of his hands and started to unfold it. I scanned through the letter as fast as I could. He was being signed by Manchester United as a striker.

"It's the third offer they've sent me because I didn't respond to the other two," he said. "I was waiting until everything with Don was over. But I have to decide by tomorrow…"

"This is your dream." I waved the paper at him. "This is everything you've always wanted. How have you not responded to this?"

He shook his head. "You're my dream. Soccer is a very very distant second."

"Don't you want to go?"

"Only if you'll come with me."

"Miles, I'd follow you to the ends of the earth. You know that. Of course I'll go with you."

"What about college?"

"Are you kidding? I'll take classes online. I meant what I said earlier. I hate New York City. I don't want to go back there. Let's go to England!"

He looked so happy. "Really?"

"Yes, really! We'll just get Liza to ship all our stuff over there instead of here. What is the temperature over there? Could I ask my dad to come with us?"

"Thank you." He leaned forward and kissed me. "And to answer your questions: cold and yes."

I laughed. Coming back here had been wonderful. But we needed a fresh start. More distance between Don would be nice too. I had moved around a lot as a kid. But I had never gotten to choose the place. England was somewhere I'd always wanted to go. "When do we leave?"

"As soon as possible. We'll need to find a flat."

I laughed. "This is going to be so much fun." I looked down at his other hand. It was still closed in a fist. "What was in your other hand?"

"Nothing much." He opened his palm and tossed something at me.

I caught it in my hand. I looked down and it felt like my heart stopped. It was a diamond ring.

"Summer Brooks."

I looked up and he was kneeling on one knee. *Oh my God.*

"I'm not the boy you used to know. But my feelings for you have never changed. I've always been in love with you. Always. And I'll never stop loving you. You're my whole world, Summer. I'm not me without you."

"Miles." My heart was so full it felt like bursting.

"I talked to your dad after dinner. He gave me his blessing. And I didn't want to wait another second to ask you. We've been apart for so long. And we were never meant to be apart. We've always been written in the stars. Marry me, Summer."

"Yes! A million times yes!" I threw my arms around him and he caught me. He was always there to catch me.

He was right about everything. We weren't kids anymore. We had been through so much. There was a darkness in me that was forged in flames. His darkness was carved in ice. But I was wrong before. I didn't burn because of it. And he didn't freeze. Neither one of us broke. Our love for each other made us strong enough to see the light again. Strong enough to hope. To dream. To find happiness in a world of chaos. Because we were both made of steel.

LETTERS FROM MILES

Want to read more about what Miles was up to while
Summer was in foster care?

Letters from Miles contains the letters he sent Summer over
the years they were apart. The letters that she never re-
ceived…

To get your free copy of *Letters From Miles*, go to:

www.ivysmoak.com/carved-in-ice-amz

TEMPTATION

Meet your new book boyfriend!

James Hunter gave up his billionaire lifestyle in NYC to become a professor. But he never expected to be teaching such a beautiful student...

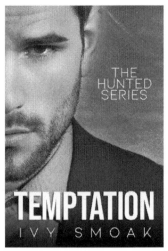

A NOTE FROM IVY

When I first started thinking about Summer's story, it was going to be a light-hearted superhero novel. But as I fell in love with these characters it became so much more. My husband always jokes around with me about how I turn all my stories so dark. (Also…when I started this series he wasn't my husband yet. So how cool is that?!) But I don't think happily ever afters are quite as effective if there isn't some pain along the way.

I always knew how Summer's story would start and how it would end – with her and Miles together. But this was quite the journey. This particular book was one of the hardest I've ever had to write. And this series made me cry more tears than I'd like to admit.

I hope you enjoyed seeing who was behind the mask and that you fell in love with these characters as much as I did.

IvySmoak

Ivy Smoak
Wilmington, DE
www.ivysmoak.com

ABOUT THE AUTHOR

Ivy Smoak is the international bestselling author of the *Made of Steel Series* and *The Hunted Series*. When she's not writing, you can find her binge watching too many TV shows, taking long walks, playing outside, and generally refusing to act like an adult. She lives with her husband in Delaware.

Twitter: @IvySmoakAuthor
Facebook: IvySmoakAuthor
Goodreads: IvySmoak

Recommend *Carved in Ice* for your next book club!

Book club questions available at:
www.ivysmoak.com/bookclub

Made in the USA
Columbia, SC
17 September 2020